The Dating Do-Over

Cathy Spencer

Comely
Press

Published by Comely Press
www.comelypress.com

ISBN: 978-1-926486-01-7
eISBN: 978-1-926486-00-0

Cover design by Design Your Cover
http://www.designyourcover.co.uk

During the Women's Liberation movement, women were told that they could have it all. Later, they discovered that having it all was exhausting. This book is dedicated to all those women who still haven't figured out what they want.

Discover other titles by Cathy Spencer:

The Anna Nolan Series:
Framed For Murder (2014 Bony Blithe Award winner)
Town Haunts

Also by Cathy Spencer:
The Affairs of Harriet Walters, Spinster
Tall Tales Twin-Pack, Mysteries
Tall Tales Twin-Pack, Science Fiction and Fantasy

ACKNOWLEDGMENTS

Many people helped me to research this book, and if there are any errors, the fault is mine. Wayne Stoltz and Charlotte Clarke answered my questions on farming and horses. Fellow author and physician Tom Combs provided information on heart disease. My husband, Reid Spencer, was my go-to guy on home renovation, plus I've soaked up tips from watching all those shows on HGTV. Kate Spencer and Luke Gold-Ruvolo helped choose locations since it's been a few years since I've lived in Toronto. I am also grateful for the input of my discriminating beta readers, Barbara Ledger and Debbie Welland, and for my patient editor, Kate Spencer.

Chapter 1

Viviane Nowak hummed as she toted the bulky grocery bags up the last few stairs to her second-floor apartment. She was looking forward to impressing her boyfriend, Kyle, with a gourmet dinner. Pausing to unearth her keys from the abyss that was her purse, she wrestled the door open and kicked it shut behind her. Oops, the message light was blinking on the phone. Carefully depositing the bags on the living room floor, she plunked herself down on the sagging couch, kicked off her shoes, and called voice mail.

"You have one new message. Message received at 10:15 a.m.," the automated voice intoned.

"Hello, Mr. Weaver? This is Dennis calling from Superior Jewelers on Thursday morning. Just wanted to let you know that the special item you ordered came in and is ready for pick up. The number here is 1-800-555-0199. Let us know when you're coming. Talk to you soon. Bye!"

Viv inhaled sharply and punched in the number on her phone, her heart fluttering with excitement as she waited for the call to connect.

"Hello, Superior Jewelers? Is this Dennis? Hi, I'm calling on behalf of Kyle Weaver. You left a message for him on his home phone. He was on a flight from Vancouver this morning. He's been by the store already? Oh, that's great. I was afraid he wouldn't get the message in time. By the way, I'm Kyle's girlfriend. I don't suppose you could tell me what the 'special item' is he ordered? What's that? Yes, there are lots of secrets on Valentine's Day. No, I understand. Okay. Thanks. Bye."

Viv ended the call and sat still while the information that Kyle had special-ordered something from a jewelry store sank in. Three seconds later, she was bouncing up and down and shrieking with joy while the sofa springs groaned in protest. Forcing herself to calm down, she called one of her two best friends. The phone rang twice before it was picked up.

"Julie, guess what," Viv blurted.

"Heddo?"

"Olivia, is that you? It's Viv. Where's your mommy, honey?"

There was the sound of footsteps crossing the floor and a voice saying, "Did you answer the phone, Olivia? Give the phone to me, honey," while the two-year-old squawked, "Heddo? Heddo?"

Finally, a voice said, "Hi, it's Julie."

"It's me. You'll never guess what happened."

"What?"

"There was a phone message for Kyle from a jewelry store when I got home."

"Really? What'd it say?"

"It said that the 'special item' Kyle had ordered was in."

"What do you think it was? Wait, you don't think?"

"I do. I think that Kyle bought me an engagement ring!"

"Oh, sweetie, that's fabulous! I'm so happy for you! How romantic."

"I know. It's just perfect. The most wonderful man in the world is going to propose to me on Valentine's Day. This is going to be the happiest day of my life."

"What about the job interview? Has he called yet?"

"No. We agreed not to talk about it until he got home from work. He doesn't want anyone to suspect he's applied for a new job until he's sure he got it."

Something clattered to the floor in the background, and Julie said, "No, Olivia, wait for mommy. Viv, I've got to run," she said, returning to the conversation. "I promised Olivia we'd make cookies, and she's getting antsy. But I'm so pleased for you. It's about time Kyle proposed."

"I know, but he's been worth the wait."

2

"Uh huh. Call me tonight, if you get a chance. Let me know if Kyle got the job, and what the ring looks like."

"I will, if I can, but I've got a feeling that we'll be doing some pretty heavy celebrating."

"I bet. See you at school tomorrow."

"Bye, Julie."

Viv put down the phone and stared around the apartment in a happy daze. It had been their little love nest for the past six years. Sure, the walls needed a fresh coat of paint and the furniture was mostly shabby hand-me-downs from their university days, but Kyle had insisted that they not go into debt buying new stuff until he had finished articling and she had a permanent teaching job. Later, when their careers were established and they could afford a roomier apartment, he had convinced her to spend their money paying down his student loans ahead of schedule so they could save on the interest. He was so smart with money and so disciplined; not like her, having trouble sticking to a budget. She was lucky that Kyle was planning for their future.

She smiled at the place fondly; they had made a lot of happy memories here. Part of her would be sorry to say goodbye if he got the job in Vancouver. It would be really tough leaving her friends and her father behind, not to mention the kids at school, but entertainment law was a competitive field, particularly here in Toronto, and this opportunity could be a real boost to his career. Oh, she could hardly wait until Kyle got home and told her what had happened!

Viv glanced at her watch. Five fifteen! Less than two hours to prepare dinner and do her hair and make-up. She wanted to look especially pretty for when he proposed. This was going to be a memorable evening for both of them, one they could share with the grandkids someday. Scooping the bags up off the floor, Viv trotted into the kitchen to start dinner.

Chapter 2

Viv pulled the mustard-and-rosemary-encrusted rack of lamb from the oven and set it on the counter to rest before resetting the temperature to 375°F. The individual cappuccino soufflés were in the fridge ready to go into the oven ten minutes before they were ready for dessert. The Scallops Yakitori was on the table. Potatoes mashed – check – brussel sprouts with bacon on low on the burner - check – Spanish red wine breathing on the table – check. It was all good.

She rummaged through the cutlery drawer for the box of matches and hurried to light the two white candles on the table. It looked like a page out of a decorating magazine with its white linen cloth and the red placemats and napkins she had picked up on sale after Christmas. The smoke from the blown-out match curled toward the ceiling while Viv took an appreciative sniff from the wine bottle. *The Toronto Life* wine critic was right; she really could smell raspberry, chocolate, and vanilla in the bouquet.

Viv heard a key turning in the lock and tossed the matches back onto the kitchen counter. Running her fingers through her hair, she started toward the door with an eager smile as Kyle stepped into the apartment.

"Kyle!" she sighed, wrapping herself in his arms and snuggling against his chest. He smelled deliciously of musky cologne, and his black alpaca overcoat was soft against her cheek. He dropped his briefcase and overnight bag on the floor and pulled her onto her toes for a kiss.

"I've missed you, Sugar Lips. Boy, something smells good." He let her go. "I'm starving – I haven't had anything except a bagel since breakfast." Depositing his scarf and coat on a chair, he put an arm around her waist. "Wow, you look hot in that dress! Did you just get that?"

"Uh huh. From the money Daddy gave me for Christmas, so it didn't cost us a thing. Do you like it?" Viv twirled so that Kyle could appreciate the dress, a red metallic with skinny straps and a short skirt.

"I've always liked you in red. You should wear it more often." He drew her to the table and lifted the casserole lid. "What's this?"

"Scallops Yakitori."

"Looks great." He nabbed a skewer and tore a scallop and mushroom from the end with his teeth. "Good."

"Never mind about the food." Viv turned him around to face her. "Tell me about the interview. Did you get the job?"

"I sure did." The grin on his face was huge.

Viv threw her arms around him and kissed him. "That's fantastic! I'm so proud of you!"

"Thanks, baby. All my hard work is finally paying off." He patted her bottom. "Come on, let's eat."

She released him, and they sat down at the table. He bit into another scallop while she beamed at him.

"Did they give you a start date?"

He nodded, picking up the wine bottle and sniffing. "March 1st. What's this?"

"It's a 2010 Ribota. But that doesn't give us much time. I've got to give notice at school, and we have to let the landlord know."

He poured wine into their glasses. "Don't worry about it. Let's not spoil dinner with the details. It looks like you've made another fabulous meal." He handed her a glass and picked up his own. "Happy Valentine's Day, Viv."

She clanked her glass against his. "Happy Valentine's Day, sweetheart."

Kyle ran his spoon around his dessert cup and licked it before dropping it onto his plate. "That was so good, but I ate too much." He leaned back in his chair and patted his flat stomach. "I'm going to have to go for an extra-long run tomorrow to burn this off."

Viv spooned some of the chocolate sauce from her cup and let it melt onto her tongue. "I can think of a good way to start burning calories tonight, if you like," she said, playing with the spoon against her teeth.

"Come here, Sugar Lips."

She sashayed around the table and slid onto his lap. Bending to reach his mouth, she kissed him with a tantalizing slowness, feeling the rush of heat from his lips course all the way down to her toes. When the kiss had ended, he bit the dress strap off her shoulder and nuzzled her skin with his lips. It tickled, and she giggled.

"Don't think I forgot about getting you something special for Valentine's Day," he said in a husky voice. The other strap slipped from her shoulder while Viv squirmed against him.

"I know. There was a phone message from Superior Jewelers when I got home," she said in a breathy voice.

He lifted his dark head to gaze into her eyes. "So, you think I bought you jewelry this year?" One of his eyebrows arched as he smiled teasingly at her.

"I've been wondering what it was ever since I got home from work."

"Well," he said, sliding a brown velvet box from his jacket pocket and holding it up on the palm of his hand for her inspection, "I'd better not keep a lady waiting."

Viv gulped. Ohmigod, the moment she had been waiting for was finally here! She held her breath as Kyle lifted the lid. Nestled inside were two golden drop earrings with diamond-encrusted hearts. Her own heart plummeted.

"Pretty, aren't they? The store only had them with emeralds, so I had to special order them to get diamonds. Do you like them?"

"I don't understand." Viv dragged her eyes from the earrings to stare at him.

Kyle frowned. "You don't like them?"

"No, sweetheart, they're really nice. I just thought that with the new job and the move to Vancouver and all, it might be something different." She looked away, feeling disappointed and small. "I thought you might want to propose to me tonight."

Kyle stood up, forcing Viv to scramble from his lap.

"Look, we need to talk."

"What about?" She was suddenly apprehensive, and began fidgeting with the ring she wore on her right hand. It was a single pearl with two diamond chips on either side. Daddy had given it to her on her sixteenth birthday.

He drew Viv to the couch and they sat down. "This new job is going to be a great opportunity for me, you know. It's going to make my career."

"I know. Jenkins, Weber, and Chan handle some of the biggest sports stars in Canada. They're a great firm, and you'll do a wonderful job for them. You're not having second thoughts, are you?"

"Are you kidding? I'm so ready for this. Plus, I've been wanting to make a fresh start somewhere, and Vancouver is just the city to do it in."

"Then what's the problem?"

Kyle took her hand and gazed into her eyes. "I'm going to Vancouver on my own."

Viv's stomach sunk. "I don't understand. Do you mean you're going ahead to find us a place to live?"

He shook his head. "We've been together a long time, Viviane."

"I know. Six years."

"Yeah. It's time we decided where this relationship is heading. I think it would be best if we spent some time apart to really think things through. We were awfully young when we got together, you know. Just kids starting out after school."

Viv's bottom lip started trembling. "You mean, you don't want to get married?"

"Not now. This job comes with a whole lot more responsibility. I'm going to have to focus one hundred percent to be on top of my game. I can't be worrying about anyone else. You want me to be a success, don't you, Viv?"

7

"Well sure, Kyle."

He nodded and flashed her one of his dazzling smiles. "I knew you would. You always want what's best for me." He started to rise from the couch, but she snatched his arm and tugged him back down again.

"But maybe I can come visit you in a couple of months, after you get settled." Her eyes searched his face for reassurance. It couldn't be over between them. "We could talk then, see where we are."

He paused, one knee on the couch. "I think it best if we made a clean break, don't you? You're young, Viv. You want marriage and kids. I can't do that now, but I wouldn't want to hold you back if you found someone else. It wouldn't be fair to you."

He raised her hand to his lips and kissed it before standing. "Let's make this as painless as possible, shall we? I'll come by tomorrow to pick up my clothes while you're at work." He glanced around the room. "Most of this stuff is junk, anyway, so you can keep it or donate it to charity. I don't want it."

He threw on his things and picked up the briefcase and overnight bag. "I'll put my apartment key through the mail slot when I'm finished. Take care of yourself, Sugar Lips. You'll always have a special place in my heart."

He was out the door just as the tears brimmed over and cascaded down her cheeks.

Chapter 3

It was after midnight when there was a brisk rap on Julie's front door. She rushed to answer it before her daughter woke up.

"Where is she?" Sabrina asked, bursting through the door.

"Shhh. Olivia's asleep. Viv's on the couch." Julie nodded toward the living room. "Thanks for coming on such short notice." She closed the door behind her friend.

"Not a problem. I ditched my date early. It was no biggie – he was just a 'better him than nobody' date for Valentine's Day." She slipped off her coat and handed it to Julie.

"Whoa! That's what you wear for a 'better him than nobody' date?"

Sabrina smiled and twirled, her auburn curls flying from her shoulders. She was wearing a cream-coloured halter dress with two strands of pearl beading accentuating her exquisite back.

"I thought I'd throw the poor guy a bone. After all, he bought me five courses at Café Vert."

Julie whistled softly. "Olivia and I had homemade chicken fingers and sweet potato fries for dinner," she said wistfully.

"Sounds good to me," Sabrina said as she followed Julie into the living room.

Viv was sprawled in a corner of the couch with her eyes closed. She was wearing grey sweat pants and a "Hello Kitty" t-shirt, a treasured Christmas gift from one of her Grade 1 pupils. Her long blond hair was pulled back into one of Olivia's scrunchies, and her face was puffy and red from crying. An empty wine glass sat on the coffee table next to her.

"Oh, hon, I'm so sorry." Sabrina sat down on the couch and pulled Viv into a hug. Viv sniffled, opened her eyes, and rested her head on Sabrina's shoulder.

"S'okay, Bri. I felt bad before, but not anymore. I don't feel anything anymore. I'm dead inside." Sabrina glanced over her head at Julie, who frowned.

"That bastard, Kyle," Sabrina sputtered. She rubbed Viv's back in tight, angry circles. "I never liked him. He took advantage of you, Viv. Of your beautiful, generous, loving nature. You're too good for him – you always were."

"S'not true." Viv detached herself from Sabrina's arms while peering blearily at her. "Kyle took care of me. I was hopeless before him. He taught me stuff. Like how to roast a chicken. How to do the laundry. He even did my taxes." Her face crumpled. "Now who's going to do my taxes?" she sobbed, collapsing into Sabrina's arms. Julie snatched a bunch of tissues from the box on the table and mopped Viv's face.

"You don't need Kyle, Vivvie," Sabrina said over her weeping. "An accountant can do your taxes."

Viv stopped crying and lifted her head to peer at her friend. Sabrina nodded encouragingly.

"S'right," Viv said with a sniff. "Who needs stupid old Kyle?" But her face fell, and she toppled back onto the couch. "Who am I kidding? I do!" she wailed.

Sabrina stood up and pulled Julie a short distance away to where Viv couldn't overhear them. "How long has she been like this?" she whispered.

Julie checked her watch. "Almost two hours. She was hysterical when she got here, so I gave her a glass of wine. But we've almost polished off the bottle, and I've only had one glass."

"She can't go back to her apartment like this."

"No. She can stay with me for a couple of nights. I'll tell the school tomorrow that she's sick – let her sleep it off – but we'll have to figure out a better plan over the weekend. I just don't have enough space for her here."

"She can move back in with me, temporarily. It'll be tight, but we'll make it work." Julie nodded gratefully, and they returned to the couch, taking a seat on either side of their soggy friend.

"Sweetie, you're going to sleep here tonight," Julie said. She stroked Viv's hair. Viv nodded and wiped her face with her sleeve. "Stay home tomorrow. I'll tell them you're sick."

Viv shook her head. "No, I gotta go in. Tomorrow's Super-Star Friday."

"Super-Star Friday? What's that?" Sabrina asked, looking at Julie.

"Every Friday, one of Viv's students dresses up like his or her hero. Viv takes the kid's picture and puts it on a special wall of fame."

Viv hiccupped. "Tomorrow's Noah. He's gonna be Spider-Man. Can't miss it. Can't let him down." She sighed and slumped against Julie's shoulder.

"Don't worry, sweetie. You get some sleep, and I'll wake you up in time for work. How's that?"

Viv nodded without opening her eyes, exhausted from her ordeal.

"Good." Julie slid out from beside her and went to fetch a throw while Viv nestled her head on a pillow and fell asleep immediately.

"Poor thing," Sabrina whispered as Julie draped the throw over Viv. "I'd like to kick Kyle right where it would get his attention. Didn't she have any inkling that this was coming?"

Julie shook her head. "Totally blindsided."

Sabrina sighed. "Sometimes I just hate men."

"I've got no use for them whatsoever," Julie replied.

Chapter 4

"Viv, Happy Easter! Sabrina, nice to see you again. It's been too long," Gabe Nowak said. He threw open the door to his semi-detached house in the Annex. Viv was busy flapping her umbrella in a flurry of raindrops, but Sabrina stepped inside with a smile and a quick kiss.

Viv hurried to give her father a long, damp hug. "Happy Easter, Daddy," she said, rising on tiptoe to kiss his cheek.

"You should come around more often – I've been worried about you."

"Sorry. I've been busy at work."

"Sure, sure, I understand." In a heartier voice, Gabe added, "Let me take your coats, ladies."

"Thanks, Gabe," Sabrina said. She slipped out of hers to reveal a daffodil-yellow silk shift, and his square, ruddy face brightened.

"Don't you look lovely, sweetheart."

"Thanks. You look pretty dapper yourself." Gabe was dressed in a blue-and-cream-checked shirt and navy dress pants tailored to mask his paunch. He bowed to acknowledge her compliment.

"Here you go, Daddy." Viv handed him her coat. She wore a black-and-white-striped sweater and black pants that bagged on her petite frame. Gabe brushed her cheek with his hand.

"You look lovely, too, Peaches. Come on, everyone into the kitchen. Magda's been cooking up a storm, and she'll be offended if you don't start stuffing yourselves immediately." He put his arms around the young women's shoulders and led them down the hallway into the kitchen.

The daylight filtering through the French doors overlooking the dripping garden made the room feel bright and airy. Magda was pulling a rosy ham from one of the stainless-steel ovens, and the aroma filled the room. The ham was large enough to feed a dozen people, not the four who had gathered to celebrate the holiday together. She hoisted the roasting pan onto the range top and turned with a grin on her flushed face.

"Viviane!" Magda rushed forward with the oven mitts still on to hug the young woman. She rocked Viv back and forth with her bare, muscular arms before holding her out for inspection.

"What have you been doing? Starving yourself?" She took off a mitt to pinch Viv's arm, making the young woman squawk.

"No, of course not," Viv said, rubbing her arm. "But now that it's just Sabrina and me, I don't cook as much as I used to."

Magda tsked. "No point crying over that worthless Kyle. Put on a pretty dress and go dancing. Show the young men in this town what a treasure you are." She turned to Gabe. "Am I right?"

Gabe tried to keep a straight face as his daughter scowled. "Who am I to argue? You're always right, Magda."

The housekeeper nodded. "You bet. As for you young lady," she said, eyeing Sabrina, "you're skinny, too, but you've got great legs. Those shoes you're wearing are murderers." Magda's own feet were encased in pink bunny slippers, but her floral skirt ended a saucy two inches above her knees.

"I think she means 'killer,'" Viv said.

"Why, thank you, Magda. That's the nicest thing you've ever said to me." Sabrina pointed the toe of her white stiletto with its splashes of black, green, yellow, and pink.

"Let's not talk about her shoes," Viv muttered.

"Why not?" Magda asked.

"They're 'Rouge.'"

"Oops! Well, they're still beautiful." Viv shook her head, but Magda put her arm around Viv's waist and pulled her toward the island crowded with serving dishes and platters. "Come on, beautiful girl, help me get the food on the table so we can eat."

The table was decorated with pussy willows and a vase of pink and purple tulips, plus a red or purple Easter egg with an intricate geometric design in front of each plate. Magda passed a serving bowl to Gabe.

"What's this?" he asked.

"Cranberry and low fat feta with greens. Take some."

He spooned some onto his plate, but took two servings of scalloped potatoes when Magda wasn't looking.

"I'm trying to get your father to eat more green vegetables. The doctor says his cholesterol is too high."

"How high is it, Daddy?" Viv asked with concern in her voice.

"Ah, don't worry about it. With all the exercise I'm getting flipping houses, it's not a problem."

"What are you working on now?"

"A duplex in Cabbagetown. We're converting it back into a single-family home. I'm working with a new contractor."

"The cowboy," Magda interjected.

"He's a cowboy?" Viv asked.

"Nah. Magda just calls him that because he lives on a horse farm near Oakville and drives a pick-up truck. His name is Tom Lockhart. Good man. A carpenter by trade, and he does nice work. Mike Birch from the bank recommended him."

"How do you like early retirement, by the way?" Sabrina asked, nibbling some greens from her plate. She had skipped the potatoes and loaded up on salad, braised red cabbage, and fresh asparagus. "It's been – what – over a year now? Do you miss working at the bank?"

"Sometimes, like when I discover asbestos in the walls, or have to dig up a front yard to replace the sewer pipes. Managing a mutual fund portfolio is clean work, if you don't mind wearing a suit and sitting on your ass all day." He shrugged. "It was getting old. Time to have some fun. What about you, Sabrina? Still happy climbing the corporate ladder?"

Sabrina fluttered her fingernails in the air. They were painted a shiny black with gleaming gold tips. "Real estate banking works for me. I don't like getting my hands dirty."

"Like slinging drinks in your mother's bar?"

"That would mean living back in Newfoundland. No thank you. That's why I went to university here in Toronto." She pointed her thumb at Viv. "I wouldn't like looking after Viv's kiddies all day, either. But *chacun à son goût*."

Gabe turned to his daughter. "How's work?"

"Good," Viv said, spooning some mustard onto her ham. Magda's home cooking was making her hungrier than she'd felt in weeks. "The kids keep me sane. Six is such a fun age. It's when they start recognizing simple word patterns and figure out that five and three make eight. There's a new discovery every day, and I'm there to see it. I wouldn't earn my living any other way."

Her face lit up as she spoke, and Gabe smiled at her affectionately. Viv had been such a loving kid, mothering all her playmates even before she was old enough to start kindergarten. A grade school teacher was all she had ever wanted to be, and her love for children and learning shone through her eyes. Despite her setback with Kyle, she was a lucky woman, if only she knew it.

"And how's it going, you two, living back together again?" Gabe asked. "You've got a condo just outside the Distillery District, don't you, Sabrina?"

"Three blocks away. It's great having Viv back again." Sabrina smiled at her friend. "Just like old times."

"Sometimes I worry that I'm cramping your style," Viv said.

Sabrina shook her head, but before she could say anything, Gabe interrupted. "You know, I've been thinking about that, Peaches. Why not move back in here with Magda and me? We've got tons of space, and you can have your old room back."

Magda had got up to fetch a basket of rolls from the kitchen. "I'd love to have our beautiful girl back again," she said over her shoulder. "You wouldn't have to worry about a thing, Viv. I could cook for you and do your laundry, just like I used to. We could have girl talks again!"

Viv glanced at her father's hopeful face. She had to admit, moving back in would have its advantages. After sleeping on the futon in Sabrina's office for seven weeks, she was longing for a real bed and some privacy. Sabrina was seeing a new man pretty regularly, and it was awkward when the two of them were feeling amorous in the one-bedroom condo, especially since the office didn't have a door.

On the other hand, how pathetic would it be, a thirty-one-year-old woman moving back in with her father? It wasn't as if he needed her anymore, not with Magda living in.

Gabe had hired Magda to be their housekeeper when Viv was only ten. Magda had kept the house clean, looked after the laundry and the shopping, been there when Viv got home from school, and cooked supper every night. It was handy having her live in, especially when Gabe was away on one of his overnight business trips. Magda became like a mother to Viv, helping her survive the insecurities of adolescence and dating, until Viv had graduated from high school and was ready to start university. She had refused to stray further afield than the University of Toronto, however, not wanting to be too far away from her father, but ready enough for her first taste of independence to move into residence.

Could she stand being coddled by these two again, and having heart-to-hearts with Magda? Viv shuddered. At least Sabrina left her alone to mope in private, but Daddy would probably invite men home for dinner, anxious for her to start dating again. It might be cramped at Sabrina's, but at least she wasn't being smothered by good intentions.

"I don't know. I'll think about it," she said, reaching out to take Gabe's hand. She didn't like lying, but it was better than hurting his feelings. "It's sweet of you to ask," she added. He smiled and squeezed her hand.

"Who's got room for dessert?" Magda asked, setting down a traditional Polish Easter cake, a white-frosted lamb kneeling on a plate of green-tinted coconut.

At the end of the afternoon, after the young women had thanked Magda for the fabulous meal and Viv had kissed her goodbye, Gabe escorted them back down the hallway. Viv and Sabrina each carried a pink straw basket brimming with chocolate and marshmallow eggs, jelly beans, and a chocolate bunny. The rain had stopped, and sunlight poured onto the grey slate floor when Gabe opened the door.

"Don't be strangers, girls. Come visit an old man now and then."

Viv hugged him and kissed his cheek. "I promise, Daddy," she said. "Sorry I haven't felt much like visiting these past couple of months."

"I just want to see you happy again, Peaches." He kissed both her cheeks. "Don't forget to go out and have some fun now and then."

Sabrina slid her arm around Viv's waist. "Don't worry, Gabe. I'll make sure that she does."

Chapter 5

Viv was stretched out on Sabrina's couch flipping through a Vogue magazine on a Saturday night two weeks later. Sabrina bustled into the condo, tossed her jacket into the closet in the foyer, and sat down on the bench to unzip her knee-high leather boots.

Viv turned a page and called out, "How was dinner?"

"Great." Sabrina dropped her boots onto the floor and padded past the kitchen into the living room. She paused with her hands on her hips to study her friend. Viv was dressed in grey sweat pants, a nubby blue cardigan, and sweat socks. Again. Sabrina shook her head in disgust.

Viv looked up. "Who did you eat with tonight?"

"Trina and Barb from the office."

"I thought you were going to a club afterward?"

"I am. Trina told me about a great new cocktail bar called The Shoe Horn. It's part bar, part shoe store. She tried it last night and loved it so much that she asked us to go back with her tonight."

"Where is it?"

"At College and Ossington."

"Why'd you come all the way back here? Did you forget something?"

"Yeah – you."

"What?" Viv was paying attention now.

Sabrina stomped into the room and leaned over her. "I'm giving you just fifteen minutes to get your ass off my couch, put on something that doesn't make you look like a bag lady, and brush your hair. I called Julie, and she's going to meet us at the bar in an hour."

Viv sat up, her eyes narrowing and her face red. "I do not look like a bag lady!"

"You do, and it's got to stop. It's time for the Sabrina O'Sullivan two-step program to restart the human heart. Step one is to go out with women friends. Step two is to go out with a man." She brushed a strand of hair away from Viv's face. "Believe me, hon, I've felt low on more than one occasion, but I've never given up the way you have."

Viv glared at Sabrina. "I have *not* given up. I'm just going through a grieving period. Everyone knows that you have to grieve after a major break-up."

Sabrina glared back. "For two months, every minute you haven't been at work, you've been on that couch. Your butt has even left an imprint."

"Where?" Viv stood up and turned around to look. Sabrina locked her arm through Viv's.

"Look, you've got to start going out again, and tonight's the night. You'll like the Shoe Horn. It's just a bunch of women getting together for pretty cocktails and fabulous shoes. No men. It'll be easy."

Viv's shoulders drooped. She felt guilty, having imposed on Sabrina for two months already. She didn't want to be a drain on their friendship, but she still felt so vulnerable.

"I know you and Julie are worried about me."

"Your dad's worried, too. I promised him I'd get you back on your feet, and I will."

"Just not tonight, okay? I'm really not up to it."

"Nothing doing," Sabrina said, marching her toward the guest bathroom. "We're going to start with make-up and hair."

"I'm not going!" Viv protested.

"Shut up." Sabrina pushed her into the bathroom. "So much to do, so little time."

An hour later, Sabrina and Viv were inside the Shoe Horn.

""What do you think? Isn't this fabulous?" Sabrina shouted. "Oh, wait. There's Julie. Over here!" she bellowed, waving her hand over her head.

Viv stared around the room; she was suffering from sensory overload. A live jazz trio played in a corner while waiters ferried colourful cocktails from the white leather bar to the chattering women sitting on tufted couches. Shoes were displayed on the white, silk-lined shelves fastened to all four walls. Glittering mirrors slanted up from the floor, allowing the customers to check out their trendy footwear as they strutted up and down the red carpet running the length of the room. A two-tiered, circular chandelier with white and pink crystals was suspended from the ceiling, adding to the glamour. Viv searched her purse for her bottle of headache tablets, and downed two.

Julie pushed through a group of women bottlenecked in the entrance to catch up with her friends. The pixie cut that emphasized her dark, liquid eyes was spiked, giving her an edgier than normal look.

"Wow, you look fabulous," Sabrina shouted into her ear.

"I thought I'd dress up for a change," Julie hollered back. She was wearing a cropped jacket, a magenta silk blouse, black jeans, and studded ankle boots. "You look pretty good yourself. Love your dress, too, Viv."

Viv nodded. Fortunately, Sabrina had forced her to wear something nice, or else she would have felt underdressed as well as overwhelmed. The trio's set came to an end, and she relaxed as the noise level decreased enough to allow conversation.

Sabrina pointed to a couch on the other side of the room. "I think we can squeeze in over there." Viv and Julie nodded, and the three friends threaded through the crowd of chattering women. When they arrived at the couch, its two occupants smiled and shoved over to make room for them.

Viv sighed as she sat down and dropped her purse on the floor. It had taken a lot of arguing and arm-twisting to convince her to come tonight. Maybe Sabrina had been right to call her a wimp. Maybe it was taking her too long to stop grieving and get on with her life. Not that she was ready to start dating again, but at least she was sitting on a different couch. And this wasn't such a bad place. Better to be stuck in a shoe store with alcohol than endure another round in the bathroom with Sabrina.

"Now that you two are settled, I'm going to say 'hi' to Trina and Barb," Sabrina said. "Be back soon." Viv was staring after her when a gorgeous young waiter suddenly materialized right before her.

"Hi. What can I get you?" Viv stared at him. He was adorable with long, blond bangs falling into his eyes and an endearing smile. She couldn't help returning it.

"I'll have Sex on the Beach." She winced, colouring. Would he think she was coming onto him? It was a Freudian slip, but her id had better just pipe down. She peeked up at the waiter, who seemed unfazed.

"Mojito for me," Julie said. She grinned knowingly at Viv.

"Great. I'll be right back with those." He produced a pad from his shirt pocket and tore off two sheets. "Have a browse through the shoes, and if you see anything you like, write down the tag number on these. Your shoe server, Kelly, will be happy to help you." He nodded at a frazzled-looking young woman kneeling beside a stack of boxes on the far side of the couch. She glanced up, and Viv smiled at her. When Viv turned back to the waiter, he was gone.

"What a cutie patootie!" Julie nodded at the young man's retreating back.

"Yeah." Viv frowned as Julie wiggled her eyebrows. "Don't be so obvious. And stop worrying. I'm depressed, not dead."

"Good to know you still have a libido. I was beginning to wonder."

"Very funny. Come on, as long as we're here, let's check out the shoes." Viv grabbed Julie's elbow and tugged her to her feet. Together they studied the display behind the couch, a brand name collection of chic summer sandals.

"Check out that pale green crocodile wedge with the ankle ribbon," Julie said.

"I don't know. I'm not convinced that I can get away with wedges. If I wear three-inch-thick soles, I end up clomping around like Frankenstein's monster. I'd have to be as tall as you to carry them off." Viv pointed at the shoes next to the wedges. "How about those pink-and-white striped kitten slingbacks?"

"They're nice." Julie leaned closer to study the price tag. "Whoa, $900!"

"I'm not saying that I can afford them, but they *are* Manolos. They're worth it."

"Maybe, but my car needs a new battery." Julia glanced over Viv's shoulder. "Here comes the waiter with our drinks."

"My treat." Viv pulled out her credit card. As a single parent with mortgage payments, Julie didn't have much disposable income. And Toronto was the most expensive Canadian city to live in, next to Vancouver. *Vancouver*, she thought with pain. *Kyle.*

Taking a gulp of her drink, Viv rejoined Julie on the couch. Kelly, their shoe server, hurried out with another armful of boxes for the two women sitting beside them. Julie glanced at the woman next to her.

"Nice."

The sturdy blond frowned, her pant legs rolled halfway up for a better look at the shoes she was trying on. "You don't think the ankle strap makes my calves look fat, do you?" Her voice was unexpectedly deep.

"Hardly. You've got great calves. Strong and defined. I bet you're a dancer."

The blond perked up. "I am, one of the stars at Dora's Divas."

"Hey, didn't I see you on their float at the Pride Parade last year?"

"You did. I was Madonna."

Julie did a double-take. "I remember you. You were lip-synching to 'Material Girl.' You were terrific!"

The blond nudged her friend, who was trying on a pair of last season's boots. "Hey, Vanessa. We've got a fan here."

Julie offered her hand and introduced herself. Soon all three were talking about the shows at Dora's Divas until Vanessa changed the topic to an upcoming gall bladder operation. Viv got bored and wandered off to see what had happened to Sabrina. A really attractive red-plaid purse distracted her, however, and, veering toward the table, she came face-to-face with a display of Rouge shoes.

Of course. A designer store like this was bound to carry them. Pursing her lips, Viv took a step closer to study this season's specimens.

She had to admit, the old woman hadn't lost her touch. The summer collection was a confection of pastels featuring floral cut-outs and charming bows. They looked so delicate that it was hard to believe they were crafted from leather, but that was part of the magic. The shoes were the height of feminine indulgence, and priced accordingly.

Viv felt a hand on her shoulder and turned to see Sabrina gazing down at the collection. They exchanged an awed glance, and turned back to stare at the shoes.

"They *are* beautiful," Sabrina said, daring Viv to contradict her. Viv remained silent and sipped from her drink. Sabrina picked up a blue pump with a pearl-grey toe. "How long has it been since you've seen Véronique, by the way?"

"Not since I graduated from teacher's college six years ago."

"Hmm. You know, this collection is a real departure for your mother. Her shoes are usually so bold, so dynamic, but these are girly and pretty. If I didn't know better, I'd say she designed them with you in mind. They're perfect for someone with your looks."

"Yes, Mother has that effect on people. You think she's doing something special just for you when, all along, it's all for her." Viv turned her back on the display. "Come on, let's go find Julie and have another drink."

The music started up again as Viv linked arms with Sabrina, making civilized conversation impossible. Sabrina frowned, but allowed Viv to tow her away.

Two hours later, Viv snuggled under the futon covers while Sabrina turned off the living room lights. Viv felt pleasantly tipsy and drowsy, as if she were floating on a pink, fluffy cloud from one of her old *Slumberland* picture books. She giggled. It had been a long time since Daddy had read her a bedtime story.

Sabrina stopped to lean against the wall outside the office. The space was just large enough to hold a computer table and the futon. Viv used the table to stack her clothes and a few books.

"I heard you laugh," Sabrina said. "I haven't heard that in a long time. It sounded good. Did you have fun tonight?"

"I did. You were right about the Shoe Horn."

"I'm glad, Vivvie. Maybe next weekend we'll go out to dinner with a few friends. Night," she said as she walked away.

Talking about going out with friends reminded Viv of Sabrina's plan to forget Kyle. Her pink cloud turned grey, and she felt morose. Before Sabrina could disappear, Viv called, "Why did Kyle leave me?" It was a question she had asked herself many times over the past weeks, usually with tears in her eyes. She wasn't crying now, and maybe Sabrina could provide some insight.

Sabrina hesitated before turning around. She said, "Men like him are always on the lookout for the next best thing."

Viv sat up and put her arms around her knees. "What do you mean?" she asked in a small voice.

Sabrina sighed and walked back to perch on the mattress beside Viv. "I've got some friends in Vancouver, hon. I heard that Kyle is seeing one of the partners at his new agency."

Viv gasped. "It can't be true." She paused to think. "Wait a minute – I thought all of the partners were men."

"There's a Grace Chan."

"Oh." A few more seconds passed before she asked, "When did they start dating?"

"When he flew out for the second interview. My friend saw them together at a restaurant one night."

"Maybe it was just part of the interview process? Maybe they were . . ."

"No, hon. They were holding hands."

"I can't believe it. Kyle would have told me if there was someone else. He was always honest with me."

"No, Viv, he wasn't honest. Isn't it time you pulled off those rose-coloured glasses you've been wearing all these years?" Viv shrank away, and Sabrina reached for her hand. "I'm sorry, I shouldn't have said that. I'm just tired of hearing how perfect Kyle was, and how lucky you were to have been with him."

"What else do you know?" Viv's voice sounded flat.

"For one thing, your father had to help Kyle get his first job."

"I knew that. Why shouldn't Daddy have pulled a few strings for Kyle? Daddy always said he wished someone had given him a leg-up."

"Yeah, but did you know that Kyle would have been fired his first year if it hadn't been for your father?"

"No. Why?"

"Because Kyle almost lost the firm one of their authors. He made a rookie mistake with a new contract that would have cost the client tens of thousands in royalties. If one of the partners hadn't stepped in to fix it, the firm would have lost the author for sure. Your father had to do some serious wining and dining to stop them from throwing Kyle out on his ear. Gabe convinced them that everyone is entitled to a second chance. Then he sweetened the deal by making a sizable donation to the author's pet charity. But I'm not surprised that Kyle didn't tell you."

"No, he didn't. Neither did Daddy. But why did Daddy tell you?"

Sabrina shifted uneasily on the futon. "Because your father didn't trust Kyle. He thought he was a wheeler-dealer, and that he was using your name to advance his career. Between your father and your mother, you have some pretty sweet contacts, you know."

"I know. If I had gotten an MBA instead of a teaching degree, I'd probably be a millionaire by now." Viv twirled the pearl ring on her right hand. "I know Mother was disappointed when I didn't go into the design business. Maybe Daddy is disappointed in me, too."

"Don't say that."

"Daddy didn't trust me enough to tell me about Kyle. Maybe he thinks I'm too gullible, too soft to deal with the truth." Viv started to tremble, and Sabrina pulled her into her arms.

"That's not true. You are the centre of that man's universe. He thinks you're the sweetest, kindest, most loving person in the whole world, and he wouldn't want you any other way. He knew how much Kyle meant to you, and he didn't want to upset you by talking against him." She stroked Viv's hair. "Cynical old me, I always think someone's trying to cheat me. Your father just wanted someone watching out for you, that's all."

Viv pulled away and fumbled on the floor for the box of tissues. She blew her nose and moaned, "I've been such an idiot. I spent all that money helping Kyle pay off his student loans."

"How much?"

Viv paused to calculate. "Around eighteen thousand, I'd guess."

Sabrina winced, but patted her friend's shoulder. "It's all water under the bridge. You're better off without him, no matter how much it cost. The sooner you start realizing that, the better." She kissed Viv's cheek. "Come on." Viv lay down while Sabrina drew the covers to her chin. "We'll talk some more tomorrow. Have a good sleep."

Viv nodded and closed her eyes, but it took her hours to fall asleep that night.

Chapter 6

Viv shifted the cooler into her left hand and knocked on Julie's door. Seconds later, her friend opened it.

"Viv! Come on in. Great weather for Victoria Day, isn't it?" It was unexpectedly hot for May. Julie was barefoot, dressed in khaki shorts and a short-sleeved shirt. Olivia peeked out from behind her mother. The little girl wore a gold crown to accessorize her pink leotard and sparkly tutu, her plump legs and feet bare.

Viv gave Julie a hug and handed her the cooler. "I've got potato salad with croutons and bacon in there."

"Yum," Julie said. "Let's hang out in the kitchen." She trotted away down the dark, narrow hallway while Viv closed the door and bent to kiss Olivia's cheek.

"Hi, Olivia. Love your crown."

The child nodded, feeling for her head with a grubby hand. "I got it on my birthday."

"I remember. I was there," Viv said with a smile. "You were dressed like Tinker Bell with a fairy wand." She noticed that one of Olivia's hands was closed into a fist. "What have you got in there?" she asked, gently tapping it.

The child opened her fingers to reveal a few crushed cereal squares. She held up her palm, offering them to Viv.

"Thank you," Viv said. She chose a piece that was relatively intact and pocketed it as soon as Olivia turned to run up the hallway.

Viv followed the child into the kitchen. A revolving fan on the table pushed pockets of warm, humid air around the room. Olivia collapsed on the floor in front of the sink. She pulled off her crown and chose a stubby blue crayon to begin her colouring. Julie was stirring something in a pot on the stove that spewed steam into her face, but smelled delicious.

"Boston-baked beans. To go with the burgers," she said, putting the lid back on and hoisting the pot into the oven.

"Can I help?"

"Sure. See if you can find room in the fridge for your potato salad."

Viv opened the fridge door and was trying to figure out how to stuff anything else onto the overflowing shelves when there was a knock on the front door. She looked up in surprise.

"You expecting someone?"

Julie just smiled and left the kitchen without saying a word.

Viv heard the door open and her friend say, "Josh, good to see you! Come on in, buddy."

Viv's stomach clenched. This felt suspiciously like a blind date.

Two weeks earlier, Julie and Sabrina had arranged to meet Viv at Brewsters, a downtown coffee shop. It was a damp, chilly day, and the two women were bundled in sweaters and thin pastel scarves, trying to pretend that spring had arrived. They were placing their orders at the glass display unit in front of the register when Viv arrived five minutes late from a parent-teacher meeting.

Sabrina waved and pointed to an empty table at the rear of the narrow shop. Dodging past the hungry customers lined all the way to the door, Viv claimed the miniscule table with its child-sized, folding chairs. She was looking wistfully at the occupied armchairs in front of the faux fireplace when her friends arrived bearing white china mugs and plates.

"Here, we got you a blueberry ginseng tea and a chocolate pecan cookie," Julie said.

"Thanks! You two are the best. I'm starving." Viv took the mug and sniffed the fruity fragrance before sipping. Her friends had remembered to add a dollop of honey, just the way she liked it. She sighed and said, "I'm tired of having to deal with parents." Kayla's mother had not been happy to hear that her daughter had been sent to the principal's office for biting one of her classmates.

"Tough meeting?" Julie asked.

"I'll say. Apparently Kayla's baby brother is teething, and the whole family's sleep-deprived. Her mother had to cut short a department meeting and fight rush-hour traffic to see me, and she was close to losing it. So, thanks for the treat. I really needed it." She bit into a chunk of milk chocolate in her cookie and relaxed.

Julie checked her wristwatch. "I only have an hour before my nanny leaves."

Sabrina finished checking her messages and put down her cell phone. "Okay, let's keep this short. Viv, we called you here today for a progress report."

Viv sat up in surprise. No one had said that this meeting was to be about her.

"Julie and I have been comparing notes, and we think you're doing much better than you were after the break-up."

"You really are, sweetie," Julie interjected.

"Your wine consumption is back to normal, you've stopped waking me up in the wee hours with crying jags, and you've gone out with friends three times." Sabrina paused to grin at Viv. "Congratulations, hon. You've passed step one of the Sabrina O'Sullivan two-step program to restart the human heart."

"Uh, thanks," Viv said uneasily. She sensed that something unpleasant was coming.

"So, it's time for your first date. Don't worry, we're not going to abandon you," Sabrina added, glancing at Viv's panicked face. She turned to Julie and asked, "Did Viv ever tell you how bad she is at dating?"

"It never came up."

"That's right, she was already with Kyle when you two met. But let me tell you, the guys she dated before him were certifiable disasters."

"They weren't so bad," Viv mumbled, looking down at the table.

Sabrina laughed. "Do you remember the engineer you went out with in your first year of university? What was his name?"

"Steve."

"That's right. He was a psychopath."

Viv glowered at Sabrina. "He was not a psychopath. He was just socially inept." She turned to Julie. "He came from a small town. It was his first time away from home, and he was lonely."

"Do you remember eating with him?" Sabrina asked. "He wouldn't say a word, and he clenched his knife and fork so hard that his knuckles turned white. He was really hairy, too. Not just his beard. He had this dense, black hair that grew all the way up his arms to his knuckles. And he had these really beady eyes. Cold, like a killer's."

"He did not! Stop exaggerating. Poor Steve, he was just intense."

"Intense!" Sabrina snorted. "And then there was that pot head who picked you up in the park."

"Daniel."

"Daniel! He wanted to be in a rock band, but he was the worst guitarist I've ever heard. Remember that stupid Fedora he used to wear? He'd come out of your bedroom wearing it on the way into breakfast, the dumb ass."

"He wrote me a beautiful song, though. Remember?"

"You're right! I'd forgotten about that. What was it called?"

"Diamond-Hearted Girl," Viv said wistfully.

"Why diamond-hearted?" Julie asked. "Diamonds are hard and cold."

"Because her heart sparkled and had so many facets." Sabrina sneered. "Then he borrowed two hundred bucks from Viv to cut a music demo, and we never saw him again."

"But he was sweet and really kind to animals," Viv said. "He tried to save an abandoned cat he found in an alley that winter."

"Only it was feral, and tore up the furniture and peed all over the carpet before escaping."

"Poor thing. It's probably dead by now," Viv said.

"Ooh! Did you ever hear how Viv lost her virginity?" Sabrina asked. She spoke too loudly and drew the attention of the couple at the next table.

"Shhh!" Viv ducked her head and covered her face with both

hands.

"Only that she was seventeen when it happened," Julie said.

Viv uncovered her face and glared at Sabrina. "You be quiet. If anyone's going to tell her, it'll be me." The three women leaned closer as Viv whispered, "There was this boy I was seeing in Grade 11 named Justin. He was diabetic. After we had been dating for about five months, he told me that diabetics have trouble with erections, and he was getting really frustrated. I asked if he'd seen a doctor, and he said yes, his mother had taken him, but the doctor was no help at all. Viagra was just coming out back then, but there was no way his family doctor was going to prescribe it for a teenager."

"So, little Miss Fix-it decided to help him," Sabrina said. Her eyes glinted with amusement, and Viv gave her a dirty look before continuing.

"His mother and father didn't get home from work until six. We were in his bedroom, and he started crying. He said he was afraid he was impotent, and that he would never be a father. Of course, I felt sorry for him, so I started kissing him. I had never done anything more than heavy petting before, but we ended up naked. I was sort of on top of him when it happened."

"Oh, Viv," Julie sighed.

"I remember being really excited. I was so happy for him. I thought I had cured him."

"Until things heated up again, and Justin pulled a condom from a stash in his bedside table because he didn't want Viv to get pregnant," Sabrina said. She shook her head.

"Yeah. That was a real downer," Viv said. "Not only did Justin betray me, but I was terrified that I might be pregnant until my period came."

"Enough of memory lane," Sabrina said, checking her watch. "Julie has to go home, so let's cut to the chase. We're going to help you, Viv. No more deadbeats. Julie and I are going to vet your dates from now on. Call it a dating do-over."

Viv stared from one friend to the other.

"That's right," Julie said. "We've even developed a scoring

system for potential boyfriends based on health, attractiveness, earning potential, dating history, and overall character. We don't want you ending up with a deadbeat who's got millions but doesn't care about his environmental footprint, for example."

"With my job at the bank, I can run credit checks," Sabrina added. "Of course, I know a lot more men than Julie does."

"Except I know this one really terrific guy who would be perfect for you," Julie said. "I can't wait for you to meet him. Well, what do you think? Are you excited?"

"A dating do-over?" Viv asked doubtfully.

"That's right," Sabrina said. "Because you're so bad at finding the right man. Look at the six years you just wasted on Kyle." Viv winced; sometimes Sabrina could be harsh. "We're a lot better than a dating service because we know you so well, and because we have your best interests at heart."

Viv was silent as she mulled over her friends' plan. Sabrina was right; she had made some poor dating choices. What made her think that she could do any better now?

"Come on, Vivvie," Sabrina said. "Let us help you. You want to move on with your life, don't you?"

Viv nodded.

"You want to have a husband and children, don't you?"

Viv made up her mind. "Okay," she said, reaching for Julie and Sabrina's hands. "Let's try it. A dating do-over."

Julie re-appeared in the kitchen entrance, and Viv steeled herself for whomever was behind her. God only knew what kind of specimen her gay, elementary school teacher friend had come up with.

"Viv, this is Josh Lennox," Julie said, stepping aside.

Viv gaped. Josh was about 6'2" with cropped, sandy brown hair, high cheek bones, and beautiful hazel eyes. He looked wholesome, like the boy next door, only better.

Josh nodded and said, "Hi, Viv," before looking straight past her at Olivia.

"Nice to meet you, Josh," Viv said, her head veering to follow his gaze.

His face split into a smile. "Hi, Olivia," he said. The child regarded him for two seconds before returning to her colouring book.

Josh sat down on the floor beside her. "What's that you're drawing?" Something twigged Viv's memory, and she said, "Excuse us for a minute, won't you?" before dragging Julie into the hallway.

"Josh Lennox. That's your sperm donor!" Viv said in an emphatic whisper. Julie smiled and nodded. "Well, I can see why you chose him," Viv added. "He's beautiful. And tall. I would love my children to be tall. It's no picnic being five foot three." She stopped dreaming to focus back on Julie. "Does Olivia know that he's her daddy?"

"No," Julie whispered back just as emphatically. "When Josh donated his sperm, he agreed he would have no role in Olivia's life. She barely knows him."

"What does Josh think about that?"

Julie shrugged. "He's got no choice, if he wants to see her at all."

Viv stared at Julie. This was a side of her friend that she had never seen before. Viv doubted that she could be that hard on her baby's birth daddy if their positions were reversed.

"That's kind of rough, isn't it? How often does he get to see Olivia?"

Julie folded her arms over her chest and returned Viv's stare. "Not often. I don't want to encourage him." Apparently her relationship with Josh was not open for discussion.

But Viv didn't back down when her sympathies were engaged. "Aren't you tempting fate? If Josh and I started dating, he might bump into Olivia more often."

"Not necessarily. Besides, he's still a great guy. I thought you might like him."

"I don't know. I don't think I want to get in the middle of this. It's way too complicated."

Julie shrugged. "Look, no pressure, okay? He doesn't know why

I invited him today. But really, Viv, Josh would make you an ideal husband. He's low maintenance and a real cutie patootie, as you've no doubt noticed."

Viv hesitated. The way Julie put it, what did she have to lose?

"Okay, but don't expect any special effort from me. I'll try to get to know him, but that's all."

Julie squeezed her shoulder. "Thatta girl."

The two women returned to the kitchen, where Josh was still watching Olivia colour. Viv's heart went out to him. The poor guy, how could he bear to stay away from sweet, solemn Olivia?

"Hey, it's a beautiful day," Julie said in a perky voice. "Let's not waste it cooped up inside. How about we walk over to the park?"

"Fine with me," Josh said, glancing up.

"Olivia, do you want to play catch in the park?" Julie asked.

"Yes, Mommy."

"Okay, clean up your crayons."

Twenty minutes later, Viv was sitting on a blanket in the shade of a maple tree with Julie's camera dangling around her neck. Olivia beside her, while Julie and Josh tossed a rubber ball back and forth a short distance away.

Julie called, "Do you want to play catch, Olivia?"

The child nodded.

"Who do you want to throw the ball to you – Josh or Mommy?"

Olivia pointed at Josh.

"Okay, come here, sweetie."

Olivia went to stand beside Josh while Julie joined Viv on the blanket.

"Are you ready, Olivia?" Josh asked. She nodded and held up her hands. "Okay, here comes the ball." Olivia missed the ball and had to chase after it. When she threw it back to Josh, it arched into the air and landed several feet short.

"Throw a little harder, sweetie," Julie called.

Viv was busy snapping pictures. "You and Josh play in the same baseball league, don't you?" she asked. Olivia threw the ball again. This time it landed behind her.

Julie nodded. "We're on the same co-ed team. That's how we

met. He's the catcher, and I play third base."

"He's also a high school Phys. Ed. teacher, right?"

"Yeah."

Viv put the camera down. "So, he's a teacher, and he plays baseball. You two have a lot in common."

Julie grinned. "Right. We both like girls."

Viv shrugged. "Looks like he's pretty patient."

"Come on, Viv. I catch your drift, but what's the point of letting him hang around? Olivia doesn't need a daddy to have a happy childhood."

"They say it takes a village to raise a child," Viv murmured, but Julie ignored her.

Josh tossed the ball again, this time practically dropping it into Olivia's hand, and she caught it. A huge grin erupted on her face as Viv and Julie jumped to their feet to cheer.

"Yay, you did it!" Josh shouted. "Give me a high-five, Olivia." He held up his hand, which she slapped as hard as she could.

"Ow, you're so strong!" he complained, shaking his fingers. Olivia giggled and slapped his hand again. Josh reacted by whirling around and collapsing on the ground. Olivia shrieked with laughter and jumped on his chest.

Josh pretended that he couldn't get up. Throwing his arms into the air, he strained to sit up, but collapsed after every attempt. Olivia howled, and Viv snapped picture after picture. She glanced up at Julie, whose expression was wooden as she climbed to her feet and walked over to the pair.

"Come on, let's help poor Josh up," she said. Olivia clambered to her feet and offered Josh her hand. It disappeared in his as he jumped to his feet.

"Whew, I'm thirsty," he said.

"We could all use a drink," Julie said. "Let's go back to the house and start the burgers."

A half hour later, Viv was having a beer with Josh in Julie's postage stamp-sized backyard. Olivia was playing on her slide, while Julie barbecued the burgers and carried out the rest of the food. Viv had offered to help, but Julie had told her to relax.

"So, Josh, are you from Toronto?" Viv asked.

"Lived here all my life."

"Julie tells me you're a Phys. Ed. Teacher."

"At Riverdale Collegiate." He swilled some beer and stared off into space.

"That must keep you pretty active."

"Yeah."

"Do you find it difficult motivating kids to exercise, what with the internet and all?"

"Not so much. We've got a lot of sports for the kids to choose from."

Viv nodded, starting to run out of conversation. "Do you enjoy teaching?"

"Sure."

Julie came out of the house just then carrying paper plates and plastic cutlery. Viv said, "Josh has just been telling me how much he likes being a gym teacher." She rolled her eyes at Julie, signalling for help.

"But there's more to Josh than that," Julie said. "Tell Viv about *The King and I.*"

Josh turned to look at Viv for the first time. "I belong to a community theatre group called Toronto Theatrical Productions. We're all amateurs, but they hire professional actors for the bigger roles. This spring, we're doing *The King and I.* Musicals are more expensive to mount, but they bring in bigger audiences, so we always finish the season with one."

"Guess which part Josh is playing," Julie said.

"The king?"

"Nah, I'm not good enough to play him," Josh said.

"He's playing one of the other male leads, though," Julie said.

Josh nodded. "Lun Tha. He's in love with Tuptim, the king's new concubine."

"He gets to sing two duets with her," Julie said. "Josh has a great voice. I heard him sing at a karaoke bar after a game once." She flipped the burgers, and flames flared. The entrancing scent of barbecuing meat trailed across the air to Viv.

36

"I was in *Oklahoma* last year, but I just played one of the cowboys. This is the first time I've had more than a couple of lines to say. I'm pretty nervous," Josh said, rubbing his knee.

"Don't worry, you'll be terrific," Julie said.

He glanced at her with a grateful smile. "Hey, I can hook you and Viv up with tickets if you like. If you're interested," he added hopefully.

"Sure, I'd love to come," Julie said. "You like musicals, too, don't you, Viv?"

Viv looked from Julie's raised eyebrows to Josh's eager face. She hadn't been able to get two words out of him all afternoon, but he had come alive as soon as Julie had mentioned the play.

"I love musicals. *The King and I* is one of my favourites." Josh's face broke into a sunny smile, reminding Viv of her pupils when it was their turn for Super-Star Friday. "Can't wait," she added.

Chapter 7

Julie and Viv sat in the darkened theatre watching the play unfold before them. They were in a converted church that held an audience of two hundred. The set was decorated and lit to represent a garden at dusk, with a pool and flowers in the foreground and a short bridge in behind. The actress playing Tuptim darted out from the wings, looking frightened. A man emerged from the shadows to meet her.

"There's Josh again," Julie said, elbowing Viv. He had appeared fully dressed in an earlier scene when Tuptim was presented to the king. This time he wore only breeches with a sash tied round his waist.

"Wow," Viv whispered, her eyes widening. Josh's muscular upper body was impressive. His calves were shapely, too, not like the sinewy legs of some runners she knew. He wore make-up to darken his skin, and a black wig flowed over his shoulders. He looked exotic and sexy, a look that Viv appreciated.

Tuptim was breaking the news to Lun Tha that Mrs. Anna could not help them to meet anymore, and he looked crestfallen. The downcast couple sang "We Kiss in the Shadows," and Viv was pleasantly surprised by Josh's voice. It was light and flexible on top and rich at the bottom. When the duet finished, Viv clapped enthusiastically with the rest of the audience.

The couple appeared again when Lun Tha told Tuptim of his plan for them to run away together. They sang "I Have Dreamed" clasped in each other's arms, making Viv wonder what it would feel like to be pressed against Josh's chest. Pretty fine, she imagined, with a little thrill she hadn't felt for a long time. Not since she and Kyle had begun dating, in fact. Thoughts of Kyle brought back the familiar pain, but soon she got caught up in the story again and forgot all about him.

When the show ended and Josh stepped forward for his bow, Julie sprang to her feet and whistled. Josh seemed to hear her and grinned, somehow looking both boyish and sexy. Viv felt another flutter and leapt to her feet, applauding just as loudly as Julie.

After the show, Julie and Viv waited in the auditorium to meet Josh for a celebratory drink while the rest of the audience filed out. The stage crew were cleaning up the set when Josh bounded down the spiral staircase connecting the upper level to the auditorium and loped over to greet them. His hair was wet and the make-up was gone, but the glamour still clung to him, or so Viv thought.

"You were great," Julie said, sweeping him into a hug.

"Thanks," he said, his eyes closing, and then Julie was out of his arms and pushing Viv toward him. They hesitated, and Josh hugged her. With her face pressed against his shirt, Viv could feel the muscle beneath the fabric and smell the clean, soapy scent of his skin.

"The show was terrific. You were really impressive," she mumbled into his chest.

"Yeah?" Josh pulled back to gaze into her face.

"I almost cried when you sang 'I Have Dreamed.'" She stared back at him, mesmerized by his eyes.

"Are you hungry?"

Viv nodded.

"Great. They ordered pizza between the shows, but I didn't get enough. There's a pub two blocks from here that makes great fish and chips, if that sounds good?" He turned to include Julie in his invitation.

"Lead the way," Julie said, smiling at Josh and Viv.

The threesome spent the next hour chatting about the show and Josh's cast mates before the conversation turned to family life. Josh came from a family of six with two older brothers and a sister four years younger. After three sons, his mother had almost given up on having a daughter, but Josh's father had persuaded her to try once more, and the couple had finally succeeded.

"I bet your mom was thrilled to have a girl after all you boys," Julie said. She dipped a french fry into her puddle of ketchup and took a bite.

"Yeah. I had to bunk in with my brothers after Mary was born so that she could have her own room. I still remember my mom painting my old bedroom walls pink with little white clouds and a rainbow. She even bought Mary a princess bed when she was big enough to move out of her crib. Mom and Mary are still really close – they quilt and scrapbook together." Josh speared his last bite of fish into his mouth and chewed.

"It must have been hard on you when your sister was born," Viv said. "You weren't the baby anymore. Suddenly, your sister was getting all the attention."

"It was hard," Josh said with a nod. "My brothers didn't like having me around much. There was five years between us, and both of them were jocks. I couldn't keep up with them, at first, and I was a real pain, always trying to compete." He smiled ruefully. "But later, when I was in high school, I grew, like, five inches one summer. It got to the point where my brothers couldn't keep up with me. Now they're married and have children. They keep asking when I'm going to get married." He looked at Viv. "Do your parents do that to you?"

Viv shook her head. "My mom and dad are separated. She lives in New York, so I don't see much of her. My dad used to ask me about getting married and having a baby, but my boyfriend and I broke up just a few months ago, so that's not going to happen anytime soon."

"Sorry to hear that," Josh said.

"Yeah, Viv's boyfriend was a real jerk. He broke it off after they'd lived together for six years," Julie said.

"That's rough," Josh said with a frown. "I'd never live with someone that long without getting married. After a couple of years, you'd know if you were compatible or not, so why wait? Either it works, or it doesn't." He glanced at Viv. "Sorry. I didn't mean to say that your way of doing things is wrong. That's just the way I see it."

Viv nodded while drawing patterns on the dewy table top where her iced soft drink had sat. "No, you're right. I shouldn't have let it go on so long without getting a commitment from Kyle." She glanced at Julie, who made a show of checking her watch.

"Gee, look at the time," Julie said. "It's almost midnight. I've got to get home before the babysitter starts charging double. Josh, can I ask you a favour? Viv lives fairly close to you. Would you mind giving her a lift home?"

"Sure, no problem."

"That's all right with you, isn't it, Viv?"

Viv wondered if Julie had planned to ask Josh to drive her home all along, but she didn't mind. Julie was right; Josh was a nice guy, and she liked the idea of spending some time alone with him. "If you're sure I'm not putting you out? I can always take the streetcar home," Viv said.

"Nah, I'd be happy to give you a lift."

"That's great," Julie said, taking some cash out of her wallet and handing it to Viv. "That should cover my part." She kissed Viv's cheek and gave Josh a quick hug.

"You were great tonight. I'll see you at the ball game next Wednesday. Bye." A moment later she was gone, and Viv and Josh were alone.

"Do you want anything else?" he asked.

"No, I'm good."

It was drizzling, and they jogged the three blocks to the public lot where Josh had left his car. He unlocked the vehicle and waited for Viv to slide in before closing her door and running around to the other side. Viv was shivering when he climbed in next to her. Now that her clothes were damp, she was chilly.

"You cold? I've got a jacket in the back seat, if you want it," Josh said, reaching behind her.

"You sure you don't want it? Your shirt is damp." *And sticking to your chest*, she thought, trying not to stare.

"No, I'm fine." He drew the jacket over her shoulders.

You sure are. "Thanks," she said, snuggling into it. She could smell the light, spicy scent of his aftershave.

Josh was a good driver, taking his time and leaving plenty of room for the drivers who cut in front of them as the rain pattered down. The air smelt fresh and clean, and the wet pavement reflected the reds and greens of the traffic lights.

"So, you've only got one performance left," Viv said.

"Yeah."

"You going to miss the show when it's over?"

"I always do, although it takes a few days to come down from the performance high. Mostly I miss the camaraderie of the rest of the company. We get together for a barbecue during the summer, but I won't really see them again until the fall."

"Why don't you invite some of them over?"

Josh shook his head. "I'm not the outgoing type. I would feel kind of weird doing that." Viv didn't realize just how shy Josh was until that moment, and wondered if he were lonely. It seemed bizarre that such a nice, good-looking guy could be so insecure.

"Did you ever think of acting professionally?" she asked after a pause.

He nodded. "I took a theatre class in high school, but my brothers razzed me about it all the time, so I didn't take another. Not that I thought I was good enough to become a professional actor or anything, but I knew that I wasn't going to be happy with a desk job when I got out of school. That's why I went to teacher's college and became a Phys. Ed. teacher."

"I'm sure you're a good teacher, but it's too bad about not pursuing theatre. You seem to love it, and I think you're talented."

"Thanks," he said, looking at her. "That means a lot."

He pulled up to the curb beside her building and said, "Say, would you like to come to our game next Wednesday? Julie will be there, of course, and we go out for food afterward. It's usually fun, if you're not busy."

"I'd like that," Viv said, looking back at him across the darkened interior.

"Great."

They were silent as the wipers chased the rain drops across the window.

"Oh," she said, recollecting the jacket, "you'll want this back." She wiggled out of it and handed it to him.

"Thanks." Their hands brushed as he took it from her, and Viv felt a little thrill. Knowing that Josh wouldn't make the first move, Viv leaned over and kissed his cheek. His skin was warm and a bit bristly. Viv liked the masculine feel of it.

"Night," she said, taking hold of the door handle and letting herself out. She scurried across the wet sidewalk and into the lobby, pausing to glance over her shoulder. Josh was waiting for her to get safely inside. He tapped the horn softly and pulled away.

And he's a gentleman, too, she thought, heading for the elevators.

Chapter 8

The next morning, Julie and Viv were on recess patrol. A group of young boys chased a soccer ball past them as the two friends strolled across the yard. It was their first opportunity to chat since the night before.

"So, did you have fun last night?" Julie asked.

"Yes, I really enjoyed the show. It was better than I thought it would be."

"I meant with Josh. What happened after I left?"

"Miss Nowak," a little girl said, trotting up to them, "Aidan Brooks stole my doll, and he won't give it back." She pointed across the yard at the doll thief. "No!" she screamed, her face contorting with tears. Viv looked to where the child was pointing and saw Aidan smashing the doll into the side of the building.

"Aidan, stop that," Viv shouted, running across the pavement to him. He looked up and froze, the doll suspended from his hand in mid-whack. Fortunately no damage had been done – yet.

"Why are you trying to break Mia's doll?" Viv asked in a calmer voice. She knew these two; they had been in her class last year and had bickered all the time. Aiden stared at her with sullen eyes. She could hear Mia's wails, and looked over her shoulder to see Julie comforting the little girl.

"Mia laughed when Connor got the soccer ball away from me. I fell and hurt my knee, and she laughed at me," Aiden muttered. Viv squatted to check for injuries. The knees of his jeans were torn, but there were no bloodstains.

"Does your knee still hurt? Do you want to go inside and put some ice on it?" she asked.

"No."

Viv rose and put her hand on his shoulder. "It wasn't kind of Mia to laugh at you, but you shouldn't hurt her doll. It doesn't make your knee feel any better. Come on, let's take the doll back." She held his hand, and they walked side by side to Julie and Mia.

The girl had stopped crying and was wiping her nose with the tissue Julie had provided. Viv prodded Aiden's shoulder, and he held the doll out to Mia.

"Sorry."

Mia snatched it back and clutched the doll to her chest.

"I think you owe Aiden an apology, too," Viv said.

Mia stared at the ground. "Sorry I laughed at you," she murmured. Aiden shrugged.

"Good," Viv said. "Now, you two go play until the bell rings." Aiden nodded and ran to join the soccer game while Mia trotted to the jungle gym.

"Another crisis averted," Julie said.

"So, what were we talking about?"

"Did you and Josh play nice after I left?" Julie asked with a grin.

"We got along fine. He's sweet, if a little shy. He did invite me to watch you two play ball on Wednesday, though."

"What did you say?"

"I said yes."

"Great. I was going to ask you anyway."

"Only, I'm taking it slow, Julie. I'm pretty rusty at dating, and I'm not sure if he's my type. I'm not even sure what my type is anymore."

"That's fine." But as Viv turned away to resume patrolling, Julie chanted, "Josh and Vivvie sitting in a tree K-I-S-S-I-N-G," under her breath.

"Oh, act your age," Viv said, rolling her eyes.

Fortunately, the spell of rain enveloping the city cleared, and the day of the baseball game dawned dry and balmy. Viv sat in the bleachers watching the competition along with a few other supporters belonging to the two teams.

It was a close game, and by the bottom of the ninth, the other team was up and trailing by only a run. There was one out, and one man on second base. The batter had two strikes against her when she suddenly bunted. The pitcher lunged for the ball and fired it to first. The first baseman caught it, and the batter was out. Without missing a beat, the first baseman hurled the ball to Julie on third, but it went wild, and she had to charge after it. The player who had been on second careened past third and was headed for home when Julie snapped up the ball, pivoted, and drove it to Josh at home plate. Josh caught it with a flick of his glove, and the runner was trapped, His only hope was that Julie or Josh would drop the ball as he ran between them. He was as agile as a jackrabbit, but it was no use; they squeezed him closer and closer until Julie tagged him out.

Viv jumped to her feet, screaming and cheering with the rest of the supporters. Josh and Julie high-fived, and then the players congregated on the infield to shake hands. Julie and Josh's team was in a celebratory mood when Viv joined them for beer and pizza afterward.

There were a dozen of them squeezed around the two tables the waitress had pushed together. Julie sat beside Kim, one of her teammates, with Josh on the other side. Viv sat next to him. The waitress brought pitchers of beer while the team rehashed the game inning by inning. Josh poured some beer for Viv while she laughed at the ribbing Julie was getting for being called "Princess" by the other team's pitcher.

"That's because she's special," Kim said, hugging Julie. Kim was a pretty, fresh-faced blond a few years younger than Julie.

"I'm glad that someone appreciates me," Julie said, laying her head on the young woman's shoulder. "Wow, your hair smells good," she added.

"You're probably smelling my lemon and sage shampoo," Kim replied.

"Nice." Their eyes met, and they smiled.

Josh picked up one of Julie's short curls and rolled it between his fingers.

"Your hair smells good, too," he said. "What kind of shampoo did you say you use?"

"Um, whatever's on sale."

"Your hair's so soft and shiny. Is that your real colour?"

"Well, yeah," Julie said, nodding her head and jerking her hair from his grasp. She rubbed her sore scalp and deliberately turned her back on Josh. Kim whispered something in Julie's ear, and she laughed and shoved Kim playfully.

The waitress brought two pedestalled trays loaded with pizza, and everyone started grabbing for a slice. Viv was waiting for her turn when Josh handed her a plate with a large wedge.

"Bacon, olive, and mushroom, right?"

"Right. Thanks Josh."

"No problem."

Viv was taking a bite when Kim said, "So, you and Julie teach at the same school?"

Viv chewed and swallowed. "That's right. We met four years ago when I was subbing at Withrow. Julie put in a good word for me when the school board was hiring permanent staff, and I got the job."

Kim smiled at Julie. "That was nice of you."

"I'm a terrific person. Haven't you noticed?"

Kim laughed and turned back to Viv. "But you don't play baseball?"

It was Julie's turn to laugh. "Viv isn't what you'd call 'athletic.'"

"Not true. I'm just not into team sports."

"Unlike me," Julie said. "My parents put me into every sports camp there was: baseball, soccer, and swimming. Not to mention the ballet lessons."

"Whatever you're doing, it's working," Josh said with a leer. Julie scowled at him while Viv did a double take. What was going on with him?

"I'm going to the bathroom," Viv said. She sprang to her feet. "Julie, why don't you come with me?"

"Be right back," Julie said to Kim.

"Don't be long," the pretty young woman said.

Julie rose, and Josh slapped her on the bottom. The rest of the table were laughing so hard that they missed it, but Viv noticed. She watched Julie glare at Josh.

"I'll miss you, beautiful," he said with a grin, but the smile dissolved when he saw the expression on her face. Viv was afraid that Julie would slap him, and lunged to take her friend's arm.

"*Now*, Julie," Viv said, dragging her off to the bathroom.

There were two women waiting by the stalls, so Viv pulled Julie to the sinks.

"Did you see what that jerk just did to me?" Julie whispered.

"What's wrong with him?" Viv asked. "One moment he's polite and attentive, the next he's acting like a Neanderthal. What's going on?"

Julie frowned. "Josh has been acting kind of weird over the last few games. I think it's because of Kim. We've been getting to know each other better, and it seems to bother him. I think he may be jealous."

"Jealous? I thought he was just your sperm donor?"

"He is. He knows that I would never be attracted to him."

"It doesn't make sense. Wait a minute," Viv said, grabbing Julie's arm, "is that why you introduced him to me? Were you using me as bait to distract Josh so that you could start dating Kim?"

Julie had the good grace to look away. "Look, Viv, Josh is a really sweet guy, when he's not acting like an idiot." Viv sighed and crossed her arms over her chest. "No, he really is!" Julie protested. "He's kind, reliable, handsome, he's got a good job, and he really likes kids. You two are perfect for each other. It's not like I'm asking you to take one for the team here."

Viv frowned. "But he's not interested in me. Obviously, he likes you."

"Well, nothing's going to happen between us."

Viv sighed.

"Please? You don't know how hard it is for a single mom to find a girlfriend. Just give Josh time. I'm sure he'll come to his senses once he gets to know you better."

"But what am I supposed to do with him tonight?"

Julie put an arm around Viv's shoulder. "Tell him you've got a headache and ask him to drive you home. Talk to him about his behaviour, and make sure he understands that I'm off limits. Be sympathetic and flutter those baby blues of yours. Once he realizes I'm never going to fall for him, I'm sure he'll be all over you just like that." She snapped her fingers before pushing Viv through the bathroom door.

"What if I'm not interested in him?" Viv grumbled, but Julie ignored her as she led the way to their table.

Josh jumped to his feet when he saw them. "I was beginning to wonder if something was wrong," he said.

"Viv isn't feeling well," Julie said, resuming her seat.

Josh looked at Viv. "What's the matter?"

"I've got a headache. Do you think you could drive me home?"

"Sure. No problem. When do you want to go?"

"Now, if you don't mind." Viv retrieved her purse from the floor and reached inside for her wallet.

But Josh waved her money away. "I'll take care of this." He slid some bills from his pocket and dropped them onto the table.

Nodding to the rest of the group, Viv said, "Good night, everyone. It's been fun."

"Feel better soon," Julie said as her friends bid Viv goodnight. "Give me a call later and let me know how you're feeling," she added pointedly.

"I will."

Josh escorted Viv from the restaurant. They walked to the car in silence, the daylight ebbing from the sky and a warm breeze ruffling their hair. Viv climbed into the passenger seat and waited for Josh to settle behind the wheel.

"Can we go somewhere private to talk?" she asked. "I'd invite you to my place, but my roommate might be home."

"Sure." His expression was wary. "We can go to my place, if you like. What's it about?"

"Let's just wait until we get there, okay?"

Josh lived ten blocks from Viv in a neighbourhood of bungalows and duplexes. He shoehorned his car into a spot on the street, and they walked past the well-tended front gardens to his home, a grey bungalow with white trim.

Josh unlocked the door and stood aside to allow Viv to enter first. The front room was a living room/dining room combination with a narrow hallway leading into the kitchen. Josh slipped past Viv to turn on the lamps on either side of the couch.

"Can I get you something to drink?" he asked.

"I wouldn't mind a soft drink."

"Cola okay?"

"Yes, please."

Viv had a look around while Josh disappeared into the kitchen. He had done a nice job of making the place look homey. The chocolate-brown couch sat on an area carpet on a honey-stained hardwood floor. A worn leather chair with an ottoman was angled next to the couch, and a bookcase stuffed with books and family photographs delineated the dining area.

Josh returned carrying two full glasses tinkling with ice. He set Viv's on the coffee table and sat down on the other end of the couch.

"I can guess what you want to talk about," he said.

"Your behaviour was kind of odd tonight. You acted as if you were Julie's boyfriend – a really insensitive boyfriend – so Julie asked me to talk to you. Did it bother you when Kim and Julie were flirting?"

When Josh didn't respond, Viv asked, "Are you in love with Julie?"

His face was incredulous. "What? No, that would be ridiculous."

"You know she's gay, right?"

"Of course. It's pretty hard to miss."

"She isn't bisexual, Josh. You don't stand a chance with her."

"I know."

Viv shook her head in exasperation. "Then what were you doing? You were lucky she didn't kill you when you slapped her bottom."

Josh's face reddened. "I didn't mean to offend her. I guess I was feeling a bit desperate."

"What do you mean?" Viv slid across the couch to sit closer to him.

"It's hard for me to explain. I knew that Julie was only looking for a sperm donor when she asked for my help. We discussed it a lot, and she made it clear that she didn't want me to be a father to her baby. I thought it was a good idea at the time, having someone who was part of me to live on after I was gone. I just didn't realize how hard it would be after Olivia was born." He paused, and Viv waited for him to continue.

"The first time I saw her was through the glass window at the maternity ward. I snuck in – Julie didn't want me at the hospital. When I spotted Olivia, she was waving a tiny hand in front of her face. She seemed to be watching it with these big eyes. I – I don't know. I just . . ." His voice faltered to a stop.

Julie laid her hand on his arm. "You fell in love with her?"

Josh nodded. "She's part of me. Hell, she looks just look my mom. Julie didn't invite me to see her until the first Christmas, when Olivia was five months old. Julie let me hold her, and Olivia held onto my finger and blew bubbles. I didn't know I would feel this way," he said, tension in his voice.

"How often have you seen Olivia?"

"Just three times. The first Christmas, last Christmas, and at the barbecue."

"That's it?"

Josh nodded. "Sometimes I drive by the house before I go to bed at night just to make sure they're okay." He sighed. "I don't blame Julie. She's just sticking to her side of the bargain. But when I see her with Kim, it's like one more person's getting between Olivia and me. If Julie lets someone into her life permanently, she's never going to need any help from me. Maybe she won't let me see Olivia anymore. I thought that if I acted like Julie and I were involved, Kim might back off." He finally looked at Viv. "Please tell Julie I'm sorry. I know I have no right to interfere with her love life."

"Look Josh, I know how hard it is to love someone who doesn't love you back. And I know it's not the same as being Olivia's father, but you could have a wonderful family of your own. A caring man like you would make a great husband and daddy."

"That's not going to happen."

"Why not?" Josh stared at the carpet. "Are you gay?"

"No."

"Then what's the problem?"

"I'm not interested in men or women."

Viv hesitated. "I don't understand."

He glanced at her sideways. "I'm asexual."

"Oh." She struggled to think of something helpful to say. "Have you ever . . ?"

"Tried? Yes. A couple of times with women. Nothing happened. I tried to have a sexual relationship with a man once, but I couldn't get into that, either. I don't know why. I just don't get aroused."

"Have you seen a doctor about it?"

"Yeah. He tested my hormone levels. Said that there was nothing wrong with me, that it had to be psychological."

"What about counselling?"

Josh shook his head. "How's counselling going to change me, Viv? Has it ever made a gay man straight, or a straight man gay? I've been reading about this on the web, and there are people like me who just don't care about having sex with others. It doesn't mean that there's anything wrong with us."

"No, of course not," Viv hastened to say.

"Look, I haven't talked to anyone about this besides my doctor. Not to my family, not to Julie. I told you because I wanted to explain why I acted so dumb tonight, and because I wanted you to understand why I'm not going to be your boyfriend."

Viv nodded.

"But I'm okay with the way I am. I don't feel incomplete or anything. I'm even a bit of a romantic." He smiled weakly. "That's why the situation with Olivia is so painful. She's likely to be the only child I'll ever have who's a part of me."

He got up to pace around the room while Viv watched.

"Josh, I don't know what to say, other than I'm sorry that Julie won't let you get closer to Olivia."

He paused to look down at her. "I know there's nothing you can do. And please don't say anything about this to Julie. She'll only think I'm trying to pull a fast one. Just tell her I'll stop acting like an idiot around her and Kim."

"I won't say anything about you being asexual," Viv said, rising. They stood face-to-face in front of the couch.

"Thanks. You know, it's been kind of therapeutic talking to you. You've been awfully sympathetic. I hope that we can stay friends."

"Sure. I'd love to see you in your next show, for one thing."

"I'd like that, too." He glanced at his watch. "It's getting late. Let me give you a lift home."

"That's kind of you. Thanks."

On the drive home, Viv considered Josh's situation. It wasn't fair that Julie kept him at an arm's length, but Viv understood why. Julie came from a big, boisterous, Italian/Irish family that was really close. But although her mother and father loved her, they were very conservative, and got upset when Julie broke the news that she was gay. Their relationship deteriorated even more when both parents objected to her plan to give birth by artificial insemination. Angry that her parents didn't approve of her, Julie cut them out of her life.

Even Viv and Sabrina, who had been supportive throughout the pregnancy and Olivia's birth, had to be careful not to say anything that could be interpreted as judgemental. Not that they would, because Julie was a great mom, but she was stubborn and sometimes carried a grudge. It was good that Julie was finally ready to share her life with someone; just not for Josh, if it meant that he would be cut out of Olivia's life.

After Josh dropped her at the lobby door, Viv sighed. What was she going to say to Julie? She couldn't tell the truth about Josh's behaviour, or the real reason she wasn't going to date him. That wasn't her secret to share.

It was too bad, though. Josh had looked so good on paper. Julie had shared his score, a healthy 44 out of 50 on the dating do-over scale.

Well, Sabrina was going to have to come up with someone better. Viv had given it a lot of thought, and realized that she was either attracted to a man who needed mothering, or to someone who swept her off her feet and dominated her. Which wasn't a huge problem unless the guy was taking advantage of her, as Kyle had.

Come on, Sabrina, it's up to you! Viv thought as she reached the condominium door and steeled herself to phone Julie.

Chapter 9

Even though Viv had made a resolution at Easter to visit her father more often, she had only seen him once since then. Deciding to surprise him after school the following week, she dropped by the two-storey he was renovating.

It was the first week of June, hot and sticky. Warm air blew through the streetcar on the ride over. Getting off at her stop, Viv peeled her blouse away from her skin before checking the address Magda had provided. The house was only a block away. It turned out to be a Victorian semi with a pick-up truck parked out front on the lawn. A man was perched on the tailgate, flipping through a pile of papers attached to a clipboard. He was middle-aged and brawny; clean shaven, but with shoulder-length dark hair pulled back into a pony-tail. He tossed the clip board into the truck, stood up, and was about to go into the house when Viv called to him from the sidewalk.

"Hi! I'm looking for Gabe Nowak. Is this the right place?" He turned in the sunlight to squint at her.

"Yeah," he said in a rich baritone. "You've got the right place. Come on in." He quickly disappeared inside the front door, and Viv scrambled after him. It was dark inside the house after the brilliance of outdoors. A drill whined close by. As she waited for her eyes to adjust, Viv heard the same deep voice drawl, "Gabe, someone's looking for you."

The drill ceased and her father said, "Who?"

Viv strode through the house, following the voices to a kitchen at the back. Her father was holding a drill in one hand and a white cabinet door in the other. His face was shiny with sweat and there was sawdust in his hair.

"Viv! Nice surprise. Did you come to check up on your old man?" he hollered, handing the drill and the cupboard door to the other man. Her father was 5'11", but the dark-haired man had him by a couple of inches. She clattered across the floor and reached out to hug Gabe, but he pulled back.

"Better not. I'm a mess. Did you just come from school?"

"Uh huh. I thought I'd see how the house was doing. Looks like it's going to be wonderful."

"Thanks. All three floors are drywalled and the hardwood's refinished. Tom and I are installing the cupboards today." He nodded at the other man, who was using a level. "Tom, this is my daughter, Viv." Tom drew a pencil line on the wall before setting the level on the floor.

"Nice to meet you, Viv," he said, assessing her with his pale blue eyes. "You're a lot better-looking than Gabe."

"Course she is. All she got from me was my blond hair," her father said, running his hand over his receding hairline. "Come on, Peaches. I'll give you the tour. He turned to Tom. "Take a break, why don't you? We've been going at it pretty hard since lunch."

Tom wiped his face with the hem of his t-shirt. "You go ahead. The lower cabinets are almost done. I want to get going on the uppers."

"Well, don't kill yourself. I know the guys are coming with the counter top tomorrow, but we'll get 'er done."

Viv and Gabe strolled through the first floor, her dad pointing out where they had knocked down the wall separating the dining room and kitchen, and the newly-tiled living room fireplace. When they reached the front hallway, Gabe smacked the staircase bannister leading up to the second floor. The wood was painted a muddy brown, and it looked like someone had put a foot through two of the carved balusters.

"Tom's going to strip and restore it. It should be a real selling-feature when it's done."

Viv ran her hand over the wood. "So, how old is Tom?"

"Eh?" Gabe paused to peer at her. "He's fifty. But don't worry. Tom works harder than a lot of guys half his age."

Fifty? Too bad. Viv found him very attractive, but Tom was old enough to be her father. She'd never date a guy that mature.

"Can we check out the second floor now?" she asked.

"Sure." Viv trotted ahead with her father following more slowly. Once upstairs, Gabe explained how they had stripped the house back to its studs to rewire and replumb, as well as to insulate to modern, energy-saving standards.

"There were four bedrooms, but only one bathroom, and the closets were puny. We lost one of the bedrooms to add a walk-in closet and an ensuite to the master. Here it is," he said, showing her into the bedroom.

It was spacious, large enough to accommodate a king-sized bed with room for a night table on either side. Viv walked to the window and saw that it overlooked the back garden. A handsome horse chestnut tree was in bloom with clusters of white flowers. She turned back, noticing the refinished floor and baseboards.

"I see that you managed to save the original wood trim."

"Yeah. I think we're going to leave it as is instead of painting over it. Come on, I can't wait for you see the ensuite. There's a nice surprise in there."

Viv walked through the closet and into the bathroom, where she saw a grand old claw-foot tub resting on the sub-floor.

"Oh, Daddy, it's beautiful. When can I move in?"

Gabe snorted and sat down on the edge of the tub. He pulled a handkerchief from his pocket and wiped his face.

"When you can come up with a million, five."

"Will you take a cheque?" Her father grunted, and Viv's smile disappeared as she observed his flushed face. "Are you feeling okay? Your colour doesn't look good. It's awfully hot in here. Have you been overdoing it?"

"Nah, I'm fine. I'm just not getting any younger. Listen, I'm glad you stopped by. There's something I've been meaning to call you about."

"What's that?" Viv was careful to lean against a patch of wall that wasn't gritty with drywall dust.

"Your mother's planning a business trip to Toronto, and she asked me to give her your e-mail. She wants to see you."

Viv's mouth opened, but nothing came out. "You're kidding," she finally said. "She hasn't contacted me for six years, and, all of a sudden, she wants my e-mail?"

Gabe shrugged.

"You didn't tell me that you've been in touch with her."

"She contacted me a year ago to congratulate me on my early retirement. She asked about you, so I told her what was going on in your life. We haven't been e-mailing regularly – just every few months or so."

"Why didn't you tell me you were talking with her?"

"I know your mother isn't your favourite person."

"I didn't think she was yours, either."

Gabe sighed. "That's a lot of water under the bridge, Peaches. You gain some perspective with age. I'm not angry with your mother anymore."

"Well, I am." Viv straightened and left the bathroom, talking to her father over her shoulder. "And I don't want to see her. I've got enough on my plate right now without having to deal with her." She stomped through the bedroom and into the hallway with her father on her heels.

"You're a grown woman. You haven't talked with your mother since that big blow-up at your graduation. You're going to have to deal with her sooner or later."

"No, I don't." Viv hurried down the staircase and passed through the first floor to the kitchen, where she had left her purse. She stopped; Tom was leaning against the wall with a can of pop in his hand. She had forgotten about him. He eyed her curiously, and she frowned and turned as her father caught up with her.

"What are you going to do, ignore your mother for the rest of your life?" he asked angrily. Viv closed the distance between them in two quick steps.

"Why not? We didn't leave her – she left us. Why should I see her when she hasn't bothered to see me more than twice in twenty-one years?"

Gabe put his hand over his face and said nothing. Viv glared at him, waiting for his answer. After a moment, she noticed that he was breathing too quickly.

"Daddy, are you feeling all right?"

The men were using a white plastic pail in the corner of the room for garbage. Gabe staggered over to it and retched. Tom put down his can as Viv rushed over to her father. He straightened up with his hands braced upon his knees.

"I'm really dizzy all of a sudden," Gabe mumbled before sitting down abruptly on the floor.

Daddy!" Viv knelt beside him. He started to sag, and she caught him by the shoulders and lowered him to the floor. Gabe's skin felt hot and dry. Tom knelt beside them and placed two fingers at the base of the older man's throat.

"Your pulse feels fast," Tom said. "Are you in pain?"

"My stomach hurt before I puked. I've got a lousy headache."

Tom looked at Viv. "Sounds like heatstroke."

"Should we call an ambulance?"

"Nah, just let me lie here till my head settles," Gabe said.

Viv glanced at Tom, who shrugged. He fetched a folded drop cloth and slid it under Gabe's head while Viv dampened a cloth with water from a jug and cleaned his face.

"That feels good."

"You shouldn't be working so hard in this heat."

"Do you think you could drink some pop?" Tom asked. "I'll get you one from the cooler."

"In a minute. After the nausea passes."

Tom fetched a cold can of ginger ale for Viv, and set another one on the floor beside Gabe.

"It's there when you want it."

They rested for a quarter of an hour until Gabe had recovered enough to sit up and sip his soft drink.

"Feeling any better, old man?" Tom asked.

"Don't 'old man' me. I'm only eleven years older than you," Gabe growled.

"Well, young man, are you going to be able to haul your ass up off the floor, or am I going to have to carry you to the truck?"

"What?"

"I'm taking you home. You're done for the day."

"Wait a minute. What about the cabinets?"

"I'll finish them when I get back. Next time it's so hot, we'll hire a crew to do it." He took Gabe's arm. "Come on, time to get up."

Viv took her father's other arm and they pulled him to his feet, where he hovered unsteadily.

"You're not going to be sick again, are you?" Viv asked.

"I don't think so."

Viv glanced at Tom. "I'll drive Daddy home in his car if you can help me get him into it," she said.

Tom looked her up and down. "How do you think you're going to get him out of the car once you get him home? You're – what – five foot three?"

Viv's eyes widened in surprise. "That's exactly right. How did you know?"

"I used to have a wife your size. Sorry, darling, but you're kind of small to handle a man the size of your father."

Viv bristled. She had looked after her dad since she was a little girl, and she could look after him now. "Magda can help me with him, if I need her."

But Gabe put an arm around her shoulders and said, "Better let Tom take me home, Peaches." He reached into his pocket and pulled out a key ring. "If you'll drive my car, Tom can take me in his truck."

"Just give me a minute to clear out the passenger seat," Tom said. He hurried out of the kitchen while Viv fumed beside her father.

"Sorry about this," Gabe said. "I guess I'm a little out of shape."

Viv's face softened. "Not a problem, Daddy. But tell me, when was the last time you had a complete physical?"

Gabe thought for a moment. "Not that long ago. A couple of years, I think."

"I worry about you, you know. Promise me you'll go see your

doctor and get checked out. Blood work, EKG – the works. If you're going to start doing manual labour at sixty, I want to make sure you're up for it."

Gabe snorted. "You're not even living with me anymore, and you're still bossing me around."

"Someone's got to do it. Magda gives in to you too often."

"Look, I promise I'll make an appointment tomorrow. Just get me home for today."

"Good. Let me know what the doctor says."

Tom's work boots echoed through the house.

"Viv, what about your mother?" Gabe asked. "Can I give her your e-mail address?"

She gazed at him with unconcealed exasperation, but with her father looking so exhausted, she caved. She didn't want to upset him when he wasn't feeling well.

"All right. Go ahead and give her my e-mail address, if it means so much to you. But tell her that I'm not keen on seeing her again."

"Good girl," her father said as Tom returned to the kitchen.

Tom jerked his thumb toward the front door. "Let's get moving. I've got a lot of work to get done today.

Chapter 10

It took Viv almost two hours to drive her father's car to his house and make her way home again on the streetcar. When she walked into the condo's blessed air conditioning, she was hot and tired. Sabrina was sitting at the kitchen island eating curried chicken salad and drinking an iced tea. Viv plunked down on the stool beside her and kicked off her pumps from her aching feet.

Sabrina turned to look at her. "Tough day?"

"Yes. I went to see daddy at the new house, and he got heat stroke. I just finished helping to take him home."

"Is he okay?"

"I think so. Magda's there to look after him. I'm making him go to the doctor for a complete physical, though."

Sabrina nodded and ate her last forkful of food. "Good idea. There's some more chicken salad in the fridge if you want some."

"Thanks. Maybe later."

"Maybe you should eat now. Rick's coming over in half an hour." Rick Wilson was the new man in Sabrina's life; they had been dating for three weeks.

"Okay. I'll take a shower and make myself scarce. Are the two of you staying in tonight?"

"No." Sabrina climbed down from her stool and picked up her dirty dishes. "And he's not coming alone. He's bringing a friend for you. We're making it a foursome."

"What?" Sabrina walked into the kitchen and opened the dishwasher. "I thought we were done with blind dates after Julie tried to fix me up with Josh."

"No, we agreed that Julie wasn't going to set you up with any more blind dates. You and I are just getting started." She placed her dishes in the machine and looked at Viv, who was staring at her in dismay. "Rick got tickets for the opening of the 'Five Ages of Man' art show you wanted to see at the Freedom Gallery. So, even if you don't like the guy Rick's bringing, you'll still get to see the show."

"That's true," Viv said, perking up a little. "Gwendolyn Seer is one of my favourite photographers. I've really been looking forward to this."

"And I think you're going to like Rick's friend. I haven't met him yet, but Rick's told me all about him and shown me pictures. I've checked him out on the internet, too. He scores 40 out of 50 on the dating do-over scale. He scored a bit low on attractiveness – he's short and pudgy – but a 10 for earning potential."

Viv shrugged. "Short and pudgy sounds cuddly to me. What's his name?"

"Drew Collins."

"Good name."

"Get going, then." Sabrina checked her watch. "The guys are supposed to be here in twenty-seven minutes."

Forty minutes later, Viv was just putting on her earrings in front of the bathroom mirror when the telephone rang. She heard Sabrina answer it, and her friend's heels click across the floor as she went to the door. Their guests arrived a minute later. Viv applied a quick swish of lipstick, took a last look in the mirror, and scurried out of the bathroom, right into the foyer where Sabrina was kissing Rick.

"Hi, Viv. You look gorgeous," he said. Sabrina turned to see what Viv was wearing, and smiled approvingly. Since they were going to a gallery opening, Viv had dressed up in a sleeveless, cream-and-gold dress with inset shoulders and an above-the-knee hemline. Elegant, but alluring. Rick, who was tall and dark with a shaved head and a gold earring, looked fabulous in anything. Today he had opted for a white shirt and slim, tan dress slacks.

"Viv, Sabrina, this is my friend, Drew Collins."

"Pleased to meet you, ladies," Drew said, stepping in from the hallway. The first thing Viv noticed about him was his perfect, gleaming white teeth. The second was his build. Sabrina had been right; his stomach swelled visibly above his belt, and he stood only an inch taller than Viv in her heels. Still, with a full head of curly black hair and dark stubble on his face, he was definitely the teddy-bear type. She liked his firm handshake and noticed that his nails were manicured. Definitely someone who cared about personal hygiene, which was a point in his favour.

"Pleased to meet you, Drew," she said. "Have you and Rick known each other long?"

"Not long." Drew glanced at Rick. "About six months, isn't it?" Rick nodded. "We have season's tickets side-by-side at the Leafs' games. Although I hear that you and Sabrina have been friends a long time."

"About ten years. We were in residence together for our first year of university, and then we shared an apartment for three years until I moved out."

"And now you're back together again."

"Temporarily. Sabrina's letting me crash here until I find a place of my own. The competition for an affordable, one-bedroom apartment is pretty fierce, and it's been taking me a while."

Sabrina embraced Viv with one arm. "I'm not in a hurry to lose you," she said. "So, would you gentlemen like to come in for a drink, or go to the gallery first?"

"The gallery first," Drew said. "We can get a drink afterward. I left my car around the corner, if we want to drive."

"Aren't we going to walk?" Viv asked. "It's only three blocks."

Drew nodded at Sabrina's shoes with their four-inch heels. "In those shoes?"

"Don't worry about me."

Rick smiled. "I have to carry her when it's more than three blocks."

"Why do you think I wear them, handsome?" Sabrina wrapped her hand around his muscular forearm and grinned. Turning back to Drew, she added, "If you like, you can leave your car in the underground parking. We have visitor spaces."

"Perfect. Shall we?" Drew smiled and offered Viv his arm.

They took the elevator down to the lobby, where they stepped out onto Parliament Street and strolled around the corner. Next to the sidewalk was a gleaming, Mediterranean-blue sports car that looked like testosterone on wheels. Drew steered Viv toward it.

"Like it? It's a Maserati Quattroporte."

"It's beautiful," she said with a smile. *Boys and their toys.*

"Let's all go down to the parking garage so that you can see how she rides."

"She's a sweet ride," Rick added.

Drew unlocked the car and held the front passenger door open for Viv while Rick helped Sabrina into the back. Viv felt like royalty sliding onto the butter-soft black leather. After the men had climbed inside, Drew started the engine with a roar and checked over his shoulder before slipping into the traffic.

"I wish I could take you out for a run and really open her up," Drew said. "It's a sin to drive her in Toronto traffic." He paused at a stop sign, revving the engine a couple of times to demonstrate its power.

Sabrina gave Drew the combination to key into the entry pad when they reached the door to the underground parking. Drew parked as far away from the other cars as possible and patted the hood before they left, as if the car were a faithful pet. Once they were back on Parliament again, the couples walked in two pairs with Viv and Drew in front. It was a treat for Viv to walk beside a man whose stride matched her own; she had always been hurrying to keep up with Kyle. She was sure there must be other advantages to dating a shorter man, too.

"Nice evening," she said.

"Looks like it's going to be a hot summer."

"Do you have any special vacation plans this year?"

"As a matter of fact, I'm flying to Chicago in a week and a half to surprise my parents for Father's Day."

"That's nice. I bet they'll be excited to see you. Do you visit them often?"

"Two or three times a year. I don't have any family here in Toronto."

"You're originally from Chicago?"

"I grew up there, but I've lived here ever since attending York University."

They made other small talk as they walked down Mill Street and passed through the Distillery gate. Even though it was a Wednesday evening and the stores were closing, there were still lots of people milling about the red brick streets. Viv and her friends strolled past the rustic, brick-and-stone buildings where whiskey had been produced during the Victorian era. A sign on the sidewalk outside of the Freedom Gallery advertised the art show opening. Drew held the door open as the friends walked inside.

The interior retained its original industrial style with concrete floors, brick and plaster walls, and an open ceiling revealing duct work and wooden beams. The space was L-shaped, divided into a rabbit's warren of rooms with two open spaces in the middle. Rick handed their tickets to an attendant at the door, and a waiter offered them a glass of white wine from a tray. The couples mingled with the other well-heeled guests, perusing a collection of plastic and paper maché sculptures until they reached a sign announcing the "Five Ages of Man" exhibit.

Viv read aloud from her pamphlet. "Gwendolyn Seer took photographs of her subjects for fifty years to record the transition from youth to old age. Gwendolyn revisited the participants every ten years to capture the changes. The eldest subject is now ninety-eight." She looked up. "What a broad artistic vision. She must have come up with the idea while she was in her twenties."

The foursome stopped to study the first collection of sepia-tinted photos. In the first picture, a young woman wore a simple white wedding dress with a circlet of daisies atop her tangled long, blond hair. Her feet were bare, and she was grinning as she waved a peace sign at the photographer. In the second picture, the same woman, wearing a pair of knee-high black boots, hot pants, and an orange turtle neck sweater, was being chased across a lawn by two children and a dog. In the third, the subject was stretched out on a lawn chair under a tree, her hair short and wavy where it peeked out from under the brim of a straw hat. Her head was tipped back and her eyes were closed, as if she were sleeping. The fourth picture was singular. The woman was standing at a podium dressed in a dark suit. She was captured with her mouth open and her eyes blazing, one hand gripping the podium while she gestured with the other. The wrinkles around her eyes and mouth were more evident now. In the fifth and last photo, the woman wore glasses, had silver-coloured hair, and a saggy jawline, but there was the same grin and twinkle in her eyes as she cuddled a baby in her lap.

Viv shook her head as she studied the pictures. "Beautiful."

"Wait'll you see the soldier over there," Sabrina said, touching Viv's shoulder and pointing at the wall ahead of them. The friends browsed through the portraits together, weaving past the other admirers until they reached the entrance to a small room. Standing inside was a diminutive, white-haired woman dressed in a navy pant suit, a strand of pearls dangling from her neck. Her hands were clasped over her rounded stomach as she chatted with a gaunt, middle-aged woman in a red cocktail dress and a silver-haired man in a black suit.

"That's her," Viv whispered. Her friends paused to stare, Viv's eyes shining with admiration. "That's Gwendolyn Seer."

Drew took her arm. "Would you like to meet her?"

Viv's eyes widened. "Do you know her?"

"No, but that doesn't matter. Come on, I'll introduce you." He led her forward with Sabrina and Rick trailing behind them. They waited until the elderly woman looked up and smiled.

"Mrs. Seer?" Drew asked. The photographer's companions turned to stare at him.

"Yes?" she said, tilting her head to one side.

"I'm Drew Collins, and this young woman is your biggest fan, Viv Nowak."

"Mrs. Seer will be addressing her audience in twenty minutes," the gentleman said. He stepped forward as if to shoo them away, but the artist offered Viv her hand.

"Are you a photographer, dear?" Viv took the wrinkled hand carefully, but the older woman had a surprisingly strong grip.

"Yes, but I'm just an amateur." Mrs. Seer nodded, studying Viv with lively, intelligent eyes.

"I thought as much. I noticed how you were looking at my portraits. What kind of pictures do you take?"

"I'm a grade-school teacher. I photograph my students."

"Children are wonderful subjects. They're so transparent."

"Yes," Viv said. "They want to share their dreams with you, and they still believe in magic."

"Some people never grow out of that. Perhaps you will share your photographs with the world someday? In an exhibit like this." Mrs. Seer gestured around the room.

"Oh no, my pictures are just for fun."

"Sometimes those are the best." The elderly woman patted Viv's hand. "Now, if you'll excuse me, I think my publicist and the gallery owner are about to tell me where to stand and what to say about my photographs. But it was lovely meeting you, dear."

"Thank you. It was entirely my pleasure," Viv said. She backed away, bowing. Stopping in the middle of the next room, forcing people to swerve to avoid her, she took Drew's hand.

"That was awesome! Thank you for introducing me to Mrs. Seer. I would never have had the nerve to do that on my own."

"It was easy," Drew said with a smile. "Celebrities like to be fawned over. Did I ever tell you about how I met George Clooney at the Toronto International Film Festival?"

Viv's eyes widened. "No!"

They stayed at the gallery until Gwendolyn Seer had spoken, and then left in search of a drink. Drew took Viv's arm, and Rick and Sabrina followed, exchanging a smile. They turned down a side street on their way to an outdoor café. There were lemon-yellow tables with white wooden chairs. Circular, black metal lampshades with candelabra bulbs were suspended from a web of wooden beams overhead. The foursome sat down beneath a sky of wispy pink and purple clouds and ordered their drinks. Viv smelled barbecuing meat and suddenly remembered that she hadn't had anything to eat since lunch.

The young waitress returned with the glasses of Lagavulin Drew had insisted on ordering. "I'm not much of a scotch drinker," Viv had protested, but Drew had laid his hand over hers and said, "Trust me. There's nothing like it."

"Can I bring you menus?" the waitress asked.

"Is anyone hungry?" Drew asked.

Viv nodded. "I'm famished."

Rick turned to Sabrina. "I could eat. How about you, honey?"

"I wouldn't mind an appetizer," she said.

"What is that delicious smell?" Viv asked the waitress.

"That's our Guinness-smoked ribs. Specialty of the house."

"We'll all have that," Drew said with a dismissive nod at the waitress. Viv saw Sabrina raise her eyebrows at Rick, but she didn't care. With such a simple order, the food might come faster.

"So, Drew, what do you do?" Viv asked. She took a cautious sip of scotch and averted her face with a wrinkled nose. Sixteen years old or not, she still didn't like it.

"I'm an executive recruiter."

"A what?"

"A head hunter," Sabrina said.

Drew shrugged. "Call it what you like. I help people make the most lucrative use of their talents. You have to be a pretty good judge of character to do my job, and I'm the best. I make a very good living at it, too." He rested a hand on Viv's shoulder. "For example, I would say that Viv is brimming with potential. How do you earn your living?"

"I'm an elementary school teacher, so I'm not really the kind of person you'd be interested in. Sabrina's more up your alley. She's a real estate banker."

"Really," Drew said, eying Sabrina. "Rick didn't tell me. Interesting."

"Sorry, Drew. I'm happy where I am."

He drew a card from his pocket and passed it to Sabrina anyway. "You never know."

She shrugged and rose to her feet. "Just need to wash up before dinner. Coming, Viv?"

"Sure," Viv said, standing. She followed Sabrina to the washroom, where they fixed their hair.

"So, what do you think?" Sabrina asked in a low voice.

Viv frowned. "It's hard to say. There are things I like about him, but other things make him seem a bit conceited."

"Like what?"

"Oh, trying to impress us with his car and his Lagavulin."

Sabrina shrugged. "Some guys try a little too hard at first. I think it was really sweet of him to introduce you to Gwendolyn Seer."

"So did I, but he did force himself into her conversation."

"It took guts to do that, and he wasn't rude about it."

"It didn't look as though you were happy with the way he ordered food for everyone," Viv added.

"Well, I have to admit that did rub me the wrong way."

"I didn't mind. I like it when a man takes care of me."

Sabrina snorted. "Where were you during the sexual revolution?"

Viv shrugged. "Just because I like a man to take care of me doesn't mean that I can't look after him, too. We all have our different strengths." Sabrina stared at her without saying a word, and Viv began to feel doubtful. "Do you think I'm too dependent on men?"

"Are you kidding?" Sabrina sighed and squeezed her friend's shoulder. "Just make sure that a man has your best interests at heart before you let him look after you, okay?"

Viv nodded. "I'll be careful. I've learned my lesson."

"I know, hon," Sabrina said with a rueful smile. "C'mon, let's get back to the boys."

Drew picked up the dinner tab, and when they arrived back at the condo, Sabrina invited them in for an after-dinner drink. She and Rick sat on one of the couches, Rick with his arm around her, while Drew and Viv sat on the other. They became immersed in a long discussion about the future of public education, but Rick was preoccupied with drawing lazy circles up and down Sabrina's arm. Sabrina watched him through half-closed eyes, practically purring. At last his hand rested on her shoulder, and he leaned in for a kiss that went on for several seconds. Viv and Drew's conversation petered to a stop as they watched. When the kiss ended, Sabrina stretched self-indulgently, yawned, and glanced at her watch.

"It's almost midnight. I've got an appointment tomorrow morning at nine. Time for bed, eh, hon?" Rick smiled into her eyes.

"No, don't leave," Sabrina said as Drew started to his feet. "You and Viv take all the time you want. Viv can let you out later."

The amorous couple rose, and Sabrina pulled Rick from the living room. "You remember the code for the underground parking pad, don't you?" she called to Drew.

"1236."

"What a terrific memory. Night."

"See you," was all Rick had time to say before the bedroom door shut.

Viv stared after them. What kind of stunt was that to pull? It might give Drew the wrong idea. She glanced at him as he sat down beside her, so close that their knees touched.

"Well, this is cozy." His arm glided around her shoulders, and he snuggled Viv against his side. She could smell the brandy on his breath.

"It certainly is." Viv laughed nervously. She felt Drew's other hand on her knee.

"You have the most beautiful blue eyes," he murmured.

"Thanks."

"And your lips," he added, "have a pretty little pout" – he touched her bottom lip – "right here." His mouth hovered near, about to follow. Viv averted her face, and Drew nuzzled her neck instead.

"You smell so good."

"So do you," Viv said shakily. "What scent are you wearing?"

"Mmm?" He was distracted because his hand was on her thigh. Viv pushed him away and jumped to her feet.

"Drew, you're going too fast!" Her sudden movement made him tumble forward, but he caught himself with one hand on the couch. Looking up at her, his bangs fell into his eyes. They were mischievous eyes, like a little boy's caught with his hand in the cookie jar.

"Sorry, Viv. I didn't mean to make you feel uncomfortable. Why don't you sit down again," – he patted the couch – "and I promise to be good." Drew grinned, and Viv spotted a dimple she had never seen before.

"Well, if you promise." She sat down with her hands clasped in her lap, but Drew reached over to take one.

"I could tell you were one of those women the minute I laid eyes on you, but you can't blame a guy for trying."

"Oh? What kind of woman is that?"

"The kind with standards. The kind of woman a man could get serious about."

Viv started. "I beg your pardon?"

Drew crossed his legs and leaned back on the couch. "I told you I'm a good judge of character. I think we're going to be great together. As a matter of fact, I've got a wedding coming up in a few weeks. He's a business associate, and it's going to be pretty dull unless I have the right kind of woman with me. How about coming as my date?"

Viv pulled her hand away and began twisting her ring. "We just met, Drew. We hardly know each other."

Drew laughed. "I always move fast when I'm onto a good thing. That's why I'm so successful. Look at the two of us. I'm smart, I make good money, and I don't have any bad habits. You're beautiful, educated, easy to get along with, and you like children. And I'm sure we won't have any problems in the bedroom." He wiggled his eyebrows. "Trust me, baby, we'd be nuclear together."

He leaned in for a kiss. Viv stared at him like a rabbit hypnotized by a cobra. Her eyes closed as he came nearer, and then their lips touched. His mouth was soft at first, but grew firm and demanding. His tongue slipped between her lips as his hands caressed her back. When he finally released her, Viv's heart was pounding and her eyes were glazed.

"Wow," she said in a small, breathy voice. He looked smug and tapped her nose lightly.

"Told you so. How about dinner on Saturday night? You can come over to my place and cook. I bet you're a wonderful cook."

Viv nodded. That was three days from now. She was sure she

could come up with a terrific menu in three days.

"Great." He rose to his feet and pulled her up with him. "I'll pick you up at five so that you've got lots of preparation time. I'm not fussy, so whatever you make will be fine." He guided her to the condo door and pressed her against the wall beside it. Viv's insides melted as he wrapped his arms around her and his mouth took control of her brain again. When they broke apart, she felt light-headed.

"See you in three days, baby," he said, gazing into her eyes. "Night."

"Night, Drew."

He shut the door noiselessly behind him, and Viv leaned her forehead against it and sighed. She knew she shouldn't fall for a man so quickly, but she felt helpless with Drew. He was so persuasive – and manly. Viv tottered shakily to bed.

Chapter 11

Viv was awakened by a creaking sound, as if someone were opening a door. She lifted her head to glance at her clock radio; it was six thirty. Peering out of the office into the hallway, she saw Rick tiptoeing toward the door. He was buttoning his shirt as he walked. She laid her head back down and pretended to be asleep in case he glanced in at her. She really needed to find a place with a bedroom door. She heard him fumbling with something – probably his shoes – and then the door opened quietly and shut again.

Viv jumped out of bed. She padded to Sabrina's room, where the door was open, and crossed to the ensuite bathroom. She could hear the shower running and knocked on the door.

"Sabrina?"

"Huh?"

"It's Viv. Can I come in?"

"Sure."

She opened the door and stepped into the steamy room, fragrant with soap and floral shampoo.

"What are you doing up so early? I hope that Rick didn't wake you," Sabrina said.

"No," Viv lied. She sat down on the toilet lid. "So, I guess you had a good night."

"The best. Rick is fabulous. Need I say more? How did things go with Drew? I hope you aren't mad at me for deserting you."

"I was at first, but not anymore. I'm going to his place Saturday night to make dinner, plus we're going to a wedding together in a few weeks." Something clattered to the shower floor. "Drew says

I'm the kind of woman he can get serious about." The shower stopped, and Sabrina's head popped out from behind the curtain.

"You're kidding." Sabrina's face was anxious as she pushed her dripping hair back. Viv shook her head. Sabrina reached for her Egyptian cotton bath sheet and disappeared behind the curtain. "Aren't you moving too fast? You two just met."

"Drew's the one doing the pushing, but I don't mind. I really like him."

Sabrina muttered something under her breath, and the curtain flashed open. She stepped onto the bath mat wrapped in the towel, her mouth set in a grim line.

"Does the word 'rebound' mean anything to you?"

Viv frowned. "You think this is a rebound relationship?"

"Oh, Vivvie." Sabrina walked to the cabinet, opened the top drawer, and pulled out a moisturizer. "I'm going to make a few calls after my meeting this morning. I wanted to know what you thought about Drew before I did a full diagnostic on him. No point in wasting time unless you liked him." Sabrina massaged the lotion into her face. "I'm going to find out who he's dated and how long the relationships lasted." She pointed at Viv in the mirror. "I know that you're hopeless when it comes to new relationships, but Drew should have had more sense. Maybe he's just as loose a cannon as you are." Sabrina shrugged. "Not that you wouldn't be happy with him." She squeezed some foundation onto a sponge and dabbed it across her forehead. "Of course, if you two have children, they're going to be pygmies."

"I get my height from Grandma Nowak. I think the tallness gene skipped my generation."

"Well, maybe you'll get lucky and it'll land on your kids. Anyway, I'm going to do some checking up on Drew before you get in any deeper. Your break-up with Kyle really sucked. I'm not going through that again."

Viv walked up behind Sabrina and hugged her. "I know. I'm sorry I've been such a pain."

"Not a problem, but we don't want it to happen again." They stared at their reflections in the mirror, the statuesque redhead with the unwavering green eyes, and the pretty blond with the sweet face.

"Love you, Sabrina," Viv said.

"Love you, too, Vivvie."

Viv was in the middle of a math lesson right after lunch the next day when there was a knock on the classroom door. The children stared as Vice-Principal Daya Chopra stuck her head into the room.

"Good afternoon, boys and girls. I have to talk to Miss Nowak for a minute." She nodded at the board, where Viv had written down a simple sum. "I see you're working on addition today. Work it out in your lesson books while Miss Nowak and I talk in the hallway." She looked at Viv pointedly and withdrew.

Viv had never been called from a classroom by a vice-principal before, and felt uneasy as she followed Daya into the hallway.

"Viv, we have your father's housekeeper on the office phone," Daya said in a low voice. "I'm afraid there's a medical emergency. I'll watch your class until one of the teacher's aids can cover for you."

"Thanks," Viv called over her shoulder as she trotted down the hallway for the main office. Once she was there, the receptionist handed her the phone.

"Magda," Viv said, "what's wrong?"

"Now, don't panic, Viv," the housekeeper said in a reassuring voice. "Your father went in for his physical this morning, and they've checked him into the hospital. His EKG showed that the blood flow to his heart isn't so good, so they're going to do an angiogram to see what the problem is. That's when they inject dye into his arteries and take an x-ray. I'm at the hospital right now – the Toronto General – in the Cardiovascular Investigations Unit. That's on the second floor of the Eaton building."

"I'll be right there," Viv said. As she hung up the phone, her chest constricted with panic, but she had to hold it together for her father's sake. She dialed the number of a taxi company and asked for a cab right away.

Traffic was with them that afternoon; fifteen minutes later Viv was running up the stairs to the cardiovascular unit. She found the waiting room and spotted Magda flipping through a magazine. Magda stood up to give Viv a hug as the young woman hurried into the room.

"He's having the procedure done now. He had to wait three hours until they could fit him in and prep him." Magda pointed at the chairs, and they sat.

"When did he have the EKG?"

"At seven thirty this morning. He went early because he had to do one of those fasting blood tests, too. He was really ticked when they told him he had to come here for the angiogram. He had planned to work this morning."

Viv half-smiled. "I bet. Has he been having any chest pains that he didn't tell me about?"

Magda shook her head. "He did seem kind of short of breath climbing stairs lately, but I thought it was because it was hot, and he's been working so hard."

Viv sighed. "Thank goodness he had heatstroke on Wednesday and I talked him into the physical. Otherwise, we may not have found out about his heart until things got worse." She looked thoughtful. "If it was heatstroke." Viv glanced at Magda. "What happens after the test?"

"The doctor looks at the result while Gabe stays flat on his back for three hours. They're putting a tube up his groin, so the wound needs time to seal. If everything is okay, I can take him home. If not . . ." The housekeeper's face fell, and she looked teary. "Sorry," she said, waving her hand.

"Now, Magda," Viv said, embracing her, "don't go borrowing trouble, eh? That's what you always tell me."

"I know," she whispered, but a fat tear rolled down her cheek. She nodded and thumped Viv's back before releasing her.

"Have you had any lunch?" Viv asked.

Magda swiped at her nose. "No. First I was sitting with Gabe, and then I was waiting for you. I didn't want to miss you."

"You should have called me sooner. I could have sat with Daddy."

"What's the use of that? I didn't want to call you too soon cause I knew you'd drop everything and come."

"Well, go get something to eat. I'll be here if anything happens. I'll call you on your cell."

"Okay," Magda said. She picked her purse up off the floor and stood. "Don't drink the coffee from the machine. It's terrible. I'll bring you some."

Forty minutes later, a tall, middle-aged man wearing scrubs came into the waiting room. His face was solemn, and Viv felt a flash of anxiety.

"Miss Nowak?" he said in a deep voice.

"Yes." She jumped up.

"I'm Dr. Magoro. I did the angiogram on your father this afternoon. Please sit." Viv reseated herself, and the doctor sat beside her. "We got the result from your father's test, and I'm afraid that I'm not happy with it."

"No?" Viv shrank back in her chair, her stomach doing flip flops.

"No. There is definitely some blockage in the right coronary artery. I've discussed it with your father, and he's agreed to an angioplasty to correct the situation. That involves putting the catheter back up his groin, just as we did with the angiogram, and inflating a balloon in the artery to press the plaque back against the wall. A mesh tube called a stent is left in the artery to prevent it from narrowing again. It's a standard procedure, one I've performed hundreds of times."

Viv relaxed a little. "Has my father had a heart attack, Doctor?"

"No, not yet. Looks like we caught it just in time."

"That's wonderful news," Viv said, brightening. "When will the procedure be done?"

"Right away. He'll be taken back in shortly."

"Can I see him first?"

"No, there isn't time."

"How long will he have to stay in the hospital afterward?"

"Just overnight. He'll be awake for the procedure, just as he was for the angiogram. He'll need to take it easy for a week afterward because we want the incision in his groin to heal properly. It's also possible he might experience some heart spasms, but that's normal. We'll give him some nitro glycerin for that. Now, about that home renovation work he's been doing – he'll have to stay away from that for two weeks. I don't want him ripping out toilets while he's recovering. We'll schedule some blood work and a stress test for two weeks from today, and if everything looks good, he should be able to go back to work after that. He'll need to be more careful with his diet in future, but we'll send him home with information."

Viv smiled. "That's great news, Dr. Magoro. I guess I was expecting worse."

The doctor stood up. "Overall, your father's health is fine, but he's not a young man anymore. He should consider hiring help to do the more strenuous work."

Viv rose beside him. "Please make sure to tell him that, Doctor. He won't listen to me, or to anyone else. He tries to save money wherever he can."

"Well, health scares remind us that we're not invincible." He smiled, and his brown eyes were kindly. "I'll certainly have a talk with your father about slowing down a little." He held out his hand. "It was a pleasure meeting you, Miss Nowak."

"Thank you, Doctor. You as well." She shook his hand. "Take good care of my father."

"I surely will," he said, before walking away.

It was seven o'clock at night. Viv was sitting by her father's bedside while he shovelled chicken, rice, and green beans into his mouth. He had had nothing but liquids all day in preparation for the procedures, and he was starving. Magda had stayed until Gabe was settled into his room, and then Viv had sent her home to rest. It had been a nerve-wracking day for the housekeeper, and she looked exhausted. There was a knock on the hospital room door, and Tom Lockhart looked in.

"Gabe, how're you doing? Are you up for a visitor?"

Gabe waved his fork, gesturing for him to enter. "I'm doing

okay, now that I can finally eat. How's it going at the house? Did you finish the kitchen backsplash?"

"Yup. We just need the appliances now. So, what's been happening with you?" Tom pulled up a chair, and Gabe explained about the angioplasty while finishing the food on his tray. The contractor looked like he had come straight from work, wearing dusty, paint-spattered jeans and a t-shirt. He settled back comfortably in his chair with one foot propped on the bed rail.

"Sounds like you'll be out of commission for a couple of weeks. Might put us behind schedule."

"No it won't. I can still come to the house and help with the easy stuff, like the painting."

Viv's eyes flashed with anger. "No you won't, Daddy. Didn't you listen to the doctor? You're going to stay away from the house for two weeks. I know you – as soon as you're back, you'll be ripping out tiles and overdoing it."

"Will not. Besides, Dr. Magoro told me to try to keep my stress levels down. Do you know how stressed out I'd be, sitting at home watching another mortgage payment fly by before the house even goes on the market?"

"Tom can take care of things, can't he?" Viv turned to the contractor, who paused before answering.

"I can do most of it and bring in help when I need it, but your dad has to make some decisions first." He looked at Gabe. "You said you wanted the paint lighter on this one. What colours do you want? And what about the tile for the bathroom floors and the showers? Then there's the basement fireplace and the kitchen appliances." He peered at Viv from under bushy black eyebrows. "Your dad makes the decisions, not me."

"Don't you work with an interior designer anymore?" Viv asked her father.

"Nah, just for the first two houses. After that, you get a feel for things, depending on how you want to price the house. It's no big deal. I'll drop by the building supply centre and order some stuff. I'll do it tomorrow."

"Oh, Daddy." Viv sighed. "Look, I'll help. How about if you tell me what you're looking for, and I'll visit the building centre to pick up some samples. Then you can choose the stuff you like, and Tom can buy it." Her father looked uncertain. "I don't mind. The term is winding down, and my reports on the kids are almost finished, so I'm not that busy. Besides, you always said I had good taste. This could be fun for me."

"Well, if you're sure you don't mind," Gabe said.

"Not at all. We can start tomorrow. If it'll make you feel any better, I can help with the painting, too. How hard can it be?"

Gabe and Tom exchanged a glance. "That would be a big help, Peaches. Thanks. If you've got some paper on you, we'll make a list of things you can look for tomorrow. You can stay for dinner afterward."

"Sorry, I can't stay for dinner tomorrow. I almost forgot. I've got a date."

"Really?" Her father's face perked up. "Who's the guy?"

"A friend of Sabrina's boyfriend. His name is Drew Collins."

"What does he do?"

"He's an executive recruiter."

"Head hunter," Gabe said with a frown. "I lost a lot of good people to guys like him over the years."

"Maybe so, but Drew's a nice man, and a real go-getter. Sort of like you. He drives a beautiful Maserati Quattroporte," she added, hoping to impress him.

Tom nodded. "Nice ride."

"Kind of flashy," Gabe said. "Well, make sure he treats you well."

"I will." She kissed her father's cheek. "Now, let's get started on that list."

Viv got home about an hour later, tired, but relieved that things had worked out so well for her father. The condo was empty; Sabrina was probably out with Rick. She microwaved a low-cal entrée for herself, and pulled out her laptop to check her e-mail. There was one from her mother. Viv sighed. Did she really have to deal with it tonight, or could it wait until tomorrow? Deciding that she'd worry all night if she didn't read it, Viv clicked on the message.

Dear Viviane,

As your father may have told you, I am flying to Toronto on Monday to meet with my Canadian distributor about the winter collection. I'll be staying at the Castle Crest until Thursday, and would like to have dinner with you on Tuesday evening. I think it's time we talked, don't you? I'll make the dinner reservation. Let me know if you will come, please.

I look forward to seeing you.

Mother

Viv frowned. So like her mother. No apology, no "how are you doing," no information about what she wanted to talk about. Just a cold summons.

Viv shut down the computer. She needed some time to think before deciding how she would respond. Maybe she should finally face her mother, woman to woman. Tell her that there was nothing left between them, and that she never wanted to see her again. That would be satisfying, wouldn't it? To give the ice queen some of her own back?

Or maybe it would be better to let loose and tell her mother what she really thought of her. Ask her how she could leave her husband and daughter behind – her ten-year-old child – for a career in New York. In shoe design, for heaven's sake. It wasn't as if Véronique had left her for something worthwhile, like doctoring babies in third world countries. Who the hell cared about wearing flats instead of three inch stilettos?

And not to bother coming home for Christmas or birthdays – to send cards with cheques that were never cashed instead, not that

Mother ever took the hint. And to show up for only two hours for her sweet sixteenth birthday party. They hadn't had even a minute to talk alone before the airporter had whisked Mother away again.

Viv refused to even think about her university graduation; that always made her furious. The woman was a self-centred, selfish *bitch* who didn't deserve three minutes of her time, let alone a whole dinner.

Viv breathed in deeply and exhaled slowly. She needed to calm down. She mustn't let Véronique get to her like this. It only hurt her, not her mother. She took another deep breath and held it before exhaling.

Right. She obviously had some deep-seated emotions about her mother's desertion, and she needed to deal with them. Just like the grieving process she had read about in magazine articles, she needed some closure. Maybe it would be best to see Mother one last time. Get some things off her chest. Close the chapter on her childhood and never think about it again. She must live in the present and envision a happy future.

She opened the computer and rebooted it. When her e-mail came up, she began typing.

Mother,

I will meet you in the lobby of the Castle Crest Hotel at 7:00 p.m. on Tuesday. Yes, I agree it's time we talked.

Viv

(She had never liked the name, "Viviane." Why had Mother named her that? Mother was only half-French, after all. She'd been born in Buffalo, for pity's sake.) After a moment, Viv added a postscript.

P.S.
FYI, Daddy had an angioplasty today. The procedure appears to be successful.

There. Let her stew, if she had any compassion left in her cold, narcissistic heart for the man who was technically still her husband.

Viv shut down her computer and turned to a more pleasurable pursuit. She was going to make dinner for Drew tomorrow, and needed to consider some recipes. Was he more of a steak and potatoes kind of guy, or a salmon with raspberry coulis and couscous? Or how about spaghetti and meatballs – she made a killer sauce, if she said so herself. But maybe spaghetti was the kind of thing a bachelor made all the time for himself? Better scrap the spaghetti.

She lay on her stomach on the futon, flipping through a cookbook. It was supposed to be cooler tomorrow with a chance of rain. How about pork schnitzel and potato salad? Who didn't like that? She could team it with fresh asparagus. Done!

Glad to have made a decision, she made a list of ingredients to pick up tomorrow. Daddy was going to loan her his car to visit the building supply store, so she could pop into the grocery store on the way back. With that done, she padded barefoot into the kitchen to start the strawberry cheesecake she was bringing for dessert. She was going to impress the heck out of Drew Collins, or die trying!

Chapter 12

Viv was out early the next morning at the building supply store. The first item on Daddy's list was paint colours. She stopped in front of the samples to study the selection. There were three brands; she hadn't asked if he had a preference. She'd better pick up samples from all of them.

Daddy said he wanted a light colour for the living room and the basement rec room. Normally he went for white or off-white to keep it neutral. Let's see, there was a "White Jasmine" that looked a little denser than a pure white. Not bad, but what was that below? "Home Song" was nice, and had a touch of green. Hmm. Green was calm and serene, a pleasant feeling for a living room. This brand of paint had colours divided by room and style. Under "Casual" they had "Celery Bunch." That was nice. A little more impact than the other green, and fresh-looking. Nothing wrong with a little colour. Looking at another brand, she spotted "Posh Celery." That made her laugh.

With a dozen likely colours, Viv decided she had enough selection and moved on to carpets. Daddy wanted a nice grey for the basement rec room and bedroom, something cozy. Let's see, there were different textures of carpet: frieze (looked like shag), loop (for high-traffic areas), texture (also for high-traffic areas), and pattern (the fibres looked like a combination of loop and texture). Maybe she'd better draw a diagram of the different textures so that she and Daddy would be on the same page. She scribbled the information into her notebook.

Now, what about colour? "Comet Grey" was patterned. Ooh,

she liked the "Midnight Grey" even better with its grey, white, and blue fibres. It all depended on how dark Daddy wanted to go.

"Excuse me," she said to a passing employee. "Is it possible to get samples of these carpets?"

"Yes, if you leave your information and a small deposit."

"Great. Could I arrange for samples of these two, please?"

With the samples in her bag, there was only one more item left on her list – floor tile. Fortunately, the kitchen was already done, but tile was also required for the front entrance, the bathrooms, and the laundry/mudroom. Three very different areas of the house. Daddy would want something stylish for the entrance, something nice but easy to clean for the bathrooms (she hated those little tiles with the grouting between them that trapped lint), and something utilitarian for the mudroom. Hmm, the tile section of the store was more challenging. Porcelain, ceramic, peel and stick, premium mosaic, glass, stone, Belgian foil, and combinations. Obviously, some of these tiles weren't meant for floors. They also came in a bewildering assortment of sizes and finishes. There didn't appear to be any samples to take home, either. She'd better take some pictures with her cell, and make notes.

Forty-five minutes later and with the beginnings of a headache, she drove back to her father's house, stopping at a grocery store on the way to pick up the ingredients she needed for dinner. Gabe was dressed in sweats and sitting in his reclining chair in the bedroom. She pulled the bench from the end of the bed and placed it beside him before unearthing the samples and notes from her bag. They went through her findings, Viv discovering that her father was very logical when it came to finishings.

"Nothing cheap, Viv – I don't want to get a reputation for doing shoddy work – but nothing too expensive unless it's going in a high impact area. I always spend less money on the basement carpet, for instance. If you buy a good underpad, it still feels luxurious."

"Yes, I agree with you that this tile is prettier, but who's going to be buying the house, a man or a woman? You've got to choose something less distinctive. The buyer will add his or her own decorative touches."

"Green? We've never used green on the walls before, unless it was in a bathroom. Off-white is a safer bet." But Viv stood her ground.

"White is boring, Daddy. I'm not asking you to paint the living room fire-engine red, but "Nature Mist" is a lot more modern than white. You can paint the dining room white. It's got that dark wainscoting."

"I don't know." Gabe frowned at the colour sample. "It's kind of bright."

"How about 'Valley Mist' then? It's more neutral and very soothing. I'd like to come home to a living room painted that colour."

"Well . . ." he said, pursing his lips. "You're twisting the arm of a sick man, you know."

Viv batted her eyelashes at him.

"All right. Let's live a little. 'Valley Mist' it is."

Viv hugged her father and shouted, "Yay! Tell me how much paint to order, and I'll get it delivered this afternoon. Then I can paint the living room tomorrow."

"Thanks, Peaches. You've been a big help."

"You're welcome. I'd be happy to help some more. It's been fun. Just let me know what you need." She knelt down on the floor and gathered the samples back into her bag. "I'll just drop off these carpet samples and order the stuff you want before I head home to get cleaned up."

"Right. You're cooking for the head hunter tonight."

Viv stood up, brushing off her knees. "I wish you wouldn't call Drew that. It makes him sound like a cannibal."

Gabe snorted. "Let's hope not. Still, I'm glad your friends are helping you to date again, although I don't know about this scoring system thing they're using. I always just followed my gut when it came to finding a woman."

"Ahem," Viv said pointedly, sitting down on the arm of his chair.

"Yeah, I know. You think your mother and I were a mistake. But we got you out of it, so how wrong could we have been?" Viv bent to kiss the top of his head. "And she's not the only woman I ever dated, I'll have you know."

"That's okay, Daddy. I don't need to know about your love life. Unless," she said, bending down so that her face was level with his, "you want to tell me if there's anything going on between you and Magda?"

He pantomimed locking his lips and throwing away the key. "A gentleman never tells."

"Fine, Casanova." She shrugged. "I just want to know if the two of you are ever going to get married."

"I'm still a married man."

"Hah. Speaking of which, I'm going to see Mother for dinner on Tuesday."

"Hey, that's the best news I've heard all week!"

Viv stood up. "Well, don't get too excited. I'm finally going to get a few things off my chest with her."

"Just listen to what she has to say first."

"Do you know why she wants to meet with me?"

Gabe squirmed in his chair. "I admit, Véronique ran it past me first. But I prefer she tells you what's on her mind."

Viv sighed. "Whatever. It doesn't really matter." She kissed her father's cheek. "Take it easy, and I'll see you soon. Bye, Daddy."

As she walked out of the room, Gabe called, "Give my regards to the head hunter. Tell him that after three dates, he gets to meet the father!"

"Sure, sure," she said, waving her hand.

Drew was bang on time when he rang Viv from the condo lobby.

"I'll be right down," she said, ending the call and retrieving the grocery bags from the kitchen counter and the homemade strawberry cheesecake from the fridge. When she reached the lobby, Drew was waiting for her next to the elevators.

"Here, let me carry those for you," he said, taking the shopping bags.

"I'll hold onto the dessert. I don't want it to slide on the plate."

"What is it?"

"Strawberry cheesecake. I made it myself."

"You can make strawberry cheesecake?"

"Uh huh."

"Will you marry me?"

Viv giggled as they left the complex and walked around the corner to Drew's beautiful car. He tucked her inside, and she balanced the cheesecake on her lap all the way to his downtown apartment.

"I like to be in the centre of the city," he said as he drove down the ramp to the underground parking. "Everything I need is here at my fingertips. And the view of the city skyline is the best. I can even see the CN Tower."

He unlocked the door to his twenty-second floor apartment and led Viv inside. The six hundred square foot space was divided into three rooms, with a galley kitchen just inside the door, an L-shaped living/dining room, and the bedroom. The living area was furnished with black leather and chrome, plus a state-of-the-art sound system. The apartment definitely needed a woman's touch.

Drew set Viv's supplies on the kitchen counter and took her hand. "Let me show you the view from the living room." He guided her past a gas fireplace with a huge flat screen TV hanging over the mantle, and pulled back the blinds on a floor-to-ceiling window.

"Wow, that's spectacular," she said, looking out at the glass and steel skyscrapers.

"There's another great view from my bedroom."

Drew opened the door, and Viv peeked inside. She saw a king-sized bed with a black leather headboard (more black leather), a side table with a chunky glass lamp, and a tallboy dresser. There wasn't room for anything else, except for another floor-to-ceiling window.

"I like to lie in bed at night with the lights out and look out over the city."

"That sounds wonderful."

"Well, that's the apartment. Do you approve of it, milady?"

"It's very handsome."

"Thanks. Can I get you a drink? Some white wine or sparkling water?"

"I'd love a sparkling water. Do you have any lime?"

"I certainly do. Coming right up."

Viv watched Drew pour a couple of club sodas over ice and chop a lime into quarters. Squeezing the juice from one section into each glass, he tossed the rind into the garbage. The other sections went into a storage container in the fridge.

He's neat, Viv thought. *We won't get into arguments about leaving wet towels on the bathroom floor.* They leaned against the counter sipping their drinks.

"Now, why don't you take a seat at the dining room table and tell me more about yourself while I start dinner," Viv said.

"Okay." Drew sat down at the glass-topped table with his drink. "There's not a lot to tell. My father is an architect and my mother is a retired nurse. I've got a younger sister who's working on a master's degree in civil engineering. I'm the only one in the family who went into business."

"What brought you to York University?" Viv asked, rummaging through the cupboards for a pot to boil the potatoes in.

"My grandmother lived in Toronto, and we used to visit her from time to time. Plus, the MBA program at York has an excellent reputation. I did my undergraduate degree at home in Chicago, but I wanted to go someplace else for grad school. Toronto didn't seem like a foreign place, plus I had Gran here in case I got lonely."

"That's pretty perceptive for a young man. But I thought you said you didn't have any family here in Toronto?"

"She passed away during my second year."

"Oh, I'm sorry. That must have been rough, losing your grandmother while you were still in school."

Drew nodded. "It was. I still miss her."

"Sorry, but do you have a vegetable peeler?"

"No. I don't eat many meals at home, so my utensils are pretty basic. I've got an electric can opener, a toaster, and a coffee maker." He pointed to the appliances on the counter.

Viv smiled. "Doesn't matter. I can use a knife. So, what happened after graduate school?"

"One of my profs helped me land a marketing job with an information technology company, so I was able to get a work visa to stay in Canada. I moved from marketing to sales, and left the company after five years to work for Royal Recruitment. I've been with them for six years, recruiting managers in the information technology and energy sectors. I love it. It's an exciting field to be in."

"It sounds exciting. You must be a real people-person."

"That's right. Being around people gives me a charge."

Viv nodded while she chopped the potatoes.

"How about you, Viv? What was your childhood like?"

"Well, I've lived in Toronto all my life. Daddy was in investment banking, and he met my mother while he was at a conference in New York. She was a fashion designer. They fell in love at first sight, and she moved to Toronto to marry him. Mother went back to work five weeks after I was born, so I didn't see very much of her when I was young. But Daddy made up for it by being home for dinner and tucking me into bed every night. When I was ten, Mother had an opportunity to start her own shoe design house back in New York, so she left. She's very successful, but I've only seen her twice since then."

"Wow, that sounds rough."

Viv shrugged. "I haven't missed her at all. Daddy retired from banking last year to flip houses. He loves it, but he just had a health scare yesterday." Drew's eyes widened. "Everything turned out fine. The doctor caught it before it became a problem, but Daddy needs to slow down a little."

"That must have been scary."

"It was. And to make my life more stressful, my mother is flying into Toronto on business next week. We're having dinner together on Tuesday night."

"How's that going to go?"

"I'm going to let her have it. It's about time." Viv poured water over the potatoes and set them on the stove to cook.

"Good for you, Viv. I bet you'll feel good after you've confronted her."

Viv nodded. "That's how I feel, although Daddy thinks I ought to mend fences. He says there's something she wants to talk to me about."

"What?"

"He wouldn't tell me, so I'll just have to wait and see. Not that I'm dying of curiosity or anything." She was cutting the ends off the asparagus, and stopped to look at Drew. "I guess I sound pretty callous."

"Not at all. It seems like you have every right to be angry with your mother. I can't imagine any business being more important than a ten-year-old daughter, and I'm a businessman. If my mother needed me, I'd be there in a flash."

"Exactly," Viv said, pointing her knife at Drew. "I teach Grade 1, so I know how crucial those early years are to a child's formation and sense of well-being."

"It's amazing how well-developed you are, given the circumstances."

"I owe it all to Daddy. If it hadn't been for him, I'd be a mess."

"Which you certainly are not." Drew smiled approvingly.

"Thanks." Viv smiled back. It was nice to have someone on her side, someone who thought she was well-developed.

Dinner went very well. The pork schnitzel was crispy and tender, the potato salad and asparagus were tasty, and Drew ate two servings of strawberry cheesecake. He insisted that she put her feet up and listen to music while he cleaned up the kitchen and put the leftover food away. Afterward, he joined her on the couch with a bottle of port and two cut-crystal glasses.

"They're lovely," she said, holding up a glass to admire it in the sunlight.

He poured some of the ruby-coloured drink into their glasses and held his up for a toast.

"Here's to the beautiful blue eyes of milady. I am lost within them."

"That's lovely, Drew," Viv said. He was such a romantic.

They sipped the wine with their feet propped on the coffee table and blues music playing in the background. Drew flicked on the gas fire with a click of the remote, and laid his arm around her shoulders. Viv snuggled against him with her head resting cozily in the crook of his arm. Finishing the last of his port, Drew took Viv's glass and set it on the table. Viv smiled up at him, and he stroked the side of her face.

"I could get used to this," he murmured, leaning in to kiss her eyes, her forehead, and her mouth.

"You don't think we're moving too fast, do you?" Viv whispered between kisses as her pulse quickened.

"No. Do you?" His finger traced a lazy line from her ear to her collar bone, and then to the top button of her blouse.

"I don't know. I've got such mixed feelings. I'm still hurt by the way my boyfriend treated me, but it feels nice to be appreciated by another man."

Drew nodded as he undid the first button. "I've been there myself, Viv. Having someone disappoint you can be hard on the ego. You start to worry if it was something you did, but I know you weren't to blame. It was your boyfriend who didn't see what a good thing he had." His fingers caressed the skin between her breasts as they slid down to undo the second button.

"Still we're neither of us kids, Viv. We know what we want." She felt his fingers undo the third button as his tongue teased her lips open for short, silky kisses.

Viv pulled her head back. "That's true, but Sabrina was just saying that I ought to be careful of having a rebound romance." She glanced down as Drew pulled her blouse open to expose her lacy pink bra. His velvety lips trailed down her throat to the upper swell of her breast, and she sank back against the couch.

"Love is dangerous, there's no denying it. But you have to gamble big to win big." He slipped her top off one shoulder, nipping her white skin with his teeth.

Viv groaned, and the phone rang. Drew reached over top of her to pick it up from the side table.

"Sorry, I just have to take this call." He sat up. "Hello?"

Viv's eyes opened.

"What did you say? No that's not right. His plane's not arriving until tomorrow." Drew listened for a moment. "No, I could have sworn. Hang on a minute." He fished his cell from his pocket and flicked past screens.

"That's right, I booked the eleven twenty flight for tomorrow morning. What do you mean, he changed the flight?"

Viv pulled her bra strap back up on her shoulder.

"The meeting's tomorrow?" Drew stood up and started pacing the floor. "Who authorized the change? No one told me. Did someone change the hotel reservation? What the hell! No, no, I can fix it, but this is going to cost money. Look, his plane is landing in" – he checked his watch – "fifty-five minutes. If I drive like a maniac, I can make it. Get on the phone to the Hyatt and change the reservation. Right. I'll see you tomorrow."

He slammed the phone back onto its base and stared at Viv, seeming to see her for the first time in minutes.

"Baby, I'm really sorry. Someone screwed up the dates on this business meeting, and I've got to run to the airport to pick up the client."

"That's all right. I don't mind," Viv said. She sprang to her feet and began searching for her shoes.

"I'm really, really sorry. I don't even have time to drive you home." He snatched up her purse from the kitchen counter as she slipped into her sandals.

"No problem. I can catch the streetcar home." He clicked off the fireplace and walked her to the apartment door.

"I'll be leaving right behind you. But listen, thanks so much for tonight. You let me know how the dinner with your mother works out, will you?"

"Sure. I'll call you."

He opened the door and kissed her quickly. "You're an angel. I'll see you later, baby."

The door shut behind her, and Viv paused to pull the purse strap onto her shoulder and smooth her hair. Wow, that had been a close one. If the phone hadn't interrupted them, she might have made love with Drew. She didn't know if she was ready to trust him that much, but her body had certainly reacted as if it did.

The elevator bell dinged, and an elderly woman with coiffed silver hair stepped out, supporting herself with a cane. She smiled at Viv as she thumped down the hallway, and as they passed, gave Viv a large wink. Startled, Viv hurried into the elevator and caught her reflection in the mirror. The front of her blouse was still hanging open, revealing her pink push-up bra. Flushing as bright as her underwear, Viv fumbled to close the buttons, and rode the streetcar home in a flood of embarrassment.

Chapter 13

With Sabrina and Rick out of town for the weekend, Viv decided to get over her shame from the night before by doing her laundry and cleaning the condo. The place was sparkling by noon, and she left to take the streetcar to the house her father was renovating. It had poured rain all morning, but there was a break in the weather when she reached her stop, and she jogged the block to the house. It was spitting rain when she let herself in with the spare set of keys. She was pleased to see that Tom had covered the living room floor with a drop cloth. Rolling up the sleeves of the old shirt she was wearing, Viv got to work. She was bouncing her head in time to the music on her iPhone when a hand fell on her shoulder.

"Aagh!" She jumped back, flailing her roller at her attacker. Tom held up his hands.

"Easy," he shouted above the music in her ears. He gestured at the wall she was painting a lovely shade of Valley Mist.

"What are you doing here?" she demanded. Her heart was pounding in her chest. He mouthed something she couldn't hear.

"Wait a minute." Viv dropped the roller onto her paint tray and removed the ear buds.

"I said, horseback riding was a washout with all this rain, so I came to see how you were making out. What the hell are you doing?"

"I'm painting. What's wrong? I taped the trim before I started, just like Daddy told me."

"But you have to prime the walls first. You can't just paint on top of drywall. And what are you doing with green paint?"

Viv turned to study the wall. The green was a little darker than it had looked on the colour card, but the lady at the paint counter had told her to expect that. It did look kind of blotchy, though.

She looked back at Tom. "How do you prime a wall? Daddy didn't tell me to do that."

"With primer. I left it here with the paint the store delivered. Didn't you see it?"

She squatted down to study the labels on the tubs. She had just assumed that it was all paint. Spotting the primer, she sighed and straightened.

"I'm sorry, I didn't know you had to prime first. Have I ruined the wall? Should I put the primer on top of the paint?"

"No, too late for that." Tom sighed and stepped up to the wall to study her work. "Just put another coat on top and hope it looks all right." He turned to look at her with those piercing, pale blue eyes. "You ever painted before?"

Viv frowned. What was he implying, that she wasn't doing it right?

"Actually, no."

He nodded. "Let me show you." He picked up one of the two poles from the floor beside the tubs and handed it to her. "Screw that onto your roller. How were you going to reach the upper part of the wall?"

"I was going to use a ladder."

"Put some paint on your roller," he said, nodding at her paint tray.

She dipped her roller into the puddle of paint and spun it back and forth on the tray to distribute it.

"Show me how you paint."

Feeling foolish, Viv approached the wall. The extra length of pole felt awkward as she painted up and down, and painted over the strip again just to make sure.

Tom unfolded his arms from his chest and reached for the pole. "Not enough paint, Viv. Watch." He rolled the brush back and forth in the green liquid, rolled it on the tray once, and lifted it. Stepping forward, he painted a "v" on a part of the wall that she hadn't covered.

"You don't have to paint in straight lines. Branch out a bit, like this." He swiftly covered a large patch, stopping his roller a couple of inches from the top of the wall. "I'll finish that with a brush. Don't want to get paint on the ceiling. You keep working on this wall while I prime the others."

Viv dipped her roller as Tom had shown her and tried to duplicate his work. They painted in silence, Viv finishing the rest of the wall in half the time it had taken her before. Even so, Tom had already finished priming the second wall and was onto the third by the time she looked up.

He must have sensed her eyes on his back. "How'd you get Gabe to go for green?"

She shrugged. "He wasn't keen on anything but white at first, so I showed him some of the brochures with rooms decorated in themes. You know, 'Traditional,' 'Modern,' 'Country.' Valley Mist came from the 'Casual' style. I liked a different shade that was even brighter, so we compromised on this."

Tom nodded and continued priming the wall. "I haven't been able to talk him into anything but white before." He turned to look at her. "I like it."

Viv smiled and painted the second wall. When Tom had finished priming and repainted the wall she hadn't primed, he painted the area where the walls met and took out a ladder to do the brush work next to the ceiling. By the time Viv finished with her roller, he was painting the last strip.

He climbed down the ladder to stand beside her. "What'd you get for the dining room?"

"White." She grinned. "And white for the hallway and the bathroom. Although I did talk Daddy into using green again in the mudroom."

"Let's get at 'er."

By six thirty, Viv was paint-spattered, sweaty, and stiff, but the first floor walls were painted. Tom showed her how to clean her roller in the sink, and they tidied up together before calling it a night. She noticed that he looked a lot cleaner than she did and didn't seem half as tired. He must be in great shape, to do the hard labour that he did.

Tom waited for her at the front door. When they stepped out onto the porch, Viv saw that it had stopped raining and the sun was peeking through the yellow-grey clouds. She stretched and rotated her shoulders to ease their stiffness as Tom locked up.

"Come on, I'll drive you home," he said. His truck was parked out front on the street.

"Thanks. I'd hate to be seen on the streetcar like this."

She followed him to the truck and waited for him to toss old receipts, a sawed-off piece of wood, the saw, and some crumpled food containers into the back seat.

"The truck gets a little messy during a project. Hop in." He headed around the truck and climbed behind the steering wheel. "Where do you live?"

She gave him directions, and they pulled away with the windows rolled all the way down to let the wind blow through. Viv took her damp hair from its holder and shook it out to let the breeze dry it.

"You hungry?" Tom asked. "There's a burger place in the next block with a drive-through. You don't even have to get out of the truck."

"I'm starving, and I don't want to cook when I get home. Thanks."

Ten minutes later, they were parked behind the restaurant with cheeseburgers, fries, and icy-cold colas. Viv tore open two pouches of ketchup for dipping her fries. Tom opened a couple of mustard pouches, poured his fries into his hamburger container, and dribbled mustard over them.

"That's unusual." She pointed at his food. "I've never seen anyone put mustard on fries before."

"You ever try it?" She liked his slow drawl.

"No."

He held out the container, and she sampled a fry. It was tangy with the mustard.

"Not bad," she admitted. Tom nodded and shoved three fries into his mouth at once.

"But I still prefer ketchup." She dipped a single potato daintily into her mound of sauce.

Tom finished eating much sooner than Viv. He leaned his head back on the head rest and closed his eyes. Viv studied his profile. It was a strong face with a straight nose and a square jaw. There was a little grey mixed among the black next to his sideburns, but none in the rest of his long hair.

"This was your day off, wasn't it?" she asked.

"Yup." His eyes were still closed.

"That's pretty devoted of you."

"I saw to some things around the farm first. I wanted to see how you were doing."

"Checking up on me, you mean?"

One side of his mouth tilted up, and he looked at her without lifting his head. "You don't seem like the kind of woman who's had a lot of experience with house renos."

She met his eyes for a second before taking a bite of her burger. "You're right." After chewing and swallowing, she added, "I'm curious. What kind of woman do I seem to you?"

His answer was immediate. "The kind who likes to help out her daddy so he won't worry as much."

She nodded, pleased. "And I did a good job with the painting, once you showed me how?"

"Not bad. You stuck with it longer than I thought you would."

She tossed her napkin into the food container and squeezed it shut. "I'm not a quitter, Tom."

He grunted.

"Plus, I'd like Daddy to see that he can renovate houses without doing as much of the work himself. So, any way that I can help out during this job, I'd like to. I can come over after school most days, and on the weekends. Just not Tuesday night. I'm having dinner with my mother then."

Tom sat up and turned the key in the ignition before glancing at her. "You can help with some things, Viv, but on others, you'd only slow me down. The most important thing with a reno is to stay on schedule. If you can keep your dad on track with the decisions, I'll take care of the rest, even if it means hiring extra help. Still, if you want to come over now and then, I guess there's stuff I can find for you to do."

Viv frowned. "You make me sound like one of my six-year-olds. Come on, I'm a quick learner, and, like I said, I'm no quitter. Give me a chance, Tom."

He looked at her out of the corner of his eye. "If you think you're up to it, Viv, I can teach you a few things." He held out his right hand, and she smiled and shook it.

"Done."

Chapter 14

"Hey, Viv, I've got some good news," Julie said in the lunch room on Monday. She had just heated up some chili in the microwave and sat down at the table beside Viv to eat it. Viv was taking a bite from her egg salad sandwich.

"What is it?" She looked up, licking mayonnaise from her lips.

"Do you remember me telling you about Fred Shiner, the University of Toronto ancient history professor I met last year?"

"The one with the cat with the funny name?"

"Constantine. Anyway, Fred's going to Greece for a year on sabbatical. He's leaving next week. The man who was supposed to be renting his house just backed out with some health problem or other, so Fred's desperate for somebody to rent his house right away. It's furnished very nicely, plus it's only six blocks from school. You can walk it in ten minutes."

Viv put down her sandwich. "What's he asking for the rent?"

"Only a thousand a month, plus utilities."

Viv's eyes opened wide. That was amazingly low for a house rental.

"What's the catch?"

"There's no catch. Fred's pretty finicky about who he rents to because he's got a lot of antiques. You'd have to water his plants and take care of his cat. I hear that Constantine's a little difficult to get along with, but he's only a cat. I was over there once, and I didn't even see him."

"I can get along with a tarantula for a furnished house six blocks from school and only a thousand. Is it detached?"

"Yes."

"Two-storey?"

"Two and a half."

"When can I see it?"

"Tonight. I told Fred we'd come over after dinner. He's very excited to meet you. I talked you up a bit."

Viv smiled broadly. "Thanks, Julie. It sounds like a wonderful opportunity."

"That's all right. I owe you." She looked across the table at a third grade teacher who was reading a novel and picking at her salad. The woman was notorious for spreading gossip. Julie leaned forward to whisper in Viv's ear, "Because of Josh."

"You don't owe me for Josh. I enjoyed meeting him," Viv said in a low voice. "It's too bad he reminded me so much of my first boyfriend. The resemblance was uncanny. I just couldn't warm up to Josh after what Justin did to me." She faked a shiver of distaste.

"Well, if the chemistry isn't right, there isn't much you can do about it. As my Italian grandmother used to say, 'You don't visit a garden that has no flowers.' Whatever that means. But Josh must have liked you a lot if he pretended to be coming onto me just to make you jealous." She elbowed Viv. "It wasn't very mature of him, but you must have felt good when you found out. That Josh liked you so much, I mean."

"I did," Viv said with a rueful smile. "Now, tell me more about the house."

It was seven when Viv got off the subway at Broadview and walked the three blocks to Wolfrey Avenue. The house was not far from the corner. There were two towering apartment buildings across the street, but they had a lot of green space around them and didn't make the residential neighbourhood feel crowded. The houses on Fred's side of the street all seemed well looked after, too.

Fred's house was a red brick with beige trim, plus a handsome bay window on the second floor. Viv studied the house from the sidewalk. The yard was enclosed by a low stone retaining wall, and had a flowerbed of tall grasses and perennials off to one side. A flagstone sidewalk led past a weeping pea to the wide front porch.

Viv rang the doorbell and waited. The door was opened by a tall, slim man with stooped shoulders, a headful of grey hair, and a Van Dyck beard.

"You must be Viv," he said. He had a bright, clear voice perfectly suited to reaching the back of a lecture hall.

"I am. And you must be Dr. Shiner."

"Call me 'Fred.' Come in," he said with a bow. His dark eyes swept her from head to toe as she stepped inside. The vestibule was painted a rich burgundy, while the hallway was papered in a blue-and-green peacock pattern. A white wooden staircase with a green runner rose from the front hallway to the second floor.

"Julie and Olivia are in the parlour." He indicated the first room to the right with a sweep of his hand. Julie was seated on a red, Queen Anne-styled couch with a curved back, round arms, and slim feet. Olivia was dressing one of her dolls on an oriental rug of faded reds, blues, and greens.

"Hi, Viv," Julie said. Olivia glanced up and smiled before returning to her doll.

"Please, sit anywhere you like," Fred said.

Viv gazed around the cluttered room. In addition to the couch, there were two high-backed chairs in floral upholstery. Just beyond the chairs was a beautiful fireplace with a frame of white vines and flowers. A mirror mounted in a matching frame hung over the mantle. To the left of the fireplace was a stained-glass window of yellow flowers with green stems and a border of blue and yellow squares. Beneath the window sat a mahogany writing desk and a wooden chair with a petit point cushion. An overflowing bookcase filled an alcove in the back, while several round side tables bearing ferns, statuary, and knick-knacks were interspersed with the furniture.

"Such a lovely room," Viv said. *What a lot of dusting*, she thought. She joined Julie on the couch.

"I'm glad you like it," Fred said. "I inherited the house from an aunt twenty-five years ago, and I've been adding to the decor ever since." He seated himself in a wing chair and crossed his legs. "Julie tells me that you're looking for accommodations?"

"That's right. I've been staying with a friend for almost four months since the break-up of a long-term relationship. I didn't want to remain alone in the old apartment. My friend has been very kind, but her condo really isn't large enough for the two of us."

"I quite understand. Better to start over again somewhere fresh. What about furnishings?"

"None of them were worth keeping. All I have are my clothes and a few personal items, mostly books and photographs."

"That would suit me very well. As you can see, there isn't room for additional furnishings. Tell me, how do you get along with cats?"

"Just fine. My boyfriend and I didn't have pets – our apartment was too cramped – but I've babysat other people's cats."

"Viv looked after my orange tabby when I was in the hospital having Olivia," Julie piped.

"Marmalade, wasn't it?" Fred asked.

"That's right. We lost her a year ago."

"I'm so sorry. How terrible for you." He looked down at Olivia, who was redressing her doll in a doctor's scrubs and lab coat with a tiny stethoscope. "Although you do have the consolation of the child."

"That's right," Julie said, hiding a smile.

Fred returned his attention to Viv. "Well, why don't I take you on a tour of the house? I'm sure we'll encounter my Siamese, Constantine, on one of the beds. He likes to take an after-dinner nap before his evening playtime."

"That would be great," Viv said. She jumped to her feet, eager to see the rest of the house. Fred showed her a casually-furnished office across the hall, a separate dining room with a large walnut table and a side board filled with china and crystal ("I do love to entertain"), and a kitchen. The kitchen was a disappointment. It was galley style with a stove and fridge that had seen better days, and cupboards painted a dingy blue. It did have a dishwasher, however, and a view of a fenced backyard with a flower garden and stone patio.

The house's only bathroom was on the second floor, a four-piece with pink tile. There were three bedrooms, each with a queen-sized bed and handmade quilt. The master had the bay window Viv had spotted from the street, plus a flat screen TV, and a collection of DVDs in the bookcase beneath it. In the middle of the bed sat Constantine, cleaning his front paws. He had a dark face with almond-shaped blue eyes, a cream-coloured body, and chocolate-coloured legs and tail. He stopped cleaning himself to meow petulantly.

"Hello Constantine," Fred said, sitting down on the bed and stroking the cat's back. The sleek animal climbed onto his lap and purred as Fred scratched behind his ears. Viv followed Fred into the room; Julie and Olivia had stayed below.

"This is Viv. Can you say hello?"

"What a handsome animal," Viv said. "He looks young. How old is he?"

"Just eighteen months. I've had him since he was a kitten."

Viv offered her hand to the cat, who hissed and disappeared under the bed.

"Constantine is very attached to me, but he takes a little time to warm up to other people. I'm sure you and he will get along magnificently once he knows you. He's such a loving, companionable animal." From beneath the bed the cat protested, producing a meow that sounded like a baby's cry.

"Yes, Constantine, I know you're there. I'll find your laser pointer in a little while. He loves chasing that," Fred said. "Let me finish showing you the house."

The third floor attic was devoted to storage ("I've never bothered with the attic . . . the house is too big for one person as it is"), and the basement was low-ceilinged, dark, and creepy, but contained a washer and dryer. Viv considered that a luxury after years of schlepping her stuff to a laundromat.

Leaving the house, Fred led the way to a detached garage at the rear of the garden. He unlocked the padlock on the garage door and levered it up to reveal a yellow, 1973 VW Beetle.

"Her name is 'Daisy.' She was my aunt's car. I take her to the shop for check-ups, but I don't drive her very often. You're welcome to use her, if you like. I forgot to ask – you do drive, don't you?"

"I have a licence. I don't drive much, living here in Toronto, but I appreciate the offer." Fred nodded, shut the car back up in the garage, and returned to the house with Viv.

"What do you think? Could you see yourself living here?" he asked. They were back in the living room, where Fred was serving tea from a silver service and lemon poppy seed cake he had baked himself on china plates.

"I certainly could," Viv said. "It's a beautiful house, and so convenient to work."

"I wouldn't rent my house to just anyone, but Julie recommended you. She said that I could trust you to keep all my treasures safe and to take excellent care of Constantine. You understand that he must never be allowed outside. I couldn't bear to think of him being hit by a car, or attacked by a dog."

"Of course not. Cats should be kept indoors, where they're safe."

"Exactly. I have a manual here with Constantine's routine and his vet's phone number, as well as instructions on lighting the furnace, what to do if the water heater leaks, a maintenance plan for the indoor and outdoor plants, and my contact information in Greece. We've already discussed the rent and utilities. There's a lease here, if you want to take the place. You could move in on Saturday." He lifted a coil-ringed manual to expose the four-page lease.

"I would be delighted to look after your home and Constantine during your sabbatical," Viv said. Rent cheques were produced, but Fred insisted they review the lease paragraph by paragraph before allowing Viv to sign. When she had, he handed her two keys on a pewter fob.

"Welcome to your new home," he said with a smile.

Chapter 15

When Viv got back to Sabrina's condo that night, she noticed that the lights were on in her friend's room and the door was ajar. Viv tapped on it with her fingernails.

"Sabrina, are you alone?" she called.

"Come in."

Viv walked inside and found Sabrina sitting up in bed with her computer balanced on her knees. "Just trying to finish some work for tomorrow," her friend said.

"How was your weekend with Rick?"

"Not great. We broke up." Sabrina kept her eyes on the screen, but they were suspiciously pink.

"You're kidding! I'm so sorry." Viv perched on the edge of the bed as Sabrina shrugged. "What happened?"

"Rick said I was too engrossed in work to invest enough time in our relationship. That was what this weekend was about, finding more time to spend together. I guess it was too little, too late."

"That's sad." Viv patted Sabrina's leg beneath the covers. "Rick seemed like a good guy."

"He is, but any man who gets involved with me has to appreciate how important my career is. I'm never going to be a mommy or a housewife. Rick's in banking, too. He knows that you have to make an extra effort to get noticed. He must think that only men want to succeed."

"Is there anything I can do?"

"No. I'll be fine." Sabrina glanced up. "What's been happening with you?"

"Big news. I found a house to rent, and I'm moving in on Saturday."

"What!"

Viv told Sabrina all about Fred Shiner and his urgent need to find a tenant. "The house is gorgeous, if a little fussy with all his antique furniture. But it's big and cheap and close to work, and the neighbourhood is great. You've been really generous, letting me stay here all this time and helping me to get over Kyle, but it's time I moved on. I just wish I wasn't leaving right when you and Rick have broken up."

"Don't worry about me. I don't have anywhere near the emotional investment that you had with Kyle. But how did your date with Drew go on Saturday night?"

"It started well. I told him about my mother and how I'm having dinner with her tomorrow night, and Drew seemed so understanding. We were getting pretty cozy on the couch after dinner when he got a business call. Someone rescheduled a meeting from Monday to Sunday without telling Drew first. He had to run to the airport to pick up the client. Otherwise, we might have – you know."

Sabrina put down the computer and belly-flopped onto the mattress beside Viv. "So, you have chemistry with Drew that you didn't have with Josh?"

"For sure! But I have to admit that I felt a little sluttish leaving his apartment. An elderly lady in the hallway looked at me as if I had been making a booty call."

"What's wrong with that? We've all done it. By the way, I made those phone calls to check up on Drew. His dating history looks fine. He's away on business a lot, but he still managed to hook up with three women in the past four years. The last one he dated for six months before they broke up. Things seemed pretty amiable on both sides."

"That's good to hear."

Sabrina grinned. "So, are you going to sleep with him?"

Viv hesitated. She normally didn't get intimate with men she didn't love, but Drew had a charisma that was hard to resist.

"I think so, but didn't you say I was moving too fast?"

"Yes, but now that I've checked him out thoroughly, we know that you're not wasting your time with him. If you want a husband and a family, Drew seems like a safe bet."

"He is big on family. He's flying out to Chicago this weekend to see his parents for Father's Day."

"If you find him attractive, I say go for it."

Viv grinned. "Well, thank you for your blessing."

"You're welcome. Are you going to see each other this week?"

"I'm not sure, but he did tell me to call him tomorrow after I see Mother. He wants to know how our meeting goes."

"Good. Are your ready for that, by the way?"

"As ready as I'm ever going to be."

Sabrina frowned. "Don't be too quick to write Véronique off. Remember, a woman doesn't have the same opportunities to get ahead in this world that a man has. Sometimes you have to make compromises."

"But you mom runs a bar, and she still managed to keep you around when you were a kid."

"Sure. I knew how to pull a beer by the time I was eight. But remember, my mom didn't have a choice. There was no one else to look after me after my dad died."

Viv shook her head. "No, I'm not falling for that. My mom could have taken me to New York if she had wanted to."

"Your dad would never have let you go."

"Of course not, but she didn't even try. She could have worked out a visitation schedule with him. I could have stayed with her in the summer and with Daddy during the school year."

Sabrina shrugged. "I don't know. There are always two sides to a story. Make sure you hear her out before you cut her out."

Viv sighed. "That's what everyone keeps telling me. Look, I promise to listen. I just don't believe she has anything to say that will validate ignoring me for all those years." Viv kept her eyes lowered as she traced the floral pattern in Sabrina's duvet with her finger. "I just don't."

"Poor Viv," Sabrina said, rubbing her friend's shoulder.

When Viv swept through the double doors of the Castle Crest Hotel the following night, she was ready for battle. She looked cool and regal in her cream and gold dress with a silk shawl draped over her shoulders and her hair in a braided updo. She paused to look around the lobby. It was two stories high with Corinthian columns, a glittering crystal chandelier over the armchairs, potted ferns, and a tinkling marble fountain. Véronique was not waiting for her in one of the chairs, however, so where was she? Viv strode to the reception desk to find out.

The concierge glanced up at her. "Good evening, madam."

"Good evening. I'm looking for Véronique Roux."

"Would you care to have a seat? I'll ring her room."

But the elevator bell dinged, and Viv turned to look. A woman emerged. Slim – not as tall as her white-columned dress would have her seem, but taller than Viv – with black hair capping a fine-boned face and grey, doe eyes. She wore her trademark red shoes: four-inch stilettos with snakeskin on the heel, toe, and ankle strap. Her eyes found Viv and lit up with pleasure.

"Viviane!"

"Mother." Viv waited for Véronique to come to her. Which Véronique did like a model strutting down a runway.

"You look beautiful," her mother said. She took Viv's hands and kissed both cheeks. Viv caught the scent of white jasmine as she felt her mother's cool skin against hers.

"You look well, Mother." In fact, Véronique looked extraordinarily well, without a misplaced hair or a wrinkle on her youthful face. Viv had seen photographs of her mother over the years in magazines. A wrinkle would never mar the face of the creator of Rouge Shoes. On the other hand, there was a hint of her mother's sixty-plus years at her jawline and throat.

"I've made a reservation for us in the Wedgwood Room. I thought it would be nice to stay in tonight."

"That's fine."

"Good. It's this way." Véronique slipped a manicured hand

through her daughter's arm. Feeling that it would be churlish to pull away, Viv allowed it to remain. Her mother guided her across the lobby to a pair of opaque glass doors so perfectly balanced that they opened at the mere touch of her hand.

"Good evening," the maître d' said with a bow.

"Reservation for Roux," her mother murmured.

The maître d' checked his list and nodded.

"Follow me." He led them to a table for two with comfortably-upholstered armchairs. Viv slipped into her seat and glanced around the room. It was painted Wedgwood blue with delicate china plates mounted decoratively on the walls. Sunlight slanted through the mullioned windows, creating a diamond pattern on the blue-and-green tiled floor. The maître d' fussed with napkins and menus before retreating to his station.

"Such a feminine room," Véronique said. She turned to her daughter. "It's wonderful to see you again. Thank you for agreeing to come."

Viv nodded and picked up her menu, glancing through it distractedly. She had imagined this encounter so many times without considering that there would be a meal to eat first.

Their waitress appeared and introduced herself. "May I get you something to drink?"

"I'll have a Vodka Gimlet. Viviane?"

"I'll have the same." Viv didn't care what she drank. The waitress nodded and disappeared.

"Tell me, dear, how is your father?"

Viv glanced up and saw real concern on her mother's face.

"He's fine. The angioplasty was preventative. He needs to rest for a couple of weeks and watch his diet."

"That's what Gabe said in his e-mail, but you know how your father is at making light of situations. It's good to hear you confirm it."

"You e-mailed Daddy after the angioplasty?"

"Of course. As soon as you told me it had happened. I've been concerned about his health since he started renovating houses. He's not a young man anymore."

"I know. That's what I tell him."

The waitress returned with their cocktails and asked if they were ready to order.

"I'll have the pear and walnut salad, and the mushroom ravioli," Véronique said.

Viv glanced down at the menu and chose the first items she saw. "I'll have the gazpacho, and an eight ounce sirloin, please. Medium rare."

"Excellent choices." The waitress left.

Viv fiddled with the bread basket, choosing a multi-grain roll before offering the rest to her mother.

"No thank you. I never eat bread."

Viv refrained from rolling her eyes as she dropped the basket on the table. She sawed her roll in half and slathered it with butter. "I never have to worry about carbs."

Her mother smiled. "You're blessed with my mother's constitution. It kept her slender all her life, despite those heavy sauces she liked to cook."

"I never met my grandparents." Viv tore off a mouthful of bread and popped it into her mouth.

"No. They returned to France after Papa retired. They're both gone now."

Viv nodded, chewing. Another missed opportunity.

"Your father told me you had a major disappointment recently. I'm sorry that Kyle turned out to be a thoroughly unreliable young man."

Viv opened her mouth to protest, but her mother's assessment of Kyle was spot on. Funny, he had seemed so trustworthy and responsible when they were together. Up until the end, that is.

The waitress served them their appetizers, and Viv swallowed a spoonful of the cold soup without tasting it. Her mother tried her salad.

"So, how are you, Viviane?"

As if you care, Viv thought, the spoon halted mid-way to her mouth. It slipped from her fingers and fell into her bowl. Viv grimaced when a few drops of soup splashed onto the serving plate.

She wanted to appear cool and deadly that evening, not gauche.

Taking a deep breath, she replied, "I'm fine. I'm dating again – a businessman."

"What kind of business is he in?"

"Executive recruitment."

Her mother paused, one sculpted eyebrow raised, but returned to her salad without comment. Viv felt as if Drew had been slighted.

"He's in information technology and energy," Viv added. "Two very important sectors, you know."

"Of course."

Viv was not satisfied that her mother was sufficiently impressed, however, and began to feel perturbed. "How is *your* business doing?" she asked.

"Very well. After concentrating on the North American market for more than a decade, we're making significant inroads into Europe. We even have a shop on Avenue Montaigne in Paris."

Viv was impressed in spite of herself. She knew that some of the greatest fashion designers had shops on that street. She forced herself to say, "Congratulations. You must be very proud."

Véronique smiled and reclined back against her chair. "Thank you. It took years of hard work, but the business has never been more successful."

The waitress returned with their entrées. A steak, still sizzling, with an assortment of tiny roasted potatoes and grilled vegetables, was set before her. Viv severed a piece of meat with her knife and fork and ate it. Her mother cut a square of ravioli in half and speared it with her fork.

"Which brings me to one of the reasons I asked to see you tonight." Véronique popped the pasta into her mouth and chewed before continuing. "I plan to retire in five years, and I would like you to take over Rouge Shoes."

Viv's mouth dropped open as she stared at Véronique.

"I want you to move to New York this summer to begin learning the business. In two years' time, you should be sufficiently trained to handle the day-to-day operations. I will remain in an advisory position for another three years to assist you with the design decisions. Then I would be prepared to hand the business to you. I'm looking forward to retirement, although I haven't decided where I'm going to live yet. Perhaps half of the year in New York – I have so many friends there – and half in Italy." She paused, waiting for her daughter's response.

Viv found her voice at last. "But, Mother, I'm a school teacher, not a business woman or a shoe designer."

Véronique waved a dismissive hand. "Teaching a group of six-year-olds is hardly a profession, dear. It's glorified baby-sitting. And after this break-up of yours, I'm sure you see the importance of having a real career to provide financial security. As for not being a business woman, neither was I, when I began. I learned as I went, and I can teach you. Having the design talent is more difficult, of course. I hope that you've inherited my artistic flair, but even if you haven't, I can teach you to recognize it in others. There's a talented young woman working with me right now who could do the designing, if you're incapable. We'll just have to see how you do."

Viv was insulted by her mother's assessment of her profession, and got more and more riled as the speech continued. With great restraint, she placed her utensils on her plate and leaned toward Véronique.

"Mother, you can't be serious. I already have a career, one that I love. Someday I hope to be blessed with a family, and then I'll stay home to raise my children. That's what I plan to do with my life. I don't want to peddle shoes."

"Peddle shoes!" Véronique hissed. Two pink patches appeared on her cheeks. "Rouge is so much more than that. It's about a lifestyle of elegance and grace. I sacrificed everything for the success I have, Viviane, and now I'm handing it to you on a golden platter. Don't be so foolish as to dismiss it so easily."

"Yes, I know you sacrificed everything for your business, Mother." The fire blazing within Viv had turned icy cold, and her face appeared taut and white. "You sacrificed Daddy and me for your success. I would never do the same to my children, and I would never accept the business that caused me so much unhappiness. I don't want it, and I don't want you. Never contact me again."

She rose from the table to lean over her mother. "And I don't like to be called 'Viviane.' It's pretentious. My name is Viv. Goodnight."

Véronique sat very straight and still, only her eyes betraying her anger. Viv strode triumphantly from the restaurant, thrilled that she would never have to see her mother again.

Chapter 16

Of course, it couldn't be that easy. An hour later, Viv was sitting cross-legged on her futon with a peanut butter sandwich on a plate and her cell phone glued to her ear.

"I know, Daddy. It's a very good business. Uh huh. Yes, I understand that Mother is very upset. What? How can you take her side? Well, it sounds like you think I should give up teaching and move to New York. You know I would never do that."

As Viv paused to listen, Sabrina looked into the room. Viv motioned for her friend to enter.

"Everything you say is true, Daddy, but I've made up my mind. Let's not fight about this anymore. I'm going back to the building supply store after work tomorrow to look at tiles for the showers. Don't worry, I'll drop by the house to get the measurements from Tom first. Is there anything thing else I should look at while I'm at the store? Lighting fixtures? Okay, I'll take some pictures for you. All right, I'll stay for dinner afterward. Love you, Daddy. Good night."

Viv put down her cell as Sabrina sat down on the mattress and pointed at the sandwich.

"I thought you were having dinner with your mom?"

Viv nodded. "I did, but I didn't eat much. I was hungry by the time I got home." She took a bite of her sandwich.

"Dinner didn't go well?"

Viv swallowed and grinned. "Depends on who you ask. I had a great time." She explained about her mother's offer to pass the business on to her. Sabrina whistled.

"I heard what you said to your dad about never giving up teaching, and I agree. You're a born teacher. But what an opportunity! I'd give all my teeth to inherit Rouge. Do you think you could talk your mom into adopting me?"

Viv shook her head as she took a second bite. "You have an adorable mother who doesn't have a block of ice for a heart. Mother's not worth it, even for all her pretty shoes."

Sabrina sighed. "They're awfully lucrative pretty shoes. A girl can dream. Oh well, back to real life. Would you listen to the presentation I have to give tomorrow?"

At three fifteen the next day, Viv was finishing an art class with her students when there was a knock on the classroom door. Barbara, the school receptionist, stuck her head in.

"Guess what, boys and girls? Miss Nowak's mom is here for a visit. Say hello to Madame Roux."

Viv looked up in surprise. Barbara disappeared, and her mother sauntered into the room. She whipped large, white sunglasses from her face and said, "Bonjour, boys and girls."

"Bonjour Madame Roux," a handful of the students responded.

Véronique smiled. "What charming children! Don't mind me. I've been longing to see where my daughter teaches. I'll just have a look around while you finish up for the day." She walked to the back of the room while Viv stared after her and the children giggled. Viv returned her attention to her students with difficulty.

"All right, everyone, the bell is going to ring in ten minutes. Leave your art work on top of your desk so that the glue can dry, and don't forget to sign your name to it. Jasmine, will you take around the recycling bin, please? Put all your leftover scraps in the recycling bin for Friday's art project. Jeremy, go back to your seat, please. Jasmine doesn't need your help."

Ten minutes later, the children were lined up in single file at the door. "See you tomorrow. Have a good night," Viv called after the bell sounded. The children rushed from the room, leaving Viv alone with her mother. She stormed to the Wall of Fame where her mother was studying the portraits.

"What are you doing here? How dare you ignore my wishes. I told you last night that I never wanted to see you again!"

Véronique ignored her outburst to remark, "These photos are delightful." She pointed at a boy with his face painted to resemble a lion. "Who is he supposed to be?"

"Simba from *The Lion King*."

"Isn't he a dear with those big, brown eyes. You've captured him roaring."

"Yes. Never mind that. What do you want?"

"And this girl with the toy stethoscope who is listening to her puppy?"

"She wants to be a vet."

"Adorable. Look how serious she is."

"Mother, you can't just show up while I'm teaching."

"You took all of these yourself?"

"Yes. For Super Star Friday, when the children dress up as their heroes."

"What a marvellous idea. And these photographs are remarkable. You've got a real talent for lighting and composition."

Viv sighed. "What are you doing here, Mother?"

Véronique looked at Viv for the first time. "I had a long phone conversation with your father last night after you left the restaurant. It seems that I don't know my daughter very well. He told me what a fine teacher you are, and how you've always loved children. I thought I would come and see for myself. These portraits – I didn't expect to find them here. You're a gifted photographer, Viv."

Viv noticed that her mother did not address her as "Viviane," but was unmoved. "I'm an amateur, but photographing my students combines the two things I love."

Véronique nodded. "I can see that. I have a friend in the city who's a portrait photographer. May I take some of your pictures to her? I'd like to hear what she thinks of them."

Viv was flattered by her mother's praise, but decided to appear non-committal. She crossed her arms over her chest and did not meet Véronique's eyes. "Who did you say she was?"

"Frances Harvey."

Viv's eyes widened. "Frances Harvey! She's wonderful. She's photographed Mother Teresa and the Queen of England. The portrait she took of Nelson Mandela the year before he died was extraordinary."

"Yes, she's very good. I've known her since we went to private school together. She took black and whites of us back then with a cheap little instant camera." She leaned closer to Viv. "She asked us to pose in our underwear. Very risqué. Even then, I knew she was special." She studied Viv. "I think you have something. May I ask her to have a look at your children?"

Viv hesitated, rotating her ring. She didn't want to owe her mother for a favour, but Véronique had said that she was talented. She wouldn't be willing to show her photographs to Frances Harvey if she were lying, would she? Not even Véronique would waste the time of an important artist.

"All right. Let me get something to put them in." Viv hurried to her desk to get a legal-sized envelope.

"Wonderful," Véronique said with a sly smile.

After her mother's departure, Viv was sitting at her desk. She couldn't get over the fact that Frances Harvey would be seeing some of her photographs. She must be dreaming. If Ms. Harvey liked them, Daddy and her friends would be so proud of her.

Daddy! She had forgotten all about him. She was supposed to get the measurements for the showers, check out the tiles and the lighting fixtures at the building supply store, and drop by his house in time for dinner tonight. She checked her watch; it was four thirty. She'd better get a move on, or Tom might be gone for the day.

Viv was relieved to see Tom's truck still parked out front of the house. She knocked before entering.

"Tom?" she called.

There was no answer, but she heard a clatter upstairs.

"Tom," she called again as she trotted up the stairs to the second floor.

"I'm in here." She rushed down the hallway to the master bedroom and into the ensuite. Tom had ripped up the old linoleum and was tossing it into a box.

"Hey, Viv." He paused, his face breaking into a smile that brought out the crinkly lines beside his eyes. "Good to see you. Have you come to work?"

"Sorry, not tonight. I know I promised I'd be by to help, but I'm working for Daddy tonight. He asked me to get the measurements for the showers from you, and then I'm going to look for tile at the building supply. But I can come back to help tomorrow after school."

The smile faded. "You don't really need to, you know."

"But I want to. And I will. Tomorrow night. How about you show me how to tile, and I'll do one of the showers?"

He nodded. "Sure. That would be a big help." He pulled a tape measure from his back pocket. "You got a paper and pen?"

"Just a minute," she said, rummaging through her purse. She found a pen and the notepad she had purchased for jotting down information about the reno. "Shoot!"

Tom stepped into the walk-in shower, the tape measure rattling in his hands. "Forty inches."

"Forty inches," she repeated.

"By six feet."

"Six feet."

"By eight feet, but Gabe knows the ceiling height."

"Got it," Viv said, noting the height anyway.

"Now, you have to tile the floor and the walls in here. Maybe with all the same tile, but maybe with different kinds. Your dad might want a decorative inset on the wall, too, so give him a selection of tiles to choose from."

Viv nodded, her pen poised over the paper. "What kind of tile should I look for?"

Tom shrugged. "There's a lot to choose from. Ceramic, stone, porcelain, mosaic. There's pebble, too, but Gabe doesn't usually go for that."

"Okay," Viv said, scribbling. "Anything else?"

"Well, you're going to have to order some thinset mortar and grout. Your dad will tell you how much to get." He stepped out of the shower and looked over Viv's shoulder as she wrote. She was very aware of his nearness.

"Grout," she said, writing down the last item. She looked up into his eyes and smiled. "Done."

"Come on. Let's go do the other bathroom." Viv followed him out of the master and down the hallway to the four-piece.

"Now, here the tub and shower are combined. You'll only be tiling the wall above the tub."

"I know that," Viv said, rolling her eyes.

"I know you do, darling. Just mentioning it." He pulled out the tape. "The depth is seventeen inches. Take that from your eight feet and you get . . ."

"Seventy-nine inches," Viv said automatically. "That's six feet, seven inches."

"You're quick."

"At simple math. I hang around first-graders all day."

"Your dad was telling me that you might be giving it up."

Viv paused to stare at Tom. "When did he tell you that?"

"Let's see. I was talking to him on Sunday, after I got home. He wanted a progress report on the reno."

"He's wrong, you know. I'm not giving up teaching."

Tom had been taking measurements while she spoke. "I didn't think so, from the way you've talked. That's five feet."

"Five feet."

"By thirty inches."

Viv nodded as Tom climbed out of the tub.

"We don't have to worry about the four-piece in the basement. We're using a shower surround for that."

"Good. So we're all done here?"

"That's it." Tom clumped down the hallway in his work boots. Viv caught up to him in the ensuite, where he was wrestling with the box of broken linoleum.

"Say, Tom. I'm curious. What exactly did Daddy say to you about me quitting teaching?"

"As long as you're here, pick up the other end, will you?"

"Sure." She slung her purse over her shoulder and bent to pick up the end. The box was heavy and awkward with the loose linoleum. Tom backed out of the room first.

"He said your mom was about to offer you her shoe business in New York, which would make you a very rich young lady."

"That's true, but I don't care about the money." They trudged down the hallway with the box. "I've got everything I need, and the school board offers a good pension."

Tom started backward down the stairs, the contents of the box shifting toward him. "Careful, now." After a moment, he added, "He also said that it would give you a chance to get away from Toronto and start over again. Something about a busted romance?"

Viv grimaced. She wished her daddy hadn't been so forthcoming with Tom; it was embarrassing. Tom was taciturn and tough. She assumed that he suffered through his broken romances without a whimper.

"It's true I wouldn't mind a fresh start somewhere. Toronto's a great city, but who wouldn't want a chance to live in New York?" The majority of the weight was on Tom, but Viv struggled to hold up her end. "Just between you and me, I've always loved fashion. It would be exciting to rub shoulders with some of the world's great designers."

Tom grunted as they navigated the bend in the staircase and continued down the steps to the front door. Now that the subject had been broached, Viv couldn't seem to stop talking.

"The thing about teaching the early grades is that it's so predictable. The curriculum never varies much, or the methodology. Plus, there's so much politics in the school system. The idea of being the head of a prestigious company like Rouge is very tempting. Scary, too, but imagine being able to make all of the decisions yourself."

They navigated the box through the door and out onto the porch.

"And I think I'd be okay at shoe design. I've got an artistic bent. That's why I took up photography. Even my mother thinks my work is pretty good." She kept silent about Frances Harvey seeing some of her portraits; that was still too incredible to share. And what if Ms. Harvey didn't like her work? Best to keep quiet about it for now.

Out loud, she said, "No, the design aspect of the job doesn't frighten me."

They trundled over to the dumpster on the front lawn. Tom shifted the load up onto his shoulders and fired the box into the bin. He wiped his hands on his pants.

"But you're not going to give up teaching and leave Toronto, are you?"

Viv shook her head. "No. I'd miss the kids too much. And my friends, and Daddy. And Toronto. Sure, I have sad memories leftover from Kyle and the break-up, but I'm moving on."

"To the head-hunter. I remember." Tom grinned, and there were glints of devilment in his eyes.

"Maybe," Viv said with a grin of her own. "Drew seems like a nice man."

Tom rested a hand on her shoulder. It felt comfortable there. "If not, there're plenty more fish in the sea, darling. You're young, pretty, and feisty, and you've got a heart of gold. You won't have any trouble finding a good man to look after you."

"Thanks, Tom," Viv said, patting his hand. "Although a lot of women would take issue with being told they needed looking after."

Tom removed his hand. "I'm kind of old-fashioned that way."

Viv studied him in his worn, dirty clothes. Up close, she could see some white mixed in with the dark stubble on his cheeks and chin. He was a little battered by the years, perhaps, but confident and capable. Plus, there was humour and kindness in his eyes. She didn't mind old-fashioned. Too bad he was old enough to be her father.

"You got any sons, Tom?"

"I do. One's twenty-nine with a wife and two kids and another one on the way. The other is twenty-seven and single. Works as a fire fighter in B.C." He winked. "He'll be back someday for the farm. Might take a few years, though."

"Nah, if he's as good-looking as you, another woman will have snatched him up by then."

Tom pretended to tip a non-existent hat to her, and Viv bowed.

"Besides, I'm lousy at choosing men. That's why my friends are helping me. Drew is contestant number two, by the way."

"I'd be careful about that. Ain't no way anybody else can know what makes your heart beat faster, Viv."

Viv shrugged. "I've been wrong before, you know."

"Growing pains. You were too young. You'll know better now.

"Thanks, I sure hope so. But I've got to run. I'll see you tomorrow after school to tile the shower, all right? I promise."

"See you then. Tell Gabe that the kitchen appliances are going to be delivered by the end of the week. That ought to help him keep his pants on."

"Will do. I'll pick some pretty tiles for the showers."

"Okay, darling. See you."

Viv checked her watch as she left, and realized that she had only six minutes before the streetcar was due. As she trotted for the stop, she felt pretty good about her love life. Tom was right; she was more mature now. With Julie and Sabrina weeding out the bad choices, she was bound to find the right man this time.

Chapter 17

It was after ten by the time Viv got back from dinner with Gabe and Magda, but it had been a productive evening. Gabe had called in an order to the building supply store before they sat down to eat. The materials to tile the showers were going to be sent in the first delivery the next morning. She hoped that Tom would be pleased with their choices.

Sabrina wasn't home when she got in, but had left a light on in the living room. Viv scrubbed off her make-up and climbed into bed with a new romance on her e-reader. She was a few pages in when her cell rang. Darn! Just when things were getting good.

"Hello?"

"Hi, Viv. It's Drew. I was just calling to see how your dinner went with your mom last night."

Viv sat up in bed. With her mother surprising her at school that afternoon and with everything else that had happened since then, she had forgotten about calling Drew.

"I'm sorry. To be perfectly honest, I forgot to call, but it's been a crazy day. The dinner with Mother went fine. As a matter of fact, she offered to give me Rouge Shoes." Viv heard an intake of breath on the other end.

"You're joking. Wow. What did you say?"

"I told her I didn't want it. She expected me to give up teaching and move to New York this summer to start training. I just can't do that. It's not what I want out of life. I told Mother no thanks, and that I never wanted to see her again. Then I left the restaurant."

"That certainly took balls, Viv. No regrets today, now that

you've had time to think about it? It's one hell of an opportunity, you know."

"I know I made the right decision. But you haven't heard what happened after that."

"What?"

"Mother dropped by my classroom this afternoon just before the bell rang."

"What did she want?"

Viv paused to think. "I don't know, exactly. She said something about not knowing her daughter very well."

"That sounds like a step in the right direction."

"Maybe. Anyway, she told me how much she loved my photographs of the kids in my class. She loved them so much, in fact, that she borrowed some to show Frances Harvey. Seems they're old schoolmates."

"Frances Harvey! I know her work. You must be ecstatic."

"I have to say, I'm pretty pleased. It's terrific to think that I might get some feedback from her."

"Do you think you'll get to meet Frances?

"I don't know. Mother didn't say. That would be fantastic, though."

"Sure would. I know you have issues with your mother, but she certainly makes your life interesting."

"When she's around, which isn't very often. Hey, there's something else I forgot to tell you. I rented a furnished house from a professor who's going on sabbatical for a year. I'm moving in on Saturday."

"That's good. I know how cramped you are at Sabrina's. I heard from Rick that the two of them broke up, by the way."

"Yes, I feel badly about deserting Sabrina just when she needs me the most. She says she's okay, though."

"Rick's taking it pretty hard. Say, can I give you a hand moving this weekend?"

"What? I thought you were surprising your parents in Chicago."

"Yeah, that didn't turn out so well. My parents are going to Las Vegas this weekend. My mom's giving the trip to my dad as a

Father's Day present. I cancelled my flights, and the airline is giving me a credit."

"That's too bad about your parents, but it works out well for me. I do have a few heavy boxes of books that I wouldn't mind a hand with. Sabrina has them in her storage locker. I'm going to rent a van, although there isn't that much stuff to move. Would that be okay?"

"Nothing would give me greater pleasure, milady. What time would you like me?"

"Say, eleven?"

"Great. I look forward to seeing you then." His voice lowered. "By the way, I hated the way things ended on Saturday night."

Viv giggled. "Me, too. Did the business meeting work out?"

"It did. Threw a real kink into the beginning of the week, but it's all straightened out now. I got a great deal for the client, too. But I do want to make things up to you, so I'd be happy to heft boxes, if you'll forgive me."

"There's nothing to forgive, Drew, but all the same, thank you. I'll see you on Saturday."

"Bye, baby."

Viv put down her phone. Things were looking up. She'd found a nice house to rent cheap, her mother was showing her work to a world-renowned photographer, and her new boyfriend appeared to be a keeper. The year had started out badly, but things were finally turning around. She clicked off the lamp and slid under the covers. Who knew what good fortune tomorrow might bring?

Viv woke up five minutes before her alarm on Thursday morning. Hopping out of bed, she showered, dressed, and was scrambling a couple of eggs when Sabrina staggered out of her room. Her hair was a bird's nest, and her eyes were bloodshot as she sank onto a stool at the kitchen island.

"Coffee," she croaked, stretching out her hand.

Viv poured some milk and coffee into a mug and placed it into her friend's hand. Sabrina brought the mug to her lips and sipped as

Viv buttered some toast.

"Rough night last night?"

Sabrina nodded and winced. "Had a little too much to drink. Didn't get home until two."

"Want some eggs?" Viv held up the skillet with the cooked eggs.

"Hell, no." Viv slid the food onto her plate and sat down beside Sabrina.

"I won't be home until later tonight, by the way. I'm helping Tom tile one of the showers."

"Good for you," Sabrina muttered.

"You don't want to talk right now, I take it?"

"No, and could you go eat on the couch or something? The smell of those eggs is making me nauseous."

"No problem," Viv said, tiptoeing out of the kitchen.

The afternoon was warm, without a breeze to break the humidity. Riding the streetcar after work, Viv heard a peal of thunder and saw the first drops of rain spatter down the window. She sprinted from the streetcar when it reached her stop, running to the house as the rain started falling in straight sheets. Bolting up the porch steps, she practically tripped over a scruffy dog taking shelter from the downpour. He was a terrier of mixed breed with sad brown eyes and drooping ears. There was no collar around his neck. He got up and backed away from her, his tail waving tentatively.

"What's the matter, boy?" Viv held out her hand for the dog to sniff, but he sidled around her and darted down the stairs. Scurrying across the lawn to the sidewalk, he trotted across the street before Viv lost sight of him.

Viv shook her sodden raincoat out on the porch and stepped into the vestibule.

"Tom?" she shouted as she hung the raincoat on the back of the doorknob.

"Up here, Viv." She jogged up the stairs and found Tom sitting on the rim of the tub in the main bathroom with a trowel and a bucket of what looked like grey peanut butter on the floor beside him. Next to the bucket were packages of tiles. He smiled at her over his shoulder.

"I was expecting you about now. I just finished the first row of tiles so that the rest will be straight."

"Hey, have you seen a dog hanging around the house?"

Tom shook his head. "What's he look like?"

"Not very big. His head comes to about my knee. Grey, shaggy, with floppy ears. He was on the porch just now."

"I haven't seen him around, but I'll watch for him in case he comes back."

"Thanks. He was kind of cute. So, what do you want me to do first?"

"Climb in." Viv stepped into the tub and sat down beside him.

Tom pointed at the walls. "See those pencil lines? That's where the shelves and the inset for the pattern are going."

"Okay."

"Once I show you how, tile until you get to that line, and then call me. I'm going to work on the floor in the ensuite while you're doing this. If we both get done by the end of the day, we're laughing."

He picked up a glossy white tile. "First you need to back-butter the tile with the thinset." He spread some goop evenly across the back and scraped off the excess with his trowel, flicking it into the bucket.

"Then you press it here on the wall. Give it a good push and move it around a bit." He demonstrated for her. "Then put a couple of spacers in to keep the tiles evenly apart." He pushed in the blue plastic widgets, picked up a second tile, and back-buttered it. "You put the next tile beside it. Press it in good. And you keep on going until you get to the line." He glanced down at her. "Ready to give it a try?"

Viv picked up a tile and tried back-buttering it. "Is that enough?"

"Little more thinset." He took the trowel from her and scooped up some of the mortar, plopping it onto the tile and spreading it. "You don't want to be too stingy."

She took the tile from him and pressed it gingerly onto the wall.

"Don't be scared. You're not going to break it. Give it a good push and kind of squish it around a bit." He put his hand over hers to demonstrate. "Now put in the spacers."

Viv pushed two spacers beside the tile.

"Good. Let me see you do another one." He watched as Viv back-buttered the next tile and set it in place.

"I'm afraid it's going to fall off," she said.

"Nope, the thinset will hold it."

She added the spacers and looked for his approval.

"You got it. Keep at it. I'll see you later." Tom rose from the bathtub and climbed out while Viv bent to pick up the next tile. She had completed the second row and was two tiles into the third when her cell rang.

"Darn." She worked the phone out of her pocket with two dirty fingers. "Hello?"

"Viv, dear, it's Mother." Viv didn't reply, startled to hear her mother's voice. "Viv?"

"How'd you get my number?"

Véronique sighed. "From your father, of course. Now, listen carefully. I've got some good news."

"Yes?"

"I'm with Frances Harvey. She's just looked through your photographs and thinks they're lovely." Viv heard a voice in the background. "Frances says to tell you she's impressed, and that she'd like to talk with you."

Viv's face lit up with excitement. "That's fantastic! When would she like to do that?"

"Now. We're at her studio on Queen Street."

Viv frowned and looked up at the unfinished wall. She had promised Tom that she was going to tile the shower tonight, and she had barely started. She glanced at her watch.

"Mother, I'm right in the middle of something. It's 5:05. Could you give me until 6:30? I'll come right over then, I promise."

There was a pause. Véronique's voice was hushed when she spoke again.

"Viv, you have got to be kidding. This is Frances Harvey. If she wants to talk to you about your pictures, you drop everything and come right over."

"I know, I know. Look, tell Ms. Harvey that I'm on my way. I'll be there as soon as I can find a cab. What's the address?"

Véronique gave her the information. "That's perfect, dear. We'll see you soon."

"Bye, Mother." Viv slid her cell back into her pocket and hopped out of the tub. She hurried down the hall to the ensuite, where Tom was on his hand and knees working on the floor. Viv hated to disappoint him, but she had no choice.

"Tom, I'm really sorry. I have to go," she said.

"What's that?" He sat back on his knees and looked at her over his shoulder.

"Mother just called. She took some of my photographs to show Frances Harvey, a famous photographer. Do you know her?" Tom shook his head. "Take my word for it, she's fabulous, and she likes the pictures I took of my students. She wants to talk to me about them, but it has to be now. I've got to go. I'm really sorry." Viv waited uneasily for Tom's reaction.

He shrugged. "It doesn't matter. Go do what you have to do." He turned his back on Viv and continued tiling. Viv left the room, but hesitated. She didn't want to leave Tom on bad terms.

"Look, I'll come back tomorrow night. I really do want to help," she said, sticking her head around the door.

Tom continued working without bothering to look up. "I get that you're a busy person, Viv. But I'm working on a schedule here, and I'm behind. Just stick to helping Gabe make the decisions from now on. Get him to call me with what he wants. I'll take it from there."

Viv glanced at her watch again. Three minutes had passed since the phone call, but she wanted Tom to understand how really important this was to her. She entered the room and crouched beside him.

"Let me explain something, okay? I'm just an amateur photographer. I started taking pictures of my students a couple of years ago because it makes them feel special and important. To tell the truth, taking pictures makes me feel good, too. I'm happy with my work, but having an expert's advice would be priceless. And having Frances Harvey's approval would impress Daddy and Mother. Don't get me wrong. I know how important teaching is. But I'm an elementary school teacher. I'll never have the kind of financial success my parents have. I don't really care about my mother's opinion – she's not entitled to judge after deserting Daddy and me – but she thinks I don't have much of a career. If it turns out that I have some artistic talent – well, I'd feel pretty good about myself.

Tom stopped to look at her. "It's been a long day. I'm tired, and I've got animals to feed at home, so the sooner I finish tiling this floor and the shower, the sooner I can leave. You don't owe me anything, so stop wasting time and get going."

Up close, Viv could see the strain on Tom's face. It must be exhausting, being responsible for the reno and having all of the work to do, too. But as much as she wanted to help him, she couldn't give up this opportunity to meet Frances Harvey.

"I'm really sorry," Viv whispered before jumping to her feet. She rushed down the stairs, snatched up her purse and raincoat, and ran out onto the porch. She was moving so quickly that she didn't see the dog until she had stepped on him. He yelped, sprang down the steps, and tore across the lawn. A car was speeding down the rain-slick street toward him.

"No!" Viv cried. The dog darted into the road just as the car passed. Viv heard a "thump," and the car continued on as if the driver hadn't even noticed the small animal.

Viv raced into the street. The dog was staggering to get up, but flopped back down onto the pavement. Blood was streaming from his mangled front left leg.

"Puppy?" The dog snapped at Viv's outstretched hand, limped to his feet, and fell over. She caught him up in her arms and tore back to the house, throwing open the door and screaming for Tom as she pounded up the stairs.

"Viv?" Tom met her at the bedroom door. "What happened?"

"It's the dog I told you about. I startled him when I came out onto the porch, and he got hit by a car." Tears welled up in her eyes as she stared at the whimpering, struggling animal.

"Bring him into the bathroom where there's more light." She followed Tom inside and laid the dog on the subfloor where two work lights were set up. The dog struggled to get up, but Tom pressed him down.

"Easy now, fellow," Tom said in a soothing voice. He turned to Viv. "There's a medical kit in the kitchen, first upper cabinet on the left. Go get it for me."

Viv nodded and flew down to the kitchen, returning with the red metal box a minute later. She unlatched it and opened the top.

"There's some rolled bandage underneath the tray."

She found the bandage and held it out to Tom.

"Hold the dog while I wrap his leg."

Viv took Tom's place while he unrolled the gauze. The little animal's fur was bloody, and she could feel his ribs rising and falling as he panted. He didn't even bother to look at them anymore; that couldn't be good. Tom wrapped the bandage round and round the leg, cut off the end with a scissors, and tied a knot.

"All right, come here, fellow." He lifted the dog in his arms and rose as Viv leapt to her feet.

"Will he be okay?" she asked.

"Don't know. We'll take him to a vet right away. I've driven by one on Queen Street just a few blocks from here. Come on."

They hurried to Tom's truck, where he handed the keys to Viv. She opened the passenger's door and climbed in.

"There's a towel on the floor in the back."

Viv felt around until she located the towel and dragged it out. Opening it, she spread it on her lap, and Tom placed the dog there, wrapping him until only his head showed. The dog lay still, his head limp on Viv's knee.

Tom climbed inside the truck, started the engine, and pulled away from the curb. They sped down Harvard, turned right on Triller, and paused at a stop sign on Queen. It was rush hour, and they had to wait for a break in the traffic. Tom's fingers drummed impatiently on the wheel.

When an opening came, he made a sharp left turn and drove two blocks before careening to a stop in front of the veterinary hospital.

"You take him in. I'll find a place to park and be right there."

Viv nodded and slid out of the truck, carrying the wounded animal as gently as she could. She could see blood soaking through the towel as she hurried into the building.

"I need help," she shouted as she rushed to the receptionist's desk. The woman looked up, and then jumped to her feet.

"What happened?" The receptionist came around her desk to peer at the bundle in Viv's arms. Viv pulled the towel open, and the woman frowned.

"He was run over by a car," Viv said.

"Come with me."

Viv had a glimpse of a young woman with a cat on her lap before she was led to an examination room. She rested the dog on the table and was uncovering him when the receptionist returned with a blond woman in scrubs.

"I'm Dr. Lane," the blond said. She began making a quick inspection of the dog's injuries.

"He's a stray. He was hit by a car," Viv said.

"How long ago?"

"Fifteen minutes, maybe."

"He's going to need surgery. We'll do the best we can." Dr. Lane glanced up, looking at Viv's face for the first time. The vet's eyes were caring and intelligent. "Thanks for bringing him in."

Viv pressed her lips together, trying not to cry. If she hadn't dashed out of the house so unexpectedly, the dog wouldn't have run into the street. She was responsible for his accident. As the receptionist drew her away to the waiting room, Viv called out, "I'll pay for the surgery."

The receptionist was starting a new file on her computer when Viv felt a hand on her shoulder. It was Tom. He gazed at her expectantly, and Viv said, "The vet's taking him in for surgery now. I'm going to give the receptionist my contact information, if you'll wait for me." He nodded and squeezed her shoulder before taking a seat. Viv read the receptionist's name tag and saw that her name was "Stacy."

"What's your name, honey?" Stacy asked.

"Viv Nowak."

"We're going to have to call the dog something for our records." She looked up at Viv. "Any ideas?"

Viv stared back. She had never had a pet of her own; Magda hadn't wanted the responsibility when Viv was growing up. The closest she had ever come to having a pet was a plush German Shepherd doll she had kept on her bed when she was a child. She struggled to remember its name.

"Bruno?"

"As good a name as any," Stacy said with a smile. She took Viv's particulars and her credit card information. "I'll give you a call after the surgery. Let you know how Bruno did."

"Thanks, I'll be waiting."

Viv had turned to go when Stacy said, "Hey, thanks for bringing Bruno in and looking after him. You'd be surprised how many people would have left him on the street, or dumped him on our doorstep and taken off."

Viv remembered Bruno struggling on the pavement after the accident. How could anyone be so cruel? "You're welcome. And please take good care of him," she said.

"We will." Stacy looked back at her computer, and Tom stood up. Viv noticed the blood on his navy t-shirt and on his bare arms. She looked down and saw the stains on her own clothes. They were both a mess.

"Come on. I'll drive you home," he said. They walked back outside. The rain had slowed to a few drips that spattered their faces.

"That's okay," Viv said. "I can catch a streetcar from here. You've got work to finish at the house."

"You sure?"

Viv nodded, and Tom escorted her to the streetcar stop at the corner.

"What are you going to do about the photographer?" he asked along the way.

Viv winced; she had forgotten about Frances Harvey. She checked her watch. It was almost six. Her mother would be furious that she hadn't come. She looked up her mother's number in the call history on her cell and called as Tom watched. The phone rang only once before it was answered.

"Mother?"

"Viv, where are you? You've been incredibly rude," Véronique blurted.

"I'm sorry. There was an emergency, so I just couldn't make it. Please apologize to Ms. Harvey for me."

"I can't. She had to leave to see a client. She only had half an hour to squeeze you into a very busy schedule. I'm in a cab now, driving back to the hotel. I hope your emergency was worth it. I'm very disappointed in you."

Viv sighed. There was no point in explaining that she had blown her opportunity to see Frances Harvey on an injured stray.

"I'm disappointed, too, but it can't be helped. Thank you for trying to arrange the meeting. Even though it didn't work out, it was wonderful to hear that Ms. Harvey liked my work."

"It hasn't work out *yet*. Frances still has your prints. I'll see what I can do about arranging another appointment, but I can't guarantee anything."

"Aren't you flying back to New York today? You said you were only staying until Thursday."

"I've decided to extend my visit for another week. There are some loose ends I still have to tie up. If I'm able to arrange a second meeting with Frances, I suggest you arrive with a really good excuse for missing today's. Bring champagne and orchids. They're her favourite flower."

"Yes, Mother. Thanks for trying. It was kind of you."

"You're welcome." Her mother sounded somewhat placated. "I'm at the hotel now. Goodbye, dear." The call ended before Viv could say good night.

She looked at Tom, who stood beside her with his hands in his pockets and his shoulders hunched.

"Everything okay?" he asked.

"As okay as anything ever is with Mother. Never mind about her. If you give me your phone number, I'll call you about Bruno once I hear from the vet."

Tom recited the number while Viv entered it into her contact information. She dropped the phone into her purse and glanced up at him with a worried expression.

"What am I going to do with Bruno if he makes it, Tom? I'm about to move into a furnished house with an antisocial cat and a very particular landlord. I can't take a dog there."

"We'll work something out. Let's worry about that once we hear if Bruno makes it." She frowned, and Tom patted her arm. "Don't go borrowing trouble, Viv. There's plenty to go around for today."

She nodded and held up the bloodied towel she still carried. "Do you want this?"

He took it from her and stuffed it into a garbage can beside the streetcar stop. "That's about all it's good for now. I've got to go. Take care, Viv."

"You, too. I'll call you as soon as I hear anything."

The streetcar was coming toward her, slowing to a stop. Viv burrowed in her purse for her Metropass. When the streetcar paused, she crossed the road to the tracks, climbed onboard, and flashed her pass at the driver. He looked at it, peered up at her, and glanced away. Viv looked down; she had forgotten the blood stains on her clothes. She slid into a seat behind him and slumped down, wrapping her arms around herself to cover her shirt. As the streetcar started up, she whispered a prayer that Bruno would survive the surgery, and that she could find a home for him when he was ready.

Chapter 18

Sabrina wasn't home when Viv arrived at the condo. She changed out of her soiled clothes and took a hot shower, washing her hair and scrubbing away the blood on her skin. She was wrapped in a robe combing out her hair when the phone rang.

"Viv? Hi, it's Stacy from Lane Veterinary."

"How's Bruno?"

"He's all right, but Dr. Lane had to amputate his leg."

"Oh, no!" Viv's hand flew to her mouth. "How horrible."

"I know it's hard to take, but you'd be surprised how well a tripod does. That's what we call a dog who's lost a leg – a tripod. He'll still be able to run and be very active, once he's recovered. Dr. Lane said that Bruno's a strong dog otherwise, and that he was lucky the injuries were restricted to his leg. He'll be fine."

"If you say so," Viv said in a doubtful voice. "Can I come visit him tomorrow evening after work? I'd like to see how he's doing."

"That should be okay. We're open until seven on Friday evenings, if you can come before then."

"Fine. I'll see you tomorrow. Good night, and thanks for calling."

"You're welcome."

Viv tried calling Tom when the call ended, but only succeeded in getting his voice mail.

"Tom? It's Viv. Maybe you're on your way home now and not picking up. I heard from the vet, and they had to amputate Bruno's leg. The receptionist said that he's okay otherwise, and that dogs do fine with just three legs, but I still feel really bad for him. She said I

139

could see him tomorrow evening, but I'm going to come by the house first and tile the ensuite shower, so don't touch it, okay? I really mean it. If my cell rings while I'm there, I won't answer it, so no interruptions this time. If you want, you can come with me to see Bruno. All right, I'll see you tomorrow. Bye, Tom."

Viv spent an hour packing up her scanty belongings in preparation for the move that weekend. When she had finished, she sat in the dark on one of the couches and gazed out the living room window. Oddly enough, when she moved out of Sabrina's condo, it would be her first time living alone. Funny thing for a grown woman to say, but it was true. Would she be okay on her own?

Viv wrapped her arms around her knees. What did it say about a woman who wasn't content with her own company? That she was lonely and needy.

Come on, Viv. Count your blessings. You've got a lot going for you. A job you love, enough money to be comfortable, and a new man in your life. Plus, you're learning useful renovation skills. Besides, you won't be lonely. You'll have Constantine. Sounds like he's quite a talker.

She was about to go to bed when Sabrina came home.

"Viv?" Sabrina hesitated in the condo doorway, the light from the hallway spilling through the opening.

"I'm here, Sabrina." Viv clicked on a living room lamp and stood up.

Sabrina shut the door. "What are you doing sitting in the dark?" She dropped a couple of plastic bags on the floor and kicked off her shoes.

"I have a lot to think about." Viv padded down the hallway and told her friend about Bruno.

"I'm sorry, Vivvie. That's so sad."

Viv nodded. "What have you been up to?"

"Shopping for new clothes. Remember the Sabrina O'Sullivan two-step program to restart the human heart?" Viv nodded. "Well, this is a modified version for those whose hearts haven't actually stopped. My rejuvenation involves alcohol and shopping." Sabrina grinned, and Viv hugged her.

"We're both going to be fine. Right?" Sabrina asked. Viv nodded. "Come on, let's go have some ice cream. That's the third step. I forgot to mention it. Lots of expensive ice cream." Viv dashed away the two tears that had fallen and followed Sabrina into the kitchen.

"Tom, I'm here," Viv called the next day. She shut the front door and paused, staring at the newly carpeted stairs. "Hey, they laid the carpet today."

Tom appeared on the landing. "They did, upstairs and in the basement."

Viv bent to feel the pile. "It feels good. Daddy went with the textured finish, I see." She ran up the stairs to Tom.

He nodded. "It's a classic. Come and look." They turned and began touring the bedrooms.

"It's really coming along," Viv said.

Tom nodded. "I finished the main bathroom, the master's walk-in closet, and the cabinet in the ensuite since you've been here."

Viv smiled her approval of the main bathroom and the closet, but stopped dead when she saw the ensuite bathroom.

"Oh, Tom, it's beautiful." The granite floor felt cool to the soles of her feet as she walked to the cabinet and slid her hands over the marble counter top.

"Lovely. Two sinks."

Rolling open the top drawer, she exclaimed, "Look at all the compartments in here! I could really use this to organize my make-up." She peeked into the other drawers. "Any woman would love all this storage space."

"We like to think of the woman of the house when we do the master bath. I agree with your father's decision to go with the claw foot over a spa tub. It looks classy."

Viv studied the pristine white tub with its black iron feet and said, "It's a show-stopper." Tom nodded with a pleased smile. "Well, I'm ready to get to work on the shower if you are," she added.

He led her to the glassed-in enclosure at the back of the room. "I know you said not to touch it, but I did the floor and installed the tiles that had to be cut. There's still a lot of work to be done, so don't worry about not having enough to do."

Viv knelt on a pad beside the thin-set and the tiles. "I won't. What are you going to do while I'm tiling?"

"I've got a trifold mirror to install over the sinks, and a couple of chandeliers. I'll help you with the tiling when I'm done, and do the grout tomorrow. Once the shower's finished, that's it for the second floor. Just in time, too. Your father's coming for an inspection tomorrow."

"Don't worry, I'm sure he'll love what he sees. I'll be having breakfast with him on Sunday for Father's Day, so I'll ask him what he thinks then." She back-buttered the first tile. "What else has to be done before the house goes on the market?"

"There's still work to do in the basement. The walls are up, the ceiling's finished, and the carpet's down, but I still need to do the trim, paint, install the doors, and do the bathroom. The appliances are on order for the kitchen and the laundry. They should be here at the beginning of the week. Then there's the deck and the porch floor. And the staircase to the second floor. It needs a little tender-loving care."

Viv pushed her first tile in place, snuggling it up to the line that Tom had marked for her. "How much more time has Daddy scheduled for the reno?"

"Two weeks."

Viv glanced at him over her shoulder. "But Daddy won't be back to help for another week."

"That's right. At least he's hired landscapers to do the front and back yards."

Viv frowned. "Oh, Tom. Do you think you can do it all?"

"If nothing goes wrong, and we get a patch of dry weather. Can't do the deck in the pouring rain." He shook his head at Viv's troubled face. "Don't worry, darling. If I can't, your father'll just have to fork out money for an extra mortgage payment. Nothing to be done about it."

"You're right." Viv reached for the next tile. "You've been a saint, taking all this on for Daddy."

"Let's not forget he's paying me for my trouble," Tom said in an amused voice. "Now, I'd better get at it if we're going to finish in time to see Bruno tonight. I've been thinking about the little guy."

"Me, too." Viv pressed the tile in place. "I hope he's doing okay."

With Tom helping to finish the shower, they were able to clean up by six thirty. Finding a parking space ate up another five minutes, and it was twenty minutes before closing when they hurried inside the vet's door.

"Sorry we're late," Viv said. The waiting room was deserted except for them.

Stacy looked up and smiled. "That's okay. We've been telling Bruno that you're coming all day. I think he's been looking forward to it." She stood up and rolled her chair back. "Follow me to the recovery room."

She led them past the two examination rooms and the surgery to a spacious room with cages. A young man dressed in scrubs smiled at them as he scooped wet food into three bowls on the counter next to a sink. Two of the wire cages on the left side of the room were occupied. One of them contained a tabby with stitches on her face who glared out of her remaining eye. The other contained a Chihuahua with a cone around its neck. An old Labrador with white hairs mixed in the black fur of his muzzle limped over to greet them, his tail wagging.

"That's Duke," Stacy said. "He just had a cyst removed. You're a good boy, aren't you, Duke?" The receptionist scratched behind his ears, and the dog turned, revealing a shaved patch and stitches on the upper part of his leg.

"This is one of our veterinary technicians, Thiago Garza," Stacy said. The young man nodded. "Dr. Lane has gone home, so he'll show you Bruno. I have to close up. I'll see you later."

"Thank you," Viv said. Stacy smiled and left the recovery room.

"I hope you don't mind waiting while I feed the others," Thiago said. "Here you go, Duke." He put a bowl on the floor next to an open-doored cage, and the black dog began gobbling his dinner. Thiago opened the tabby and Chihuahua's cages, slipping in their food with a few words of encouragement, and fastened the doors behind them.

"Bruno's over here." Thiago took them to a cage on the other side of the room with a mat in front of it. "He's pretty groggy right now. The doc's putting him on some strong pain medication for the first two days. He won't be getting dinner tonight – just water."

The technician knelt on the mat outside the cage and opened the door.

"Hi, Bruno. How're you doing, buddy?"

The terrier lifted his head. There was a thick, white bandage wrapped around his chest, extending over his left shoulder where the leg had been amputated. Bruno's eyes were only half open, and his chest heaved as he panted.

Thiago brushed some fur away from Bruno's eyes and stroked his head. When he stopped, the terrier licked his hand.

"He's a tough little guy," Thiago said.

"Okay if we pat him?" Tom asked.

"Let him sniff your hand first to see if he'll let you. I understand that he doesn't know you two very well, and the medication might affect his behaviour."

Tom nodded and knelt down on the mat as the technician moved to make room for him.

"Hi, Bruno. How're you feeling?" Tom asked. He offered his fingers to the dog, who sniffed them and gave them a lick. Tom grinned, pleased.

"He recognizes you," Viv said, squatting down beside Tom.

"Glad to see you don't have any hard feelings," Tom said. He stroked the dog's head gently, and Bruno closed his eyes.

Tom looked at Viv. "You want to try?"

"Okay, but I hope he doesn't hold a grudge against me for getting hit by that car."

Viv held out her hand tentatively, afraid that the dog might bite. Bruno opened his eyes and stared at her without lifting his head.

"He's tuckered out, poor fellow," Tom said. "Try patting him."

Viv shifted onto her knees and slowly reached out to touch the top of Bruno's head. The fur felt soft and warm. She ran her fingers down his head to the base of his neck, where her fingers met the bandage.

"Poor fellow. You've sure had it rough."

Bruno whined.

"But it's okay. We're going to find you a great home, so you'll never have to live on the streets again. I promise." Bruno put a paw on Viv's arm. She stared into his sad brown eyes and was smitten. She stroked his head slowly until Bruno fell asleep.

"He's such a sweetheart."

Tom nodded.

"I'm really sorry," Thiago said. "It's ten minutes after seven, and we need to close."

"Sorry to keep you," Viv said. She stroked the dog's head one last time. "I'll see you later, Bruno." The terrier's tail thumped, and Viv smiled at Tom. "I think he likes me."

"Of course he does," Tom said. He climbed to his feet and offered Viv a hand up. They watched Thiago latch the cage.

"You can leave through the back door," Thiago said. "If you want to visit Bruno tomorrow, we'll be open until two."

"I don't know if I can make it," Viv said. "I'm moving tomorrow." She hesitated, concerned that the dog might not get much attention over the weekend if she didn't come.

"Don't worry about it. I'll stop by and see Bruno over lunch," Tom said.

"Would you, Tom? That would make me feel a lot better."

"Sure. He's a great dog." He held the back door open for Viv and glanced at Thiago. "Thanks for letting us see Bruno. Take good care of him."

"Don't worry, we will."

"We appreciate it," Viv said. They stepped out into the darkened alley behind the animal hospital.

"Come on. I'll walk you to the streetcar stop," Tom said. Side by side in their grubby work clothes, they walked down the alley and around the corner to the sidewalk.

"Thanks for coming with me, Tom. I don't know how I'll manage it, but I'm going to find a home for Bruno. Maybe my friend, Julie, might take him, although her house is so crowded already."

"Look, I'll put up some signs around the neighbourhood to see if anyone claims him, but if no one does, I'll take him."

Viv looked up, surprised. "You will?"

"Sure. I work with a rescue agency called 'Dog Angels.' We take in strays and dogs from puppy mills, or places without a 'no kill' policy. We foster them until someone adopts them."

"But no one's going to want a three-legged dog."

"That's okay. I've got a few dogs I've been fostering for a long time. Years, even. They're not going anywhere."

"Oh, Tom, you are an angel!" Standing on tiptoe, Viv threw her arms around his shoulders. She felt so relieved that she even laughed. Releasing him, she stepped back and gazed at him with bright, happy eyes. "Will you let me come and visit Bruno sometimes?"

"Sure. You can meet the whole crew."

"I'd love that. Thank you, Tom. Thanks for everything."

"You're welcome." His eyes held hers for a moment. "Good luck with your move tomorrow." He nodded and turned away.

"And good luck with Daddy's inspection!" Viv called after him.

When Viv stepped out of the building onto the sunny street early Saturday morning, she was delighted to find that the temperature had dropped and a cool breeze was blowing. Excellent weather for moving! She caught the streetcar and the subway to the rental lot before carefully navigating the van back through the traffic.

She was just shoving her suitcases and a couple of boxes into the office entrance when the phone rang. Sabrina answered it.

"Hi, Drew. We're all ready for you. Come on up," she said.

Minutes later, Drew appeared in the condo doorway in a pair of designer jeans, espadrilles, and a lilac shirt. He removed his sun glasses and grinned.

"Morning, ladies. Your muscle is here."

Viv exchanged a look with Sabrina. They were both dressed in old, ragged clothes.

"Drew, thanks for coming," Viv said, moving in for a hug. "Can I get you a coffee before we get started?"

"No thanks, I'm good. So, what do we have to move?"

Viv showed him the items in the office, and he smiled. "Hey, we'll be done in no time."

"That's not quite all," Sabrina said. "We still have to get Viv's boxes out of my storage."

"Right. Viv told me about those. No problem. I'll take these two boxes, if you two don't mind handling the luggage."

Viv extended the handles on her suitcases and overnight bag, and she and Sabrina rolled them to the elevator while Drew picked up the boxes.

An hour later, Drew's strength was flagging as he struggled to carry the final box from the elevator out into the street. Viv hurried ahead to unlock the back of the van.

"I'm sorry, I didn't realize I had so many files and books. I should have rented a hand truck."

Drew grunted, bracing the box against his chest as he rested behind the van. Viv opened the back and got out of the way. He heaved the box to shoulder height, and with an explosive "aargh," hoisted it to the top of the pile.

Drew took a step back, panting, and brought out a handkerchief to mop his dripping face. Wet patches under his arms and on his back marred his shirt's former pristine condition.

"No problem. I didn't realize you had so many boxes, is all," he panted. "You drive the van, and I'll follow in the Maserati." The car stood gleaming in the street behind them.

Viv kissed his shiny, damp cheek. "Thank you so much. I couldn't have done this without you." Of course, she and her two friends had managed to move the boxes into Sabrina's storage in the first place, but Viv kept that tidbit to herself.

"My pleasure, milady." Drew even managed a weak smile.

The shirt was discarded on the staircase bannister by the time the last box had been piled in the hallway at Viv's new home. Drew had even allowed Viv to take the other end of the book boxes, although he insisted on walking backward up the porch stairs. Viv didn't have the heart to tell him that the books were to be stored in the attic, all except for a few favourites which she meant to keep in her bedroom. She would sort the boxes out later.

"Can I get you an iced tea?" she asked.

"Sure. Just need to freshen up first," a beet-faced Drew said. Without his shirt, curly black hair covered his chest and trailed down to his waist. Not that Viv minded hair on a man; she thought it made him look virile.

"Of course. The bathroom's at the top of the stairs."

Drew stared at the staircase and drooped, but rallied to grab his shirt and haul himself up the stairs by the railing. While he did that, Viv hurried to the kitchen. She had bought some supplies to stock the pantry, dropping the bags on the counter on their arrival. Fred had left some of the essentials – flour, sugar, spices, and tea – for which she was grateful. Viv lifted down two glass tumblers and a china plate with painted roses for the date turnovers she had purchased. Rummaging in the drawers, she found two yellow cloth napkins and a wooden tray, and carried everything back to the parlour.

Drew descended a minute later, his face dry and his hair combed. He had even managed to make his shirt look crisper.

"Great house," he said, looking around. "Love the antique furniture and the windows."

"Yes, it is pretty." Viv patted the Queen Anne couch beside her. "Come and have some refreshments."

Drew collapsed onto the couch and picked up a tumbler, downing half a glass of iced tea in one gulp.

"That's better." He wiped his mouth with a napkin. "I was really parched." Viv smiled, but stared as his mouth gaped open and his nose twitched.

"Is something wrong with the iced tea?"

Drew held up one finger and sneezed. "Excuse me. I must have inhaled some dust. As I was saying, this is some house."

Viv drank her beverage and returned the glass to the tray. As she settled back again, Drew draped an arm around her shoulders.

"I'm all dirty," she protested. She squirmed under his arm, but Drew only tightened his grip.

"Not at all. You look great." Viv relaxed. If Drew didn't mind, why should she?

"So, you've rented this place for a year?"

"That's right. All to myself."

"That's terrific, baby." Drew pulled Viv toward him and kissed her. They broke apart a few seconds later, and Drew put his feet up on the coffee table. "Pfew, I admit I'm a little beat." Viv frowned, and he dropped his feet to the floor.

"Sorry, but these are all antiques." She passed the plate with the cookies. "Have a turnover." As they ate, Viv asked, "How was work this week?"

"Terrific. I took a meeting in Calgary with an oil company that wants to recruit a human resources manager. They've never used us before. My contacts are really starting to pay off."

"That's wonderful. I bet word of mouth is really important in your business."

"Fifty percent of my new accounts are personal recommendations. I . . ." He paused as Viv's cell rang in her purse beside the parlour door.

"Sorry," she said, rising to retrieve her phone. With her back to Drew, she said, "Hello?"

"Hello Viv. It's your mother."

"Mother." Viv hesitated, still startled that the woman she hadn't seen for years was calling her so regularly. "What's up?"

"What's up is that Frances Harvey is having a gathering at her studio tomorrow evening, and she's invited you. You can make it, can't you?"

"Of course! Thanks for getting me the invitation. What time?"

"Seven. It's a soiree to celebrate a photo spread that Frances did for *Ultimate* magazine. The magazine editor will be there, as well as some artist friends, Frances's PR person, and someone from the press. All good people for you to meet. Plus, Frances has very generously consented to having your photos hanging there during the party."

Viv's breath caught in her throat. She sat down on the couch beside Drew and reached for his hand.

"Mother," she squeaked.

"What is it, dear?"

Viv swallowed and tried to speak again. "Mother, you can't be serious."

"Of course I'm serious. It's very kind of Frances, I agree, but friends do favours for friends. You're not nervous, are you?"

"Not nervous?" Viv rolled her eyes.

Drew mouthed, "What?" and Viv covered the speaker with her hand. "Frances Harvey has invited me to a soiree at her studio tomorrow night, and my photographs will be hanging there."

"Good for you," Drew said.

"I'll be so nervous," Viv said, taking her hand from the mouthpiece.

"What's that? Of course, nerves are to be expected, but you mustn't let them show. You'll never have another opportunity like this," her mother said.

"You're not making me feel any better," Viv replied. Her eyes darted to Drew. "Could I bring a friend? For moral support?"

Véronique paused. "I suppose so, if he's presentable. Who is he?"

"His name is Drew Collins. He's very presentable, Mother. He recruits business executives, and he's much better at talking to important people than I am." Drew's eyebrows rose.

"Hmm. All right. Bring him along. Just make sure you're there on time and dressed appropriately. Try to wear something chic, but not too formal. You've still got Frances's address, don't you?"

"Of course." Viv searched through her purse for the envelope with the address. Phew, there it was. Her mother wouldn't be impressed if she had lost it.

"Good. I'll see you at seven sharp tomorrow night. Good night, Viv."

"Good night, Mother. And thank you."

"You're welcome."

"Oh, Drew!" Viv said, clicking off the phone.

He took one look at her face and picked up her iced tea. "Here, drink this."

She sipped from the glass, her eyes staring anxiously into his.

"This is unreal. I feel like I'm dreaming."

"What a fabulous opportunity for you, Viv! I know how much it must mean to you." She looked at him with dazed eyes while he stroked her arm. "Things may have been rocky between you and your mom, but she's really come through."

Viv nodded, and he laughed at her expression. "Come here. I'll help you get over your butterflies."

He pulled her toward him, and she crumpled against his chest. His lips tasted sweet from the tea, and she sighed. Her sigh seemed to excite him; he pulled her backwards over his lap and bent over her. As his mouth sought hers, his hands slid beneath her shirt and went straight to her bra strap. She felt him fumbling with the clasps, and then his body tightened on top of hers. He turned his head.

"Ahh choo!" Viv opened her eyes. He sneezed more ferociously a second time.

"Me-ow." Viv looked up and saw the Siamese slinking across the back of the couch. He sat down behind Drew's head and licked a paw.

Drew peered over his shoulder. "What's that?"

"Constantine, Fred's cat."

Constantine stopped licking to stare imperiously at Drew.

"Ahh choo!" Drew sat up, dislodging Viv from his lap while he lunged for a tissue on the table.

"Are you allergic?" she asked.

He shook his head and trumpeted into the tissue. "Not that I'm aware of. I've never had a reaction to a cat like this before. Ahh choo!"

Drew scrambled from the sofa, and Viv stood up.

"Look, I'm really sorry, baby, but I've got to go. There must be something about this cat's dander that irritates me. I've never been around a Siamese before. Ahh choo!"

Viv followed him to the front door. "I'm so sorry, Drew. Next time I'll shut him in one of the bedrooms so that he doesn't bother you."

"We could try that." He reached for her shoulder, but thought better of it. "Maybe if I take some antihistamine beforehand, it might help." He stepped out the screen door onto the porch with Viv following him.

"I'll still see you tomorrow night for Frances Harvey's party, won't I?" she asked. Drew trotted down the porch stairs and paused, taking in a deep breath of air.

"Of course. Wouldn't miss your hour of glory for the world. I'll pick you up at six thirty. Can't hurt, showing up in a Maserati."

Viv smiled. "You're a clever man, Drew. And thank you so much for helping me with the move. Hey, I almost forgot. I have to return the van." She was about to walk him to his car when Drew backed away.

"Better not tempt fate, baby. The sneezing just stopped. See you tomorrow night."

Disappointed to have missed out on a goodbye kiss, Viv sighed. "All right. See you tomorrow."

She watched as he slid into his car, blew her a kiss, and drove away. Viv walked back to the parlour to retrieve her purse and discovered Constantine lying on the couch.

"You're not doing my love life any good, buddy," she muttered. The cat jumped down from the sofa and disappeared under a chair.

After returning the van, Viv spent the next couple of hours arranging her things in the master bedroom and exchanged some of Fred's artwork for her own pictures. She stored the artwork, along with her luggage and some empty boxes, in the attic. She glanced at her watch – five o'clock. If she were lucky, she could catch Tom at the house before he went home.

"Hello," he said after she had placed the call.

"Tom, it's Viv."

"Hey, how'd the move go?"

"Fine. I just finished, and I'm about to take a long bath. How about you? Did you see Bruno?"

"I did. He's still dragging from the pain killers they're giving him, but he ate some breakfast this morning. We visited for a couple of minutes before he fell asleep again. I told him you sent your love."

"Thanks for checking up on him. I'll drop by to see him on Monday after I do some of the basement painting. How'd things go with Daddy, by the way?"

"Not bad. He gave you a thumbs-up on your tiling."

"Yay!"

"Yeah, he said he'd use you on a reno again. He also liked the green paint in the living room. We talked about what he wanted to do in the basement, and he decided to try a light grey on the walls."

"You're kidding. He's getting pretty trendy."

"You bet. So your design duties with your dad are finished, but much appreciated. He's raring to come back, by the way. Sounds like he's being a handful for Magda. I told him to stop being a pain in the ass and put his feet up for another week."

Viv laughed. "I bet he wasn't pleased to hear that."

"No, the old coot. But he went home without lifting a finger."

"Good for you, Tom. Stick to your guns. If you need me to read the riot act to Daddy, just give me a call."

"Will do. See you on Monday, Viv. I'll have a bucket of grey paint ready."

"Bye."

Viv went upstairs and luxuriated in the spa tub – Fred's love of antiques did not extend to roughing it in the bathroom – before putting on a sundress and scrambling some eggs for dinner. She perused Fred's instructional manual as she ate at the café table in the kitchen. Directions about the cat extended from feeding times and food temperature to his kitty litter, grooming, and play time.

Viv stopped reading when she couldn't absorb anymore. She glanced at her watch; it was a quarter to seven. Constantine's dinner time was supposed to be at six! She jumped up from the table and went to the pantry, where she chose a small tin of shrimp cat food. Picking up his food and water bowls, Viv noticed that the cat's name was engraved on them.

"Constantine? Dinner time!" But the cat didn't come. Was he sulking? Well, she wouldn't worry. Instead, she cleaned up the dishes and went outside to sit on a bench in the garden. It was a lovely spot, hidden in the shrubbery on a track of crushed white stone. Viv wasn't much of a gardener, but she recognized lily of the valley at the foot of the path. When she was ready to go inside, she broke off a sprig to rest on her pillow.

It didn't look as if Constantine had touched his dinner, and Viv had missed his playtime, too. Well, life would get back to normal tomorrow. She climbed the stairs to bed, ready for an early night. She was tired from the move, and she wanted to get plenty of sleep for her big day tomorrow. Heaven help her if she showed up at the soiree with bags under her eyes; Mother would not be amused.

Maybe she would watch TV from bed, a delightful luxury, or read from one of her favourite books. Or there were the DVDs Fred had left under the TV.

Let's see, what did he have? *Gone with the Wind* – she had seen that at a film festival. *Inherit the Wind* with Spencer Tracy. Hmm, that was about a trial. *To Kill a Mockingbird*. She had studied the novel in school, but had never seen the movie. Oh, look, a collection of Audrey Hepburn films. She had seen *Breakfast at Tiffany's*, but not *Sabrina* or *Roman Holiday*. It said that *Roman Holiday* was Audrey Hepburn's first American film. She would watch that someday, but not tonight. Too tired to watch a movie after all, Viv picked up her copy of *Bridget Jones's Diary* and climbed into bed.

The sheets were crisp and the air conditioning made it cool enough to snuggle under the quilt. She could smell the sprig of lily of the valley on the pillow next to her. Thirty minutes later, she realized that the book had slipped from her hand, and she had dozed off. Viv set the paperback on the bedside table, clicked off the lamp, and fell instantly asleep.

Sometime during the night, Viv became aware of a warm weight on her feet. "There you are, Constantine," she murmured.

And then she was asleep again.

Chapter 19

Father's Day brunch the next day was at a new restaurant called Irena's. Viv had never been there before, but her father had heard that they made the world's best potato pancakes, so she was game to give it a try. He was all smiles when Viv bent down to kiss him on her arrival.

"Sorry I'm late, Daddy. Happy Father's Day." She plunked down in the chair across from him as he smiled fondly at her.

"You're not late, Peaches. I've only been here two minutes."

She opened her purse and slid an envelope across the table to him.

"Is it a funny or a sweet card this year?"

"Sweet. I was in a sentimental mood."

He slit the envelope open. The front showed a little girl holding her daddy's hand as they strolled down a sunset-lit beach. Gabe opened the card and read the sentiment inside.

He looked up and smiled. "Thanks, Viv."

"You're welcome, Daddy." She squeezed his hand before Gabe picked up his menu.

"I'm starved. Let's see what they've got."

Forty-five minutes later, after stuffing themselves with strawberries, eggs, kielbasa sausage, and potato pancakes, they were leaning back in their chairs sipping coffee. Viv had described her new home and regaled her father with an edited version of Drew's reaction to Constantine.

When his laughter had died down, Viv said, "Tom told me that your inspection tour of the renovations went well yesterday."

"Is that so? When were you talking to Tom?"

"I called him yesterday evening to find out how Bruno was doing. Tom told you about him, didn't he?"

Gabe looked puzzled for a moment before his forehead relaxed. "Bruno. That's the dog that got hit by the car, right?"

"Yes, poor thing.

"Tom said you're paying the vet bill. That's awfully kind of you."

"It was the least I could do, considering. But Tom said you were getting antsy about coming back to work."

"He did? The fink."

"Never mind. I just hope you're not serious. Wait until Dr. Magoro gives you a clean bill of health before you go back to work. Don't push it."

Gabe looked sheepish. "Aw, don't worry. I didn't really mean it. I'm just bored, sitting on my duff at home all day."

Viv was unmoved. "I bet you've got a ton of paperwork to catch up on. You're always complaining how hard it is to get the receipts sorted out for the accountant. Why not do it now, when you've got nothing better to do?"

"Kill joy."

Viv laughed. "You know I'm right, Mr. Procrastinator."

"I have trouble making heads or tails of that bookkeeping software."

"And you a retired banker. Shame on you."

Gabe gave up his pouting. "All right, I'll give it a try."

The waitress came by the table to drop off their cheque. Gabe reached for it, but Viv swatted his hand away.

"What kind of a daughter would let her father pay for brunch on Father's Day?"

"Oops. Force of habit."

"Father's Day is the one day of the year you let me pay."

Gabe chuckled. "I guess I just can't get used to you being grown-up with a job and a bank account and all." After the waitress had taken Viv's credit card, her father added, "So, are you nervous about tonight? I wish I could come and see your photo exhibit for myself."

"I would smuggle you in if I could, Daddy, but a Frances Harvey soiree is by invitation only."

Gabe nodded. "I understand. Have a great time and call me about it afterward. I want to hear what that so-called photography expert has to say about your work. Not that your photos are anything but fantastic, in my book. And don't let anyone tell you otherwise."

"I told you, Ms. Harvey likes my work. She would hardly be hanging it in her studio if she didn't."

"All right. And give my regards to your mother. Tell her I'd love to get together for a coffee sometime. It's been too long."

"I will, Daddy."

A few hours later, Drew pulled up outside her house. Viv had been waiting for him on the porch, and scurried across the lawn to meet him.

"Hi!" She ducked inside the car and gave him a quick kiss. "I didn't want to risk you coming into the house and having another allergic reaction." Not that she had seen anything of Constantine all day.

"You look gorgeous."

"Thanks. I almost ran out to buy a new outfit." She had finally settled on a red, taupe, and black-patterned mini-dress with a side bow, which she paired with grey stiletto ankle boots. "You look handsome, too." Drew was wearing a grey summer suit with a steel-blue shirt and no tie. He looked terrific, but it had probably taken him all of five minutes to get ready.

"How're you feeling?"

"I want to get this over with, to tell you the truth."

Drew patted her hand before revving the engine. "Just stick with me, baby. I'll take care of you."

When they reached the Queen Street West address, Viv wondered if she had written it down incorrectly. There was no sign announcing the studio, and the building was nothing special. As a matter of fact, it looked like the kind of place a dentist or a chiropractor might open a practice. Viv and Drew opened the door to the building and looked around the nondescript lobby.

"Unit 102. This must be it," Viv said with a shrug. There was still no studio sign. She knocked on the door.

It was opened by a gaunt young man wearing an orange pantsuit with a helmet of Smurf-blue hair and zebra-striped glasses.

"Greetings!" he shouted over the music pulsating out the door. Boom, boom, boom went the bass, so loud that it felt like a second heartbeat.

"Is this Frances Harvey's party? I'm Viv Nowak, and this is Drew Collins."

"You're Viv! Honey, come right in, I've been dying to meet you. I just love your kids. I'm Gregory, Frances's personal assistant." He took Viv's hand and pulled her into the room.

It was like walking into an alternate universe. Viv stared at the two-storey room with its lime-green, concrete walls. Light streamed through a floor-to-ceiling glass window at the back. A steel staircase erupted from the floor and split in two at the top, leading to a balcony that ran the length of the second storey. About twenty people were swallowed up by the huge space, either sitting on the stairs chatting, or studying the photographs on the walls.

"And who did you say this gorgeous man is with you?" Gregory shouted.

"Drew Collins. Nice to meet you." Drew held out his hand, and Gregory tucked it into the crook of his arm.

"Lovely to meet you, Drew. Come on, I'll take you both to see Frances."

They moved to a quieter area on the side of the room defined by an island of white shag carpet. Frances and Véronique were seated there in canvas chairs. Both women rose to greet them, Véronique smiling. Viv felt relieved. Mother must approve of her outfit.

Frances Harvey was stout with cerise-coloured hair that sprouted, porcupine-like, from her head. She shook Viv's hand.

"So, you're Véronique's kid? You don't look like her."

"No? But perhaps she has some of my artistic talent," Véronique said.

"No doubt about it." Frances jabbed her thumb at the wall behind her, where Viv's photographs made a colourful display. "She's a little raw, but her eye is good, and I like her honesty. These kids are real."

"You don't know how much it means to me to hear you say that," Viv said. "I'm such a fan of your work."

Frances noticed Drew waiting behind Viv. "Who's this?"

Viv whirled to take Drew's arm. "Sorry. Where are my manners? This is Drew Collins. Drew, this is Frances Harvey and my mother, Véronique Roux."

"I'm overwhelmed, ladies. Such a huge admirer of both your work." Drew shook the hand that Frances offered, but paused to kiss Véronique's.

"Enchanté, Madame Roux." Their eyes met and lingered.

Véronique turned to her daughter. "What a charming gentleman, Viv. I approve."

Viv smiled, and Drew winked. Things were going smoothly so far. She knew she could count on Drew.

"I'm knocked out by the angle you used to shoot the kid who looks like a rock star," Frances said. "What made you decide to photograph him from the floor?"

Frances led Viv to the display. They spent the next half hour discussing the photographs, Viv explaining her process, and Frances either nodding or making suggestions as to how she could have done things differently. Viv appreciated that Frances never told her how she could have made the pictures better; only how they could have been different. People drifted up behind them and disappeared again, respectful of their privacy. Frances finally patted Viv's shoulder and said, "Well done, kid," before departing to mingle with her other guests. Viv remained, misty-eyed, in front of her photos.

She felt a hand on her shoulder and turned to find Drew smiling at her.

"Are you okay?"

Viv intertwined her fingers with his. "I'm so happy. Frances Harvey just talked to me about my photography. She complimented my work. It's amazing."

"I knew she would. I've been talking with your mother. She's pretty amazing, too."

Viv started. "I'm so sorry, Drew. I've stuck you with her all this time." She glanced over her shoulder to see if Véronique could hear them, but her mother was schmoozing with the other guests.

"Really, Viv, it was my pleasure. Your mother is fascinating. She was telling me about the ad campaign they're launching for the Rouge winter collection. It's a global event. Really hot stuff. It was a learning experience."

A waiter came by with a tray of champagne, and they each helped themselves to a glass. As Viv and Drew sipped, a woman wearing a navy-and-white silk suit approached them.

"Viv Nowak?"

"Yes?"

"Hi, I'm Sidnee Stavros from *Canadian Experience* magazine. I just love your pictures." She gestured at them. "I hear that you're an elementary school teacher, and that your subjects are your students."

"That's right."

"Well, your work is wonderful. I'd love to do a feature on you and your photography for our November issue. Would you be interested?"

Viv's eyes opened wide. "Seriously? That would be fabulous. The kids would be so excited, and their families, too."

"Do you have model releases?" Viv shook her head. "You'll have to get them before we can use the pictures. The form is pretty standard. I'll have it sent to you. The interview will have to be scheduled before the end of the month, before school lets out. We'll send a photographer along to take pictures, too."

Viv nodded with a fixed smile, too overwhelmed to say anything.

Sidnee handed her a card, and Viv took it mechanically. "My assistant will contact you tomorrow about the release form and setting up the photo shoot. I look forward to working with you, Viv." She held out her hand, and Viv sprang back to life, shaking it vigorously.

"Me, too. I can't thank you enough for this opportunity, Sidnee.

I'll get those model releases to you by the end of the week."

"That would be terrific." Sidnee nodded at Drew and walked away.

Viv waited until she was out of earshot before grabbing Drew's hand and jumping up and down, spilling her champagne. "I can't believe it! An article in *Canadian Experience*. Oh, Drew!"

"I'm so happy for you, baby." Drew hugged her and rocked her back and forth in his arms.

"Congratulations, Viv," a voice said from behind them. Drew stepped back, and Viv turned to see her mother.

"Sidnee told me that she was going to approach you about a magazine article. I'm so pleased for you, dear." She held out her arms, and Viv, overwhelmed with happiness, walked into them. She even hugged her mother.

"The party's breaking up," Véronique said. She pulled back to arm's length. "Frances is going out to dinner with her people. I'd love to take you and Drew out to celebrate. Would you like that?"

"That's kind of you, Madame Roux," Drew said.

Véronique regarded him with a smile. "You're too formal. Call me Véronique."

"Of course." He raised his eyebrows at Viv.

"Yes, how kind. Thank you, Mother. We'd love to."

"Wonderful. Did you come by car? Perhaps you could give me a lift?"

Fifteen minutes later, after having fervently thanked Frances for her generosity, Viv was seated in the back of Drew's car while he chatted with her mother up front. They stopped at a popular Italian restaurant just a five-minute drive from Frances's studio. Drew conducted them inside with a woman on each arm. An aproned waiter seated them at a table on a brick floor designed to look like an outdoor patio and bustled away to get their drink order.

"Well, ladies, it's been a banner day," Drew said. He was leaning back in his chair with a smile for both of them.

"It certainly has. I'm sure you think so too, Viv," Véronique said.

"It was a perfect day, Mother."

"I thought as much. There's nothing more satisfying than a discussion of one's art, unless it's other people's appreciation of it – in dollar bills." Véronique's laughter was a refined chuckle.

"Nothing truer," Drew said. "Hey, who wouldn't want to make money doing what they love?"

"That's what I've always felt," Viv added.

The waiter returned with their drinks. Drew raised his scotch in a toast.

"To doing what you love, ladies."

"To what you love," Viv echoed. She took a sip of her Daiquiri. Yum, nice and cold, just the way she liked it.

"I always knew you had it in you, dear."

"What's that, Mother?"

"The ability to see something with fresh eyes, and the talent to realize your vision. You get that from me, you know."

"Uh huh." Viv squeezed the juice from her lime wedge into her drink for a little extra zing. Lovely.

Drew and Véronique exchanged a glance.

"Would anyone like to order food?" Véronique asked. "I confess, I'm a bit hungry."

"Me, too," Viv said. Drew signaled for the waiter.

"Yes, sir?" the waiter said, hurrying to the table. "Would you care to see a menu?"

"What's the special this evening?"

"We have a nice veal with Tagliatelle and truffles."

"That sounds delicious," Drew said. "Viv and I will have that."

Viv frowned. She didn't like eating baby cow; it was disgusting. On the other hand, she didn't want to spoil the rare camaraderie she was enjoying with her mother, so she decided to go with the flow. Besides, Drew enjoyed ordering for her.

"I'd like mussels done in a tomato wine sauce with a salad," Véronique said. "And a bottle of Merlot."

"Very good." The waiter bowed and left.

"So, Véronique, you were telling me earlier that you're looking forward to retiring," Drew said.

"Yes. Hard to imagine where the time has fled, but I've been the director of Rouge Shoes for twenty-one years now. I'm not the young woman I once was." She patted Drew's hand before he could interrupt her. "No, no, it's true. The travel, the business meetings, the pressure to come up with fresh ideas. They're becoming too much for me. It's time to call it a day."

She took Viv's hand where it lay on the table cloth. "I had asked Viv to be my successor, but she was concerned about not having the business skills or the design ability to follow in my footsteps. I'll have to sell the business."

"What?" Drew gazed at Viv. "Anyone can pick up the business skills. You don't have to have an MBA, just a team of good people behind you." He turned back to Véronique. "Perhaps you'll lose some of your people in the transition?"

"I'm afraid so. Some of them have been with Rouge almost as long as I have, too. It's a great pity. But they're fearful of change. In the fashion industry, reputations can be ruined by one bad season. It's too much of a risk for some."

Drew shook his head. "That's sad."

Viv began to feel uncomfortable, as if it were her fault that Rouge Shoes was crumbling and employees would be forced to find new jobs. She took a healthy swig of her Daiquiri and finished it.

"Of course, it takes much more than business acumen to 'sell shoes,' as Viv once put it. Design ability is the soul of the business. So few have the artistic flair."

"That's right," Viv said. "Somehow you take a piece of leather and transform it into something beautiful. I could never do that."

"Now, Viv, there I have to disagree." Véronique squeezed Viv's hand and released it as the waiter returned with the wine, uncorked it, and poured a small amount into her glass. Véronique tasted it and nodded, signaling that the waiter should fill their glasses.

"As I was saying, Viv, I have to disagree with you. Having seen your photography, we all know that you have artistic talent. And real talent is not limited to just one medium. Look at Michelangelo. He worked in marble as well as in paint, and you can't find two more different vehicles."

"That's true," Drew said. "I envy you ladies your talent."

"But, Mother, to switch from photography to shoe design is such a leap. I don't make things, I just capture them."

"Nonsense. You see something – a face, an expression, a play of light – and you transfigure it into art. And look at you. You certainly have a well-developed fashion sense."

Viv felt backed into a corner as she looked from Drew's enthusiastic face to her mother's hopeful one. She took a swallow of wine to bide her time.

Her mother persisted. "You said to me the other day that I don't know you, but you're wrong. We share the same genes. A love of beautiful things. A passion for strong-minded men." Véronique smiled across the table at Drew, who wiggled his eyebrows and grinned back.

Viv stared. Wait a minute. There was something about the expression on their faces that seemed so familiar. She remembered her mother looking at another man just like that once upon a time. It was as if a wall of mist obscured her memory. If only she could only tear it away.

The memory solidified. It had happened during her graduation from teacher's college. She had stood in line with her class, waiting for her turn to walk across the stage. Her name had been called. She knelt before the university president, triumphant as he draped the Bachelor of Education hood over her shoulders. Rising and walking toward the dean, she had searched the audience for her family. Daddy and Magda had come, of course, but she had hoped to see her mother there, too. She hadn't seen Mother since her sixteenth birthday, but having her there would be almost like putting the family back together.

Viv heard a whoop as the dean handed her the diploma, and her head tracked sharply to follow the sound. It was Daddy. He knew that she had seen him, and he waved and whistled. There was Magda right beside him, beaming and clutching her hands together. Beside Magda sat a stranger, a handsome man not much older than the graduates. The sexy grin on his face caught her attention, and then he wiggled his eyebrows at the woman sitting beside him. The woman was dressed to kill in a low-necked, red dress. She took his hand and turned toward the stage. Viv grimaced at the recollection. It had been her mother. She had brought her boyfriend to her daughter's graduation, a boyfriend young enough to be her son! Drew had just reminded her of that young man.

Indignation burned within as Viv looked at her dinner companions.

"Hold on a minute. What's happening here? What are you two up to?"

Her mother's face was innocent as she gazed back at Viv. "What are you talking about?"

Ignoring her, Viv turned to Drew. "So, tell me, Drew, just why do you care so much about me inheriting Rouge?"

At least he was honest enough to appear embarrassed. "It's a great opportunity, Viv. You only turned it down because you didn't feel up to the challenge. When Véronique told me about it . . ."

Véronique recoiled, her eyes slits as she glowered at him. "Fool!"

Drew's eyes darted between the two women. Viv almost felt sorry for him.

"Be quiet, Mother," Viv said. "So, you two just met tonight and already you're a team, trying to talk me into giving up teaching and taking over the business?" She studied them suspiciously. "Unless you met earlier? But how? When I mentioned having a boyfriend at dinner on Tuesday night, Mother, I deliberately didn't give you his name." She tried to put the pieces together while sipping her wine.

She turned to her mother. "You called Daddy for Drew's name after I left you Tuesday night, didn't you? And looked Drew up on the internet."

Véronique crossed her arms over her chest and looked away. "I will not dignify your accusation with a response."

Viv grinned and pointed at her mother. "I knew it! Sometime between Tuesday and Thursday, you phoned Drew and bribed him to help convince me to take over your business. Then he called me Thursday night to find out how our dinner had gone, but he already knew."

She peered at Drew. "Wasn't that when you told me you had

called off your surprise visit to your parents?" He lowered his gaze to the table top. "Oh, Drew, you cancelled your plans with your parents to be with Véronique this weekend. That's low. But tell me, what do you get out of this?"

He looked up, attempting a smile. "It's what I was saying, Viv. My business is all about the contacts."

"And Mother has some great ones."

"Sure."

"And if I inherit the business and marry you, that would be even better, wouldn't it?" He glanced away. "See, that kind of betrayal always happens when you get involved with my mother."

"Viviane!" her mother squawked. "How dare you talk that way about me. I'm only trying to improve your life."

But Viv wasn't listening. She shook her head sadly. "All that talk about my artistic talent. I bet you had to pull in a huge favour to get Frances Harvey to hang my work at one of her soirees. When I think of the conversation we had about my photos! All along, I was just an amateur wasting her time." Viv's eyes started to tear, and she stopped to regain control.

"That isn't true! Frances genuinely liked your work."

Viv nodded ruefully. "What about the article with *Canadian Experience?*"

Her mother looked down. "I did have something to do with that."

The waiter returned to serve their dinners. The trio sat in stony silence as the plates were put in front of them. Viv looked at the veal with disgust and pushed her food away. She was disappointed, but much too angry with her mother and Drew to let tears betray her. When the waiter left, she shoved back her chair.

"Tell Sidnee Stavros not to bother having her assistant call me tomorrow. And please tell Ms. Harvey to send my pictures back to the school immediately. I'll pay for the courier."

"Viv," Drew said, rising to his feet.

"Don't bother to get up, Drew. I'll take a taxi home. And don't call me again – ever." Drew froze before sliding back into his chair.

"And you, Mother." Viv shook her head. "Daddy was right. You don't know your own daughter. Just stay away from me. Like I said before, I don't want anything to do with you or your business."

Viv stormed out of the restaurant onto the sidewalk. She was looking up and down for a taxi when her mother charged out the door behind her. Véronique's eyes were smouldering as she caught Viv's arm with fingernails that felt like talons.

"I am so bored by your attitude. Poor Viv, her mother went back to work when she was a child. Poor Viv, her mother left her and her father. Hah!"

Viv tore her arm from Véronique's grasp, and they glared at each other. A wary passerby gave them a wide berth.

"I suppose you have a good excuse for what you did," Viv said. "I would never have left my child."

Véronique laughed. "No, of course not, my perfect daughter, my daddy's little darling. You're so naïve. I bet you've never even asked your father why I left."

Viv took a step back, taken off balance. "No, why should I? You left because you couldn't pass up the opportunity to start your own design company in New York."

"That's what your father told you? Well, he lied. There was no offer. I fled to New York, back to my friends. Your father and his mistress drove me to that."

Viv's assurance faltered. "What are you talking about? What mistress? Daddy would never have had a mistress."

Véronique grabbed her arm again. "After I left, your father installed his mistress in my house – my own home – to look after the two of you. How could I return after that?"

All Viv could do was shake her head, unable to believe what she was hearing.

Her mother leaned closer. "Ask him. Ask your father who that woman is, living in my house." She looked at Viv with contempt before turning and striding back into the restaurant.

Viv stared after her, her mind reeling. It couldn't be true. Daddy couldn't have done such a thing to her and her mother. Her breath caught in her throat, and she feared that she would cry right there in the street. She had to get away.

"Taxi!"

The cab screeched to a stop in the middle of the road, and Viv scrambled inside.

"Where to, Miss?"

"Boswell Avenue."

It was time to see Daddy.

Chapter 20

Magda opened the door with a smile of welcome on her face until she saw Viv's expression.

"Viviane, what's wrong?"

Viv pushed past her into the foyer. "Where's Daddy?"

"He's in the family room watching the news."

Viv ran down the hallway with Magda scurrying after her. She rounded the corner and saw her father lying in his recliner. He took one look at her and thumped his chair into an upright position.

"Viv, what's wrong?"

Viv paused, swaying on her feet. "I just came from dinner with Mother. She told me . . . Daddy, how could you?" She tried to stop the tears from overflowing by rubbing her fists against her eyes. Gabe put his arms around her shoulders, but she pushed him away.

"Come and sit down. Tell me what this is all about," he said. Viv let him lead her to the couch, where they sat down side by side. Magda perched on the arm of the recliner.

Viv took a deep breath and said, "Daddy, tell me the truth about why Mother left us."

His gaze shifted away. "Why? What has she been telling you?"

"She said . . . She said that she ran away to New York because you had taken a mistress. Is that true?" She stared at his face, waiting for him to say that Mother was lying. Finally, Gabe looked at her.

"You don't understand how things were, Peaches." With those few words, Viv's world crashed around her shoulders. Suddenly, the vision of her father as a knight in shining armour was irreparably

169

destroyed. She groaned.

"No, listen." Gabe grasped her arms, forcing her to look at him. "Things were bad between your mother and me. She had no time for anything but her business here in Toronto. Not for me, or for you. Your mother and I were finished."

Viv scowled. "You're making up excuses. You had a marriage vow."

"I'm human, Viv. I was lonely. It had been two years since . . ." The sentence went unfinished. "There was a woman I met through the Polish club. She had only been in Canada for a year. She was kind, generous, loving – and lonely, too."

"Your father was like a knight coming to my rescue," Magda said. Viv glanced up. Magda was ashen-faced, one hand clutching at her throat. Viv tore her gaze away to look back at her father.

"I can't believe you brought her into our home."

"Don't talk like that. Magda's been a mother to you."

Viv laughed bitterly. "Some mother. Your mistress."

"We made a promise to the Virgin, Viviane," Magda pleaded. "We promised that we would live like a brother and sister as long as you were under this roof."

"Liar," Viv muttered.

"Viv!" her father barked, his face scarlet.

She stared at him sullenly. "I don't care what promises you made. You drove Mother away. How could she ever come home once *she* was living in this house?" Viv pointed at Magda, whose silent tears were streaming down her face.

"All these years I've been blaming Mother when it was you who broke up our family. I can't believe she didn't tell me before. What kept her quiet?"

"Both of us were to blame. There were men . . ." Gabe paused. "We agreed not to discuss our marriage with you."

"Well, Mother finally got tired of my fantasy of you as a good father. I can't believe how blind I've been."

"Your father was the best daddy to you, beautiful girl. You don't know the sacrifices he made."

"How can you say that?" Viv shouted. "Mother and Daddy made

a commitment to each other. We were a family. Nothing is more important than family. What kind of a woman are you, that you would come between us? You home-wrecker!"

Magda cringed away from Viv, her mouth frozen into a horrified "o." Gabe pushed past Viv to put his arm around Magda, planting himself between the two women.

"That's cruel, Viv. I never thought to hear such ugly words coming from your mouth. The daughter I know would never say such things."

"The daddy I knew wouldn't have been unfaithful." There was silence as father and daughter stared at each other, Magda hiding her face in Gabe's shoulder.

At last Gabe spoke. "Get out. Say what you want about me, but don't come back until you can apologize to Magda."

Viv gasped. Daddy was throwing her out. Was he right? Had she gone too far?

But she stiffened her resolve. Why should she be the one to apologize? What had she done to the two of them, except love and trust them?

"Fine." She tried to think of something cutting to say. "Happy Father's Day, Daddy."

Viv turned and strode away, her heels ringing down the hallway as no one pursued her. She let the front door slam behind her before disintegrating into tears on the porch.

Chapter 21

When Viv returned home, she discovered that there were messages on her phone from her mother and Drew, but deleted them without listening. There was only one person she wanted to speak to, even though it was late.

"Sabrina?"

There was a pause on the other end of the phone. "Viv? You're not usually up after eleven on a Sunday night. What's wrong?"

"It's about Mother and Daddy. Mother told me the truth behind their break up. Daddy was cheating on her . . . with Magda."

"Holy shit!"

"Yes. I just confronted Daddy about it. It's true." A nasty suspicion wormed its way into her thoughts. "You didn't already know, did you?"

"What a crazy thing to say. Of course not."

"Well, Daddy told you things about Kyle that he kept from me, so I was just wondering."

"No, Viv, he never told me that he was having an affair with Magda." Sabrina's voice softened as she asked, "How're you feeling?"

"Lousy. I thought that Daddy was the last man on earth who would cheat on his wife, but I was wrong. Speaking of cheats and liars, have you heard from Drew lately?"

"What are you talking about?"

"He and Mother were plotting against me."

"Are you drunk, or having a stroke, or something?"

"It's true. Mother was determined that I would give up teaching to take over Rouge Shoes. When she found out that I had a boyfriend, she bribed Drew into trying to talk me into it." Viv recounted the dinner conversation she had had with Drew and her mother. "You know what? Your dating do-over boyfriend rating system sucks big time."

"Come on, Viv. How could I have known that Drew was such a self-serving weasel? I'm not clairvoyant, you know. Calm down. We'll do better next time."

"Yeah, like you can find me a decent boyfriend when you can't even keep one for yourself." There was a pause, during which Viv wondered for the second time that night if she had gone too far. But it was Sabrina's fault that she and Rick had broken up, so she had spoken the truth.

"Listen, Viv, you're tired and upset, and, knowing you, probably drunk. We'd better hang up before one of us says something she's going to regret."

Viv bolted upright on the couch. "Drunk! What do you mean by that?"

"Are you kidding? You were drinking like a fish after Kyle left you. You should have had an account with the LCBO."

"Oh yeah?" Viv hesitated, searching for a retort, but it was hard to argue with the truth. She had used alcohol to dull the pain.

"Oh yeah?" she repeated. "Well, your taste in men still sucks like lemons."

Sabrina sighed. "I'm going to bed. We'll talk tomorrow." She ended the call.

Viv stared at her phone in disbelief. How could Sabrina hang up on her when she still needed to talk about her whoring, scumbag parents? And she couldn't phone Julie. Julie had a rule about not calling after Olivia's bedtime.

Viv panicked. She couldn't afford to have Sabrina mad at her with Daddy disowning her. She would just have to call back and apologize.

But Sabrina didn't pick up. Feeling uneasy, Viv tossed the cell back into her purse and trudged upstairs to bed. It had been a terrible day, and she'd only made it worse by insulting one of her best friends. She'd apologize tomorrow.

The next day at school, Viv was counting the minutes until she could talk with Julie. Sabrina could be harsh; Julie would be more sympathetic. When Viv found Julie at lunch, she pulled her to the sofa in the corner in the staff room where they could have some privacy.

"What's wrong? You look terrible," Julie said in a low voice. "Didn't you get any sleep last night?"

"Not much." Viv told her the truth about her parents' break-up.

"That's outrageous! If either of my parents had done that, they would have killed each other. Both your parents were cheating?" She stared at Viv in disbelief.

"I know! It's incredible. I'm not surprised about Mother, but Daddy . . ." She shook her head.

Julie patted Viv's back. "No wonder you look so lousy today. Oh sweetie, I'm sorry."

"That's not all of it." Viv told Julie the part Drew had played in her mother's plot to convince her to take over Rouge Shoes.

"What a dick! I hope you told him off, but good."

"Actually, he tried to phone me afterward, but I didn't return his call."

Julie nodded. "That's right. Just freeze him out."

Viv felt a little better. This was more of the kind of reaction she had been expecting. "Yes, but I think I offended Sabrina when I called her last night. I was so upset."

"Oh? What'd you say?"

"I told her that her taste in men sucked like lemons, and that she wasn't doing so well in keeping a man for herself."

Julie whistled. "Yeah, I can see that Sabrina would be a little sensitive about that."

"I know, but how could she have chosen Drew for me? I thought she had thoroughly vetted him. She must have missed something in the 'overall character' category."

"I'll say. Maybe I'd better be looking over her shoulder the next time she chooses a boyfriend for you. She knows more straight guys than I do, but I'm better at sizing people up. Josh, for example. You two would have been great together if he hadn't reminded you of your first boyfriend." She studied Viv's face. "You sure you can't get past that?"

Viv had promised not to reveal Josh's asexuality to Julie, but she felt badly that he couldn't see his daughter more often. Maybe she should encourage Julie to let him do that?

"Look, Julie," she said, "I think Josh is more upset about not seeing Olivia than he is about not dating me. It's heartbreaking, the way you keep them apart. Do you know that he drives by your house at night just to make sure that the two of you are all right?"

Julie stared at her. "No, I didn't know. That's a bit creepy."

"No it's not. He loves her."

"Well, if he has a problem with our agreement, he should have talked to me, not complained to you." Julie's mouth tightened.

Oh no, Julie was getting angry. Viv scrambled to make things right. "You don't understand. He knows he's being unreasonable, that he promised he wouldn't be a father to Olivia. He just gets scared when he sees you interested in someone – like Kim – for fear that he might get pushed out of Olivia's life."

Julie jumped to her feet, her eyes flashing. "So now he doesn't want me to see anyone?"

"Shhh. Keep your voice down." Viv glanced around the room, noticing how the other teachers were watching them.

Julie crouched down beside her, her face level with Viv's. "Look, if you're so worried about Josh, why don't you marry him and have his babies so that he'll leave Olivia and me alone?"

That made Viv angry. "Are you saying that another child can replace Olivia? That he ought to forget about her? You're not being fair to Josh."

Julie scowled. "You must think I'm a terrible person."

"No, I don't!"

"You do. That I would deprive a father of his child. Well, let me tell you, I've had enough of people telling me how to live my life. You can all just back off!"

Julie dashed from the room with Viv rushing after her. She had to trot to keep up with Julie as they charged down the hallway.

"Please, Julie, don't be angry."

"I don't want to talk to you right now." She glared at Viv. "Leave me alone!"

Viv stared after her as Julie ran down the stairs and disappeared. Damn! She had screwed things up for Josh when all she had wanted to do was help him. And now everyone was angry with her.

That reminded her that she hadn't called Sabrina yet to apologize. She glanced at her watch; it was still lunchtime. She hurried back to the staff room to pick up her purse, ignoring the other teachers' curious stares, and went outside. Rather than risk one of the children interrupting the call, she went for a walk, punching Sabrina's number into her cell as she moved.

Sabrina picked up in two rings. "Viv?"

"Look, I just want to say that I'm sorry for what I said last night about your taste in men. You have excellent taste in men. You couldn't know that Drew was a creep."

"Julie and I were just trying to help, you know." Sabrina's tone was chilly.

"And I appreciate that. I need all the help that I can get. I can't choose a good man to save my soul."

"Drew called me at work this morning. He asked me to pass along his apology. Said you hadn't returned his call."

"That's right. I don't want to talk to him."

"I told him to take a hike."

"Good for you."

"I told him that anyone who uses a romantic relationship for financial gain is a pig who ought to . . ." A truck rumbled by, covering that part of the conversation, but Viv guessed what Sabrina had said.

"You're a true friend, Sabrina. I want you to know that."

"I know you've had a rough year, Viv, especially with this latest mess with your parents, but things are going to get better. I promise."

"I know they will."

"Just wait. I predict that you'll have a great new guy in your life by New Year's Eve. I have a feeling, and you know how my feelings are always right."

Viv knew no such thing, but she wanted to keep Sabrina in a conciliatory mood. "Absolutely. Well, I hope that everything's okay between us now."

"Of course. You know that you can always count on me and Julie."

Viv decided not to mention Julie for the time being. Hopefully Julie would have cooled off by the time she and Sabrina talked again.

"You two are the best friends a girl can have."

Sabrina sniffed. "Look, I've got to finish some notes for a meeting that's starting in fifteen minutes, but I'm glad you called, hon. Just hang in there."

"I will. Thanks."

"Bye."

Viv hung up feeling better. She had had to grovel to make up with Sabrina, but at least one of her friends was back on her side. Julie was going to be a harder nut to crack; she tended to hold a grudge, which was going to make things uncomfortable until classes were over. Well, if she had to crawl like a snake on its belly, she'd bring Julie around, too.

Which left Daddy and Magda. Her mother might have been as much to blame for the break-up, but she hadn't left voluntarily. Daddy had driven her away. Maybe they could have patched things up, if only Daddy hadn't brought Magda into the house. How could he have done such a dishonourable thing? That was the one feeling about the break-up that Viv couldn't shake.

By the time she saw Tom at the reno that afternoon, Viv was still in a miserable mood. She let herself into the house and stomped down the basement stairs without more than a nod at Tom, who came out from installing the bathroom cabinet to see who was there. She spotted the pail of grey paint in the family room, poured some into a tray, and began rolling it onto the wall. Tom watched her for a minute without speaking.

"What did the wall do to you?"

"Huh?" She paused in mid-stroke.

"You're painting that wall as if you want to kill it."

"Oh." Viv let the end of her pole rest on the floor. "The past two days have been really lousy."

Tom leaned against an unpainted section of the wall. "Want to talk about it?"

She hesitated. She didn't want to talk to him about Julie and Sabrina, but he was a man of her father's generation. Maybe he could give her some insight into Daddy's behaviour?

"Why do men cheat on their wives, Tom?"

"Oh." He screwed a poll into a clean roller, dipped it into Viv's paint, and began working on the wall. Viv went back to painting her side.

"Been fooling around with a married man?" he asked. "Your father told me about your dating."

"No!" Viv stared at Tom, but he kept right on painting. "Not me – Daddy. I just found out that the reason my mother left us was because Daddy was cheating on her with Magda."

"Huh," Tom said. They painted in silence, Viv wondering if that was all Tom was going to say. Men. They stuck together.

They had finished the wall and were pausing to review their efforts when Tom spoke again. "Gabe doesn't seem like the kind of man to cheat on his wife. He must have had an awful lot of provocation."

Viv hesitated. "He says he did."

"Your father can be a stubborn, cheap, son-of-a-gun, but he's a good guy. You know that."

"I used to think so, but how could he install his mistress into the same house he shared with me?"

Tom looked her in the eye. "That any of your business?"

"I – I beg your pardon?" Viv sputtered.

"Did he wipe your nose in it?"

"No! I had no idea."

Tom nodded. "You're a grown woman, Viv. No one ever knows what goes on between a man and a woman once the bedroom door closes." He held her gaze, his light blue eyes boring into hers until she looked away.

They finished painting the family room in silence. Viv felt small for what she had said about Daddy. She'd never seen it Tom's way before. Could she be wrong?

"You want to go see that dog of yours?"

"Huh?" Viv had been lost in thought. "Sure. Are you going with me?"

"Let's clean up and get moving."

It was six by the time they arrived at the vet's. Stacy nodded to them and let them through the door into the back hallway, where they walked to the recovery area. Thiago, the technician, had Bruno out of his cage. The dog was wearing a plastic cone around his head, plus a harness. The bandage was off, and Viv could see the stitches running from the top of Bruno's shoulder to half-way down his side. Bruno was limping on his three remaining legs, and Viv's heart contracted with pity.

"Hi, Bruno. How're you feeling today?" Tom said from the doorway. The dog turned, yipped, and hobbled over to him, his tail pumping. Tom squatted and laughed when the dog butted him with the plastic cone instead of licking his face. "That to keep him from biting at his stitches?"

"Exactly." Thiago smiled. "He's doing much better today. Dr. Lane cut back his pain meds, so he's a lot more energetic, aren't you, boy?"

Viv knelt down beside Tom, and Bruno sniffed her hand before bestowing a doggy kiss upon it. "What a good boy," she said, delighted to be included in Bruno's affections.

"Come on, Bruno, let's show them what you can do," Thiago said. He circled the room with the dog limping after him, Bruno looking happy to be out of his cage and moving again. Thiago handed Bruno a treat. "We'll have him running in no time."

"He'll be able to run?" Viv asked.

"Sure. Run, climb stairs, jump. A tripod can do all the things a four-legged dog can do. Once he's found his balance, you won't be able to stop him." He led the dog over to Viv and Tom, who patted and praised Bruno.

"When will he be ready to leave?" Viv asked.

Thiago glanced at Tom. "I guess Tom didn't tell you?" Viv shook her head.

Tom said, "Because Bruno is a stray and someone might come forward to claim him, Dr. Lane is letting him stay here for the week. If no one claims him, I'll pick him up on Saturday afternoon."

The technician nodded with Bruno leaning against his leg. "We'll send him home with some instructions. You'll have to watch for arthritis developing in the three remaining legs, since they tend to get overworked. You can get him an elevated bed with a cooling mattress that would be good for his joints, if you're interested. There's a website I can give you with products for animals with amputated limbs."

"Sure, whatever helps," Viv said.

Tom smiled down at the dog. "I'm looking forward to taking you home to meet the rest of the crew."

"You've got other pets?" Thiago asked.

"Two horses, five dogs, six cats, and a raccoon I found abandoned as a kit who likes to drop by from time to time."

"Tom fosters dogs with Dog Angels," Viv said.

"I've heard of them," Thiago replied.

"I'm no stranger to animals with special needs, although I haven't had a tripod before. We'll figure things out together, won't we, Bruno?" Tom scratched behind the dog's ear, and Bruno's tail thumped his agreement.

"You'll want to keep him away from the other dogs for about a week after he gets home. Give him time to adjust and finish healing. If you have any questions or concerns, we'd be happy to help," Thiago said. "We appreciate you taking Bruno. We've all become attached to him."

"Well, I'll be back tomorrow night to check on him," Tom said, rising. "Night."

Thiago nodded and gave Viv a slip of paper with the website's address before bidding them good night. She and Tom left through the back door and followed the alley out to the sidewalk.

"Bruno looks better, doesn't he?" she asked.

"Sure. He'll be good as new in no time."

Reaching the streetcar stop, Viv said, "There's something else. I just want to thank you for talking to me about Daddy, Tom. I appreciate it."

Tom looked at her. "Did it make a difference?"

"It gave me something to think about."

"Good." He paused. "Thanks for helping with the painting, by the way. See you, Viv." He saluted, touching a finger to his forehead, before strolling away.

"Night."

As Viv watched him go, she wondered what made Tom so confident. Maybe it was something that came with age, that feeling of being comfortable in your own skin? But it was more than that, more to do with trusting yourself and your instincts. She had been so unsettled since the break-up; she wondered if she would ever trust her instincts again. As she boarded the streetcar, what troubled Viv the most was the feeling that maybe she never had.

When Viv got home, Constantine was waiting for her in the front hallway. He meowed and sniffed her leg.

"Smell Bruno, do you?"

The cat walked down the hallway ahead of her, leading the way to the kitchen. He watched as Viv filled his bowls, and ate his dinner right away. He even hung around the kitchen as she cooked her own meal, but disappeared when she sat down to eat. He was back again as the dish water gurgled down the sink, staring at her as if she had forgotten something. Viv opened the manual she had tossed aside on Saturday night to read what she was missing.

"Let's see. After dinner, I'm supposed to play with you and brush you. Hmm. There are some cat things on the shelf beside your food. Hold on a minute."

Viv rooted through the pantry and came up with a small, blue foam ball. She held it up for the cat. "Do you want to play with this?"

Constantine just stared at her, motionless as a statue.

Viv tossed the ball across the kitchen, where it rolled out the door and into the hallway. She turned to Constantine.

"It says in your manual that you like to play with your ball. Go get it, kitty."

Constantine stuck a hind leg in the air and began licking between his toes. Viv shrugged and walked to the hallway to retrieve the ball. When she straightened, the cat was watching her from the kitchen doorway.

"Okay, go get the ball." She threw it at Constantine. The ball bounced once, and the cat batted it back to her.

"Hey, that was really cute! Let's try again." Viv picked up the ball and tossed it to the cat, who let it bounce before lobbing it back just as if they were playing ping-pong.

"Well, aren't you clever." Viv threw the ball three more times, and each time the Siamese hit it back to her. Viv knelt on the floor beside him and picked up a front paw.

"High five, Constantine!" she said, tapping her finger against his foot. The cat yanked away from her grasp and meowed.

"All right, no high fives. Let's see what else you can do." She returned to the pantry and came back with a small laser pointer, aiming the little red dot on the hallway floor. Constantine charged after it, trying to catch it with his claws. Viv aimed it on the wall out of his reach, but the cat leapt after it.

Soon Viv had Constantine charging up and down the hallway, jumping up the wall, and doing back flips. Viv laughed at his antics. They spent fifteen minutes playing together until they both lost interest. After putting the pointer away, Viv removed the brush from the cupboard, picked the Siamese up gingerly, and sat down at the kitchen table. She had never picked Constantine up before, and was a little nervous that he might bite or scratch.

"Okay, Constantine?"

He just sat there, staring off into space.

Viv brushed him tentatively, but he didn't move. She had seen wiry cat brushes before, but this short-haired animal obviously didn't need one; the bristles of his brush were quite soft. She brushed him again, and then again. Constantine began to purr.

"You like that, don't you, kitty?" Viv stroked his sleek back, and he chuffed his head on the underside of her chin. "You are the sweetest cat," Viv said, giving him a hug. This was too much, however; Constantine meowed and jumped out of her arms.

"Sorry, I got carried away," Viv said. She found a pouch of treats and tossed him one. Constantine caught it in his mouth and chewed it up.

She didn't see him again until she had gone to bed and felt a soft "thump" on the mattress. Viv sensed the cat stalking to the other side of the bed. It was comforting to have the animal with her; she didn't feel so alone.

"Constantine, do you ever worry about doing the right thing?" she murmured, thinking about her father. The cat maintained his silence, however, and Viv drifted off to sleep.

Chapter 22

The kids were getting restless at school now that it was so close to summer vacation. Viv seized every opportunity to take them outside to burn off some energy, enjoying the change of routine as much as they did. Life was frosty in the staff room, however, where Julie avoided her by burying her nose in a book.

By Thursday, Viv decided to do something about it. She showed up at Julie's house after dinner with an ice cream cake. Julie stared at her blank-faced from the door while Olivia squealed.

"Yay! Cake! Cake!"

Viv knelt down to give Olivia a closer look. "That's right, honey. Chocolate and vanilla ice cream with a fudge-crunch centre."

"Let's go to the kitchen, Aunt Viv." Olivia dragged her down the hallway with Julie right behind them.

"Get three spoons and put them on the table, sweetie," Julie said.

As the child hurried to obey, Julie whispered, "That's pretty low, using my kid to make up with me."

"Whatever works," Viv whispered back. Julie shook her head and grinned.

"How did you get an ice cream cake here without it melting?" she asked out loud, setting three plates on the table. Olivia was already sitting there with a spoon in her hand.

"I got Fred's VW Beetle out of the garage. She drives a bit loud, though. I think she needs a new muffler."

"You should take her to my garage. Ask for Jimmy. He's good."

"I will. Thanks for the tip."

Julie angled the cake box closer and thrust a carving knife

through the frozen layers.

"Me first, Mommy!"

"Hold your horses, Olivia. Guests first, remember?" Olivia frowned, her spoon drooping in her hand.

"Maybe Olivia could have the first piece just this once?" Viv asked. The child looked imploringly at her mother.

"Well, just this once, if Aunty Viv doesn't mind."

"Yay!" Julie levered the first piece onto a plate and slid it to her daughter. Olivia hunkered down in her chair and went to work with her spoon.

"I've been painting the basement walls in the house Daddy's renovating every night this week," Viv said. "Tom's really up against the deadline, what with Daddy not being there."

"Your dad must be happy for your help," Julie said. Viv frowned. "Still not speaking to him?" Viv shook her head. "Well, the two of you will figure it out," Julie said, handing Viv a slice.

"Tom says that Daddy's blood work and EKG is scheduled for tomorrow. If everything is okay, Daddy plans to be back at work on Monday."

"That sounds like your father." Julie placed a piece of ice cream cake on her own plate, closed the box, and got up to stuff it into the freezer.

"Mmm, this is good, isn't it?" Viv asked Olivia. The child nodded, chocolate fudge smeared around her mouth.

"Tom and I have also been visiting Bruno at the vet this week," Viv said.

"How's Bruno doing?"

"Just great. He's chasing a ball. You'd never know he'd lost a leg just a week ago."

"Where did the leg go?" Olivia asked.

"No, honey, the dog's leg got hurt, so the animal doctor had to take it away," Viv said. Olivia looked horrified. "It's okay. Dogs aren't like people. They can get around on three legs just as well as on four." Olivia still looked uncertain, however, thrusting one of her legs forward to study.

"Really, sweetie, a dog with three legs can do anything a dog with four can do. How's your cake?" Julie asked.

Olivia smiled, diverted. "It was yummy, Mommy. Can I go play now?" Olivia's plate was spotted with mounds of melting ice cream and chocolate crunchies.

"Wait a minute." Julie took a napkin from the holder and scrubbed her daughter's face and hands. "Okay, go play. Aunt Viv and I will come out in a minute or two." Olivia skipped out the back door as Viv took a bite of the ice cream.

"This is nice, Julie. I'm glad that we made up. So, how are things between you and Kim? You two were going out after the game last night, weren't you?"

"Kim and I are getting along fine, but never mind about us. Tell me more about this Tom you keep mentioning."

Viv smiled and shifted into a more comfortable position in her chair. "Well, he's tall, lean, muscular, with dark hair tied back in a ponytail, and these blue eyes that seem to see straight through you, but light up when he smiles." Julie nodded, hanging onto Viv's every word. "He's a man of few words, but he's really comfortable to be around."

Julie smiled. "He sounds fantastic. Why haven't you asked Sabrina and me to check him out?"

"Because he's fifty." Viv laughed at Julie's expression. "Yes, he's old enough to be my father."

Julie shook her head. "You led me right into that. Too bad, though. He sounds almost too good to be true."

"If he were even ten years younger, I could really go for him. But he's already got a grown family. He wouldn't want to start another one."

"That would be too much of a May-December romance." Julie laid her hand on Viv's arm. "But don't worry, sweetie, the right man's out there waiting for you. Maybe Sabrina and I should stop worrying so much about earning potential with possible boyfriends. If you're into a man who works with his hands . . ." She let the sentence dangle.

Viv smiled dreamily. "Tom has the nicest hands, broad with long fingers. A carpenter's hands."

"If only it weren't for the liver spots," Julie said. The two women laughed and got up from the table to join Olivia outside.

By the end of the week, Viv was just plain worn out. The kids had run her ragged at school, plus she had put in all those extra hours at the house, helping Tom with the painting and tiling the basement shower. Added to that were the visits to see Bruno each night, which meant getting home much later than usual. As she and Tom had left the vet's earlier that evening, he had invited her to come out to his farm on Sunday.

"So you can see how Bruno's settling in. I'll slap a couple of steaks on the barbecue, and you can stay for supper."

"Thanks, that sounds great. I'd love to see all of your other animals, too. I'll bring dessert." He had given her directions on how to find the place, and Viv said she'd come at four.

She fed Constantine when she got home Friday night, playing with him, but skipping the brushing. Afterward, she made herself a ham sandwich, too tired to bother with anything more. Then she carried a glass of wine upstairs, looking forward to watching one of the DVDs from Fred's collection. The early Audrey Hepburn movie sounded like fun. She changed into a nighty and hunted through the cases.

There it was, *Roman Holiday*. On the cover, a grinning Audrey rode a scooter seated behind Gregory Peck, her arms clenched around his waist with the Roman Coliseum in the background.

She flipped the case over. This was Audrey's first starring role, for which she'd won the Oscar. Audrey, her hair in a tousled pixie cut, was pictured holding hands with Gregory. She looked adorable.

"Okay, Audrey," Viv said, slipping the disc into the player, "do your magic." She climbed into bed and clicked the remote to turn on the screen. Constantine settled on the bottom of the bed while Viv leaned back against the pillows.

The story was kind of a reverse fairy tale. Audrey played a cossetted princess who was on a good-will tour of European capitals. Rome was supposed to be a short stop-over, but the poor kid was exhausted from all her PR work, and had some kind of a nervous breakdown in her bedroom the first night. The countess chaperoning her called for their doctor, and he gave Audrey a sedative. They left her to sleep it off, but Audrey snuck out, determined to see some of Rome on her own. She ran into Gregory Peck, a jaded American newspaperman working in Rome. Still dopey from the drug, Audrey fell asleep in his bed. He figured out who she was, however, and with the help of his photographer friend, followed her around Rome the next day so that they could sell an exclusive story on the young princess to his newspaper. Only Audrey and Gregory fell in love, and even though it broke both their hearts, she decided to return to her duties at the end of a perfect day.

"It's so sad, but so beautiful," Viv cried as the credits ran. Tear dripped down her face as she clutched the empty wine glass to her chest. "You just knew she was going to give Gregory up. He was probably her first adult love, but she decided to do her duty rather than follow her heart. And look at her standing up for herself with her chaperones. She was going to take charge of her life and make her own decisions from then on."

Viv sat up in bed, wide-eyed in the middle of an epiphany. "She's just like me."

She crawled across the bed to the cat on her hands and knees. The Siamese opened his eyes to stare at her. Viv picked him up and cradled him to her chest. "She's just like me, Constantine." He struggled to get free and meowed, but finally settled into her arms. Viv patted him mechanically as she thought.

"Everyone's been treating me like a child ever since the break-up. Daddy and Magda wanted me to move back in with them. Sabrina and Julie told me that I was taking too long to get over Kyle and made me start dating again, even though I wasn't ready. They made fun of all the boys I've ever dated, and convinced me that they were better at choosing men than I was. *For me.* How stupid is that?"

She held the cat up to eye level. "What have I done? When did I lose control of my own life? Have I always been such a push-over?"

Constantine disliked being held like a ragdoll and struggled out of her arms. Viv didn't even notice. She lay back on the pillows, twisting her ring as she contemplated her life.

She had always liked taking care of people and making them happy, but what had happened to looking after herself? Was she too gullible, too accommodating? Was that why her relationship with Kyle had failed, because she hadn't been enough of a woman to hold him?

After being lost in thought for an indeterminate amount of time, Viv noticed that the sky outside the window was dark. Her stomach rumbled. What time was it? She glanced at the clock radio; it was twelve minutes after ten. She'd been lying there for almost an hour. Viv clicked on the bedside lamp and almost knocked over her empty wine glass. She realized that she was hungry.

She padded down the stairs and through the moonlit hallway to the kitchen. Rummaging in the fridge, she found a wedge of aged cheddar and some grapes. She put them on a tray with a box of crackers, and was about to turn off the light when she spotted the bottle of red wine on the counter. Adding it to her tray, she climbed back upstairs to the bedroom.

She needed something to cheer herself up; she was wrung out from recollecting a life full of mistakes. The second movie in the Audrey Hepburn collection was called *Sabrina*. The cover said that it was a comedy. Humphrey Bogart looked familiar, but she didn't have a clue who William Holden was. Viv shrugged; if it was an Audrey Hepburn movie, she was bound to enjoy it. She put the DVD into the machine and settled down on the bed with the tray beside her. As the movie began, she poured herself a glass of wine and munched on some crackers and cheese.

Viv opened one eye. The sunlight dazzled her, and she quickly closed it again. She groaned and snatched a pillow to put over her head.

Viv lifted the pillow and peeked out through one eye. The sunlight had shifted from her face to shine on the bottom of the bed. She tossed the pillow away and opened the other eye. Aagh. Her eyes felt like sandpaper. She rubbed them and pushed the hair out of her face. Her teeth felt fuzzy, her throat was parched, and her head was pounding.

Constantine strolled across the bed and stopped right beside her face.

"Go away, Constantine." She tried to push him away, but he rubbed his head against her hand and purred. Obstinate cat.

"What time is it?" Viv turned over, winced, and grabbed her head with both hands. Tilting her head more slowly this time, she peered at the clock. 11:12. In the morning. What day was it? She remembered that it was Saturday. Good, she didn't have to get up.

Constantine rubbed against her shoulder, and Viv looked down at him. The Siamese stared at her with unblinking blue eyes. Viv shut her own.

"Meow." The cry was insistent. The cat kneaded her arm with his claws.

"Ouch! Hey, Constantine." Viv opened her eyes and rubbed her punctured skin.

"Meow."

"All right, all right." Viv rolled over, glad that the room didn't roll with her, and sat up. She didn't feel like vomiting, so she stood up. The cat jumped off the bed and trotted across the floor, pausing to look back at her from the doorway.

"I'm coming." Viv looked at the empty wine bottle on the bedside table. That was stupid. No wonder she felt so lousy. When was she going to learn?

Her feet started moving across the floor, and she followed the cat down the stairs to the kitchen. She turned on the cold water tap, picked up a glass next to the sink, and filled it. *Bliss*, she thought, chugalugging the contents.

Constantine intertwined himself through her legs.

"Right. You want your breakfast." She fed the cat and gave him fresh water before making a cup of coffee and a piece of toast for herself. Sipping from her cup at the table, Viv tried to recollect the night before.

She remembered watching the second movie, *Sabrina*. It had something to do with Audrey going to Paris and getting a haircut, and then falling in love with the brother of the guy she had loved since childhood. Only, the brother was a lot older and not as good looking as the guy she had always loved, although he had a certain charm. Audrey and the older brother ended up on an ocean liner together at the end, so he must have won. Audrey seemed delighted with the results.

The coffee and toast were entering her digestive tract, making her more inclined to continue living. She looked at the clock on the wall and saw that it was a quarter to one. Poor Constantine. No wonder he had been so hungry.

She stopped to consider her epiphany of the night before. It was all much clearer to her now that she no longer felt like weeping. She had been a dope. Plain and simple. She had spent her childhood trying to look after Daddy, and then let boyfriend after boyfriend lead her around by the heart. Especially Kyle. She had wasted six years with him. Maybe not wasted, though. He had taught her a few things about taking care of herself. But then she had let herself be bowled over by Drew because she had missed being looked after by a man. Only Drew had been looking out for himself.

Sabrina and Julie were good friends who truly cared about her, but they were as messed up as she was. What had made her think that either one of them was better qualified at choosing life partners? Julie, who had a big chip on her shoulder, or Sabrina, who was too absorbed with her job.

She might have loved unwisely, but she was going to put that all behind her. As Tom had said, she was older now. Wiser, too, because she could see where she had made her mistakes. No more putting herself second, hoping that someone would love her back. She would follow her own instincts from now on. She would perform her own dating do-over.

Only, what did her instincts tell her about the kind of man she should choose? Viv tried to picture him. What would he look like? What did he do for a living? She closed her eyes and concentrated.

After a moment, she opened her eyes and sighed. Damned if she knew. But, hey, she'd know him when he came along, wouldn't she? Shaking her head, Viv got up to take a shower.

Chapter 23

Sunday afternoon, Viv drove to Oakville via Dundas Street, as Tom had recommended. He had an aversion to the QEW and the 403, preferring to take the back roads to avoid construction delays and heavy traffic, depending on where he was working in Toronto. At least Daisy was running better. Viv had visited Julie's mechanic the day before, and discovered that the car needed a new muffler, an oil change, new filters, and new sparkplugs. It had cost her several hundred dollars, but at least the old girl was more reliable now.

She had a banana cake on the seat beside her, baked from a family recipe given to her by a university friend. In her opinion, the recipe made the best banana cake in the world, and she was sure that Tom would enjoy it.

When she reached Trafalgar Road, she turned right, and turned right again when she spotted Lynden's Nursery. A couple of kilometers later, she saw a blue mailbox with "Lockhart" painted on it in white block letters. Turning up the dirt road and feeling each bump through the VW's struts, she paused in front of a red brick two-storey.

What a charmer! The white porch was as wide as the house, complete with a couple of rocking chairs and a porch swing to linger in on a summer's evening. The second floor had a balcony that was smaller than the porch, but had white gingerbread trim.

Viv parked next to the attached two-car garage – a more recent addition, from the look of it. The barking started as she leaned over to pick up her purse and the banana cake. An assortment of heads, coats, and tails came streaming out of the barn across the drive from the house. The dogs made straight for the car and surrounded it, a German Shepherd jumping up on the driver's door. Viv shrank back.

The screen door bumped open on the porch, and Tom strode out.

"Out of the way, you bunch of clowns," he shouted as he climbed down the three wide steps. The dogs turned and trotted to greet him, tongues lolling as they panted in the humid afternoon air. Like a ragtag honour guard, they accompanied Tom back to the car. Viv opened the door, generating another outburst.

"Quiet down," Tom hollered. He grinned as he helped Viv out of the car. "Good to see you, darling."

"Good to see you, Tom. Your house is beautiful. Say, where's Bruno?"

"He's inside the house. I'm keeping him away from this crew until he's feeling stronger. Except for Peg. She's too old to sleep in the barn, so she always sleeps in the house."

"Which one is Peg?"

"That one over there." Tom pointed at a blond Labrador sitting on the perimeter of the group. "Come meet Viv, Peg."

The dog rose and sidled through the other dogs to the car. She sat at Viv's feet and raised her right paw. Viv grinned.

"Did you train her to do that?"

"Sure. She's smart, aren't you, girl?"

Viv took Peg's paw and shook it. "Is she one of your rescue dogs?"

"Yep."

"Why? Who wouldn't want her?"

Tom patted Peg's shoulder. "She was eight when I got her two years ago, and missing a third of her teeth. Another third had to be pulled. Not many people want a dog that old, especially one with dental problems."

Viv bent to look Peg in the eye. "Well, I think you're just lovely." Peg appeared to smile, and Viv stroked her smooth head. Straightening, she added, "Introduce me to the rest, won't you?"

"Let's see." Tom pointed at the German Shepherd. "This one is Hoover, so named because he'll eat anything – shoes, wood, couches, and plastic. I had a Stetson I was fond of once, until he ate it. He's more goat than dog."

"And people don't want him because he's so destructive?"

"That, and he gets terrible gas. I make him sleep in the barn." Tom scratched the big dog's back. "You're a real goof, aren't you?" Hoover's hind leg rose to scratch his side compulsively.

"Then there's Bernie." Bernie was a beagle with only one eye, a scar running the length of his cheek from the sealed socket. One of his ears was half-chewed off as well. "As you can see, he was in a fight once." Bernie came forward to sniff at Viv's leg.

"Never mind, Bernie," Viv said. "You should have seen the other guy, right?"

"And Tank." Tom pointed to a muscular grey-and-white dog. He looked attentively from Tom to Viv.

"What's wrong with Tank? He looks perfectly healthy to me."

"Except he's a pit bull, and people are afraid to adopt him. He was raised by a couple who split up, so he's used to living with a family."

Viv offered her hand, and the dog licked it before sitting at her feet. "Good boy, Tank," she said, scratching behind his ear. "Let's see. That's four dogs. I thought you said you had five?"

"The last one's Riley. He's watching us from the barn." Viv turned and saw a cocker spaniel standing beside the door." I've been working with him since last winter. He was abused, so he's still shy with people he doesn't know."

"Hi, Riley," Viv said with a wave. She turned back and handed Tom the container with the banana cake. "I promised you dessert."

"Thanks. Would you like to come in for lemonade? It's plenty warm today."

"I'd love to." Viv's shirt was stuck to her back, and her throat was dry from the drive. There was no air conditioning inside Daisy.

"Right this way." As Tom escorted Viv up the sidewalk to the porch, she admired the colourful flower beds along the way. When they reached the porch, Tom strode ahead to open the door. Bruno stumbled up from the foyer mat and waved his tail. He was wearing a harness, but the cone was gone. Viv crouched to greet him.

"Bruno, I'm so glad to see you. How do you like your new home?"

He licked her face, and Viv smiled. She noticed that the skin around the stitches was pink now instead of red, a sure sign of healing. She stepped into the house with Peg and Tom following. The two dogs sniffed each other before Bruno hobbled down the hallway after Peg.

"Hey, his new bed arrived yesterday," Tom said. "It's nice. I'll show it to you later."

"Good," Viv said. She peered into the front room to the right of the hallway and saw furniture covered with a plastic tarp piled in the middle of the floor. One of the bare walls had three different-coloured swathes painted on it.

"As you can see, I'm doing some work on the downstairs. I stripped the wallpaper off in the living room, and now I'm trying to decide on a paint colour. I've already refinished the floor."

Viv looked down at the broad planks gleaming with dark stain. "It looks terrific."

"Thanks."

He led her across the hallway to the dining room. A chandelier hung in the centre of the room, and the broad floorboards beneath it were worn and dusty. The room was devoid of furniture except for two dog beds, one a broad pillow, the other a mattress on a platform raised four inches off the floor. Viv pressed her palm on the mattress and noticed that it felt cool.

"What keeps it chilled?"

"There's water in the core. I'll have to get one for Peg, too. She's got a touch of arthritis."

Tom and Viv followed the dogs into the kitchen, where the cupboards and counter top had been removed. Cardboard boxes were stacked neatly in a corner next to a tool box. Plates, glasses, mugs, and a silverware tray were perched on boards on top of two saw horses. The sink, fridge, and stove were still in place, however.

"I took down the wall between the dining room and the kitchen. As you can see, I haven't progressed much beyond the demolishing stage."

"How long have you been working at it?"

"About three months." Tom grinned. "You know what they say about a shoemaker's kids never having shoes."

Viv nodded. "I'm sure you haven't had much time to work on your own house with Daddy's schedule."

"You can say that again. Come on, let's get you that lemonade."

Tom set the cake on the saw horse and picked up a couple of glasses. He handed them to Viv before crossing to the fridge and pulling out a plastic pitcher. She held the glasses as he poured.

"Tom?"

"Hmm?"

"Speaking of Daddy, did you hear anything about his test results?"

"Uh huh. He's doing fine. Says he'll be back to work on Monday."

Viv had been worried about her father, but didn't want to call him. She was still too angry to speak to him. "I'm glad," she said.

Tom nodded and put the pitcher back inside the fridge. "Cheers." He gulped down half a glass while Viv took a sip.

"This is delicious. Did you make it from scratch?"

"A recipe of my grandmother's."

Viv drank her lemonade while looking around the room. "When do you plan to finish all this?" she asked.

"Your father and I should be done the reno on Harvard Avenue in a week. He's hiring extra help to do the porch and the deck so that we can finish on time. With all the overtime I put into the project, Gabe is going to pay me a nice bonus. I plan to take July and August off to finish the work here. Maybe have a little time to go fishing, too."

"I could come out now and then to give you a hand, if you like." Tom contemplated her offer as he leaned against the sink. "I have the summer off until I have to get ready for school the last week of August. I'm an experienced painter and tiler now, you know."

He shook his head. "Why would you want to work on a house in the heat of summer when you could be at a beach, or at least in an air-conditioned shopping mall?"

Viv nodded at Bruno. "To thank you for taking him. For working so hard to help Daddy finish on time." She shrugged. "Besides, I like working on old houses. It's nice to pretty them up after they've been dowdy for so long. Not that your house is dowdy," she said quickly. "I love this place. It feels so homey."

"Been in my family for four generations. She's built sturdy. Got great bones, too. Just needs to be brought into the twenty-first century without losing her charm."

"So, have we got a deal?"

"We'll see. You might not be so keen once you've worked a full day."

"Try me. Now, are you going to show me the barn?"

The other dogs accompanied Viv and Tom to just inside the barn door, where they paused to lap water from a couple of buckets. It was brighter inside the barn than Viv had expected because of a couple of windows in the front room that Tom was using as a carpenter's shop. Viv hesitated on the threshold, looking at a sideboard pushed up against the wall and an unfinished dining table in the middle of the room.

She walked over to the sideboard. The wood was lighter on top, as were the inlays on the sides and the two doors. Viv rubbed her hand over the polished wood.

"This is gorgeous, Tom. Did you make it?"

He nodded.

"What kind of wood is it?"

"The darker wood is cherry, and the lighter is maple. It's for a friend's dining room. The table goes with it."

Viv walked across the worn floor with sawdust in its grooves to eye the dining table. "They'll be stunning together. I don't know when you find the time."

"I started them plenty early. They're not promised until next month."

"Well, you do nice work."

The rest of the barn consisted of a wide-open space in the middle with a hay loft over top, plus six stalls on the far side. Two cats were stretched out on a dilapidated couch next to some covered bins. One of them sat up and meowed as Viv approached.

"Who are these?"

Tom sat down on the couch beside them and pulled the black cat onto his lap. "The grey Persian is Mitzie, and this is Tinks. They keep down the mouse and groundhog population around the barn."

Viv looked at him in surprise. "Your cats take on groundhogs?"

"With the help of the dogs. The cats flush them out, and the dogs kill them. Hoover is especially good at that."

"Yuck!"

Tinks purred as Tom petted him. "Well, you don't want the horses breaking a leg in a groundhog hole, do you?"

"I suppose not. Where are the rest of the cats?"

"They're around here somewhere."

Viv heard a stamp and a nicker. "The horses are inside?"

"My two are. I brought them in in case you wanted a ride. The other two are out in the pasture. They're boarders."

Viv grimaced. "I don't know about going for a ride, Tom. I've only been on horseback once, when I was a teenager, and I didn't enjoy the experience."

"Did you fall off?"

"No, but the horse ran away with me. I was clinging to its back for all I was worth."

Tom stood and headed toward the stalls. "Sounds like it's time you got back up again. Come on and meet them, anyway."

Viv followed Tom to a stall where a chestnut-coloured mare was waiting, her head thrust out over the closed bottom half of the door. Her mane was black and she had a white star on her forehead. Tom ran his hand down the horse's neck, and she nickered.

"This is Jenny. She's a real sweetheart, nice and gentle."

Viv put out her palm for the horse sniff. Instead, the horse's lips explored her hand, leaving saliva and fragments of hay behind. Viv frowned and wiped her hand on her jeans.

Tom chuckled. "She thinks you were offering her a treat. Here." He gave Viv a sugar cube. "I've always got some of these in my pocket. Give that to her on the flat of your palm."

Viv held up the sugar, and the horse snuffled it up with her lips and munched it.

"You can pat her, if you like."

Viv stepped closer and reached up to stroke the horse's neck as Tom had done. Jenny nodded her head, however, and Viv leaned back out of the way.

"Don't worry, she likes you." Tom gave the horse a final pat and turned to the stall next door. "This is her son, Champ."

A taller chestnut with a white blaze down his nose stuck his head out, chewing a mouthful of hay. Tom rubbed his forehead, and the horse smacked him in the shoulder with his head as Champ turned back to his manger.

"Ow." Tom rubbed his shoulder. "Not the most graceful of animals. Champ's only four. He still has time to learn some manners from his mother." Champ stuck his head out again, placidly chewing another mouthful.

Viv turned back to the mare, who was watching her. "How old is Jenny?" She stroked Jenny's neck tentatively, the horse quiet under her hand.

"She's eleven. They didn't know that she was pregnant when I bought her. Got two horses for the price of one."

The horse chuffed on top of Viv's head with her warm, moist breath. Viv laughed and said, "Hey, Jenny."

Tom leaned against the wall beside Viv, his bare forearms folded across his chest. "If you like, I could lead you around the riding ring on Jenny. There's no way she could run away with you, not that she would."

"Well . . ."

"Come on, Chicken Little."

Viv's eyebrows rose. "Is that a derogatory comment about my height?"

"Course not, Tinker Bell. What do you say?" He grinned, slow and lazy, and Viv smiled back. Maybe it was time to conquer her fear of horses.

"Well, all right," she said slowly. "She does seem well-behaved."

"Good." Tom straightened. "Come on, Jenny, let's take Viv for a ride."

He tethered the horse in the corridor to saddle her, Viv watching the process carefully. When Tom had finished, he untethered the horse, took the reins, and clucked. Jenny stepped forward beside him.

"The riding ring's out back of the barn."

The horse's hooves clopped on the concrete floor as she ambled beside Tom to the back door, Viv following behind. They emerged into the warm sunlight and strolled to the riding ring. Tom unlatched the gate, and they walked inside. Viv noticed that the floor was sand, and pointed at it with her sneaker.

"Is that in case I fall off?"

Tom snorted. "Just how're you going to fall off with me leading you?"

"You'd be surprised. Horses and I are not a good match."

"Come on over here."

With a slight grimace, Viv followed Tom and the horse to the side of the ring. Jenny was so much bigger up close.

"Okay. You're going to put your left foot into my hands, and I'm going to hoist you up. Then you're going to swing your right leg over Jenny's rump, and sit down in the saddle."

"Shouldn't you tie her up first in case she moves?"

Tom sighed. "She's not going anywhere, Viv. Trust me. Jenny is the calmest, gentlest animal in the world."

"All right," Viv said, still feeling uneasy.

Tom bent and clasped his hands together. Viv took a deep breath and placed her foot between them. With a quick movement, Tom straightened and hoisted her into the air as if she weighed nothing at all. She swung her leg over Jenny as she had been told and found herself sitting in the saddle.

"Ohmigod!" she said, clinging to the saddle horn with both hands. It seemed much higher up here than she had imagined. "Don't let me fall!" she blurted. The horse remained still beneath her.

"It's okay, darling. I won't let you fall." Tom laid a reassuring hand on Viv's knee. "Now, I'm going to adjust the stirrups. You just sit tight until I'm done."

Viv was frozen in the saddle. "Are you kidding?"

He smiled as he adjusted the left strap. "Now, put your foot into the stirrup." She didn't move, and he had to guide her foot into place. "Now I have to do the other one." He rounded in front of the horse, Viv staring straight ahead. She felt his hand on her calf.

"This will only take a moment." He did something with the strap, and Viv felt his hand on her foot. "In it goes. There, all done."

She looked down into his upturned face.

"Okay, I'm going to lead you around the ring now. You ready?"

Viv nodded once.

"Nice and easy. Here we go." Tom clucked at the horse and started forward, Jenny ambling beside him. Viv hung on to the saddle horn, feeling the horse's muscles shift beneath her. It was an easy, rocking motion that reassured her; Viv remembered thumping up and down on the runaway horse.

As Tom completed the first circuit, he looked at Viv over his shoulder. "Try gripping Jenny's sides with your knees a little. You'll feel more secure."

"Okay."

"How're you doing up there?" Tom asked as they plodded along.

"All right." She smiled briefly, and Tom smiled back.

"Good girl. Looks like you're getting the hang of it."

"It's not that bad, I guess."

Tom nodded. "Kind of like a rocking chair, isn't it?"

"Yes, only a lot higher off the ground."

Tom led them into the centre of the ring and stopped. "I'm going to show you what to do to make the horse start and turn. Don't worry, I'll still be doing most of the work, but I want you to get a feel for it. Okay?"

Viv gulped. "Okay."

"Don't look so scared, darling. Nothing's going to happen." He took a couple of steps in front of the horse, the reins dangling from his hands.

"I want you to press with both your calves to get her moving."
Viv did as she was told, and Jenny stepped forward a couple of
paces while Tom retreated. He stopped, and so did the horse.

They worked for another twenty minutes, practising left and
right turns, and stops. It took Viv a few tries to coordinate the reins
with her legs, forcing Tom to scramble out of the way on one
occasion, but by the time they had finished, Viv was beginning to
feel more confident.

Tom gave her instructions on how to dismount. "Just hold the
reins with your left hand, swing your right leg over Jenny's rump,
and step down. I'll hold the reins for you this time so that you don't
have to worry about them."

Viv ran through the procedure in her mind as she handed Tom
the reins. She soon found herself standing in the air with her left
foot still in the stirrup. She looked down.

"I can't step down from here. It's too high."

"So jump."

"Jump?" Viv licked her lips nervously, her left leg beginning to
quiver with muscle fatigue.

"Jump."

Viv shook her foot free from the stirrup and leapt, pushing away
from the horse and landing squarely on Tom's boot.

"Damn!"

She stumbled sideways, grabbing for his shirt, and Tom steadied
her in his arms.

"Sorry!" Viv peered into his face. "Are you all right?"

Tom grinned, his eyes sparkling with laughter. "Good thing
you're only wearing sneakers. We're going to have to work on your
dismount."

Viv smiled back. "I didn't do so bad for a first lesson, did I?"

"No, you did just fine."

"Thanks, Tom." She hugged him, feeling proud. "You're a
wonderful teacher." Her arms surrounded his shoulders while she
pressed her face against his neck. With all the time they had spent
alone together, she had never been so intimate with him before.
They lingered in each other's arms, and then his head turned and

their eyes met. Viv glanced away.

He released her. Now that she was on her own two feet, she felt wobbly and clung to his arm.

"You okay?"

"I guess it took a little more out of me than I expected." Tom nodded, and as he led the horse out of the ring, he wrapped an arm around her shoulders.

"You just need to develop a different set of muscles, that's all." He gave her shoulder a squeeze as they walked back to the barn, Tom moderating his stride to fit hers. "You looked pretty good up there on Jenny's back. How'd you like to swap riding lessons for some help on the house?"

Viv looked up into his rugged face and suddenly imagined what Tom would look like with all that dark hair hanging down around his shoulders. Realizing that she was holding her breath, she exhaled.

"Sure."

Chapter 24

When they reached the barn, Tom unsaddled Jenny and wiped the dust off her back with a damp sponge before returning her to her stall. Then he left, and Viv talked to the horse, praising and patting her, until Tom returned with a couple of carrots.

"Here," he said, handing Viv a carrot, "Jenny earned it. You give her one, while I give the other to Champ. Don't want him getting jealous." He broke his carrot in thirds, and Viv followed his example before offering the pieces to Jenny.

When the horses had finished their treats and Tom had checked their hay rations and water buckets, he and Viv collected the cat and dog bowls. They took them outside and hosed them clean before refilling the cats' water dishes. Viv dried the food bowls with a rag while Tom took care of the dogs' water buckets.

Magically the troupe of dogs appeared, sitting a short distance from Viv to watch. The cats came even closer, all six of them. Mitzie and Tinks meowed and rubbed against her legs.

"You'll just have to wait until Tom gets back," Viv explained to the animals. Mitzie sat down to clean herself, and Tinks stretched out at Viv's feet, as if they understood. Viv noticed Riley, the shy dog, waiting next to the carpenter shop door.

"Come, Riley," she called, but he maintained his distance.

Tom returned with the buckets, some water sloshing over the rims. He set them down just inside the barn door, where he also left the dogs' bowls once he had filled them with kibble. Only then did Riley join the other dogs to eat.

Tom opened a large tin of cat food and mixed it with dry food in two large bowls. "Here you go," he said to the cats, placing the bowls on the ground. They swarmed past him while Tom wiped off the spoon on a piece of paper towel and tossed the empty tin into a recycling bucket.

"Hey, are you hungry?" he asked Viv. "I'm starving. How about I fire up the barbecue and throw on those steaks?"

Viv glanced at her watch. "It's only five thirty."

"We keep early hours out here in the country, little lady." Tom smiled. "Do you think you could eat?"

"I think I could eat."

They strolled past the garage to the fence surrounding the backyard, the dogs following them. Tom opened the gate just wide enough to let Viv in, pushing the dogs back with his foot.

"Get away, you bunch." To Viv, he added, "I'll let them in after we've eaten."

Viv sidled past him into the back yard. Two mature trees shaded the lawn with a hammock slung between them. Right outside the house was a stone patio with a wooden awning. To the left of the patio was a vegetable garden, and just beyond it a fire pit with a couple of Adirondack chairs.

"This is what I call easy living," Viv said.

"I like it. When we were kids, we used to hound our parents to put in a pool, but I'm glad they didn't. It would have been a lot of work."

"What happened to your parents?"

"Dad's been gone – let's see – seven years now, and Mom's living in Stratford with my aunt. Mom got tired of living on the farm even before Dad passed. She's happier back in a city again. Going to the theatre and eating in restaurants now and then."

"Good for her, although I think I'd miss this once I had lived here."

Tom paused on the patio to stare at her. "And you a city girl."

"Born and bred, but it's not like it was when I was growing up. The traffic seems to be getting worse every year."

Tom started up the barbecue. "And the construction."

"Yes." Viv sighed.

Tom led her into the kitchen and opened the fridge door. "Want a beer?"

"Love one."

He handed her a plastic container holding the marinating steaks before pulling out two long-necked bottles.

"Need a glass?"

"No, I'm good."

He removed the caps and traded one of the beers for the plastic container. Viv took a swig while he helped himself to a pair of tongs and a plastic bowl from a box on the floor.

"I've got potato salad in the fridge – store-bought, I'm afraid – steak, and bread. I'm going to throw on the steaks and pick some lettuce from the garden for a salad."

"I'll pick the lettuce."

"Thanks." They went back outside together, Tom walking to the barbecue while Viv left her beer on the table and went to the garden. She squatted beside the lettuce and chose some succulent outer leaves.

"How about some spinach?" she called over her shoulder.

"Fine."

She added spinach to the bowl. "Chives?"

"Go for it." After adding a few spears, Viv assessed her collection, threw in a bit more spinach, and returned to the patio. Tom was turning down the heat under the meat.

"Thanks." He appropriated the bowl. "I'll wash this and make the salad dressing. Stay out here and enjoy your beer, if you like."

"I will. The breeze is so nice."

She walked to one of the Adirondack chairs and settled into it, stretching out her legs and crossing her ankles. The air was fragrant with the scent of orange blossom wafting over from one of the bushes. She took a swallow of beer and set the bottle on the edge of the fire pit. A robin trilled its clear, musical song. Viv leaned her head on the back of the chair and stared at the plump, white clouds drifting across the sky.

"Viv?" She felt a hand on her shoulder.

"What?" She looked up and saw Tom smiling down at her.

"Sorry, I must have fallen asleep."

He patted her shoulder. "Come on. It's time to eat."

She followed him to the patio table. There were white plastic plates, more beer, paper towel napkins, and cutlery set on it. In the middle was a plate with two steaming steaks, potato salad – still in its store container – the dressed greens with cherry tomatoes, a tub of margarine, and a cutting board with a French baguette. Viv was suddenly ravenous.

"The food looks fabulous."

Tom pulled out her chair, and she sank into it.

"Almost forgot." He strode back to the house and returned with a radio, placing it on the edge of the table. It was already tuned to an easy listening station when he turned it on.

"Perfect," Viv said.

"Dig in."

Viv thought the food was delicious, better than anything she had eaten in a restaurant lately. She and Tom didn't talk much; they listened to the music and gazed across the yard, helping themselves to seconds of the salads and bread when their plates were empty. When they had finished, Viv cleared the table and brought out the banana cake with fresh plates. She cut a generous slice for Tom and a smaller piece for herself, since she was already full.

Tom lifted a forkful to his mouth and smiled with pleasure. "I don't get much home baking these days. This is good."

Viv tasted a forkful for herself. The cake was moist and rich and the frosting was creamy but not too sweet, just the way she liked it. Tom scraped up every bit from his plate, and Viv asked if he would like another piece.

"Thanks, I'm stuffed, but it was really good. You're not going to take the rest home, are you?"

"I wouldn't dare."

He smiled again, his eyes warm. The radio began playing the song, "Me and Mrs. Jones," and he sprang to his feet, his hand out.

"Dance with me."

Viv took his hand, and Tom led her around the table, twirling her before pulling her into his arms. They swayed together, one of his hands in the small of her back and the other swinging their clasped hands in time to the music. Lowering his head to rest his face against hers, Tom crooned the lyrics in a low voice and pulled their hands to his chest.

The song was over too soon for Viv. An up-tempo song began to play, and Tom took a step back.

"Thanks for the dance, darling. That's one of my favourites." They sat back down at the table, where Viv angled her chair closer to his.

"You're a lucky man, Tom Lockhart." She waved her arm at the yard, and one of the dogs barked in the distance.

"I am blessed," he said. "I grow hay and oats for the horses, build a little custom furniture, and renovate houses. I've got everything I need."

Viv turned to him, their heads only inches apart. "Do you?"

Suddenly, a woman plopped into Tom's lap, making him jump. She was blond and leggy, her sundress hiked up to her thighs and a pair of sandals in one hand. She laughed.

"It's getting harder and harder to sneak up on you with all those dogs."

Tom turned to Viv, who was staring at the other woman.

"Viv, this is my fiancée, Shelley Huston."

Chapter 25

Shelley climbed off Tom's lap to slide into a chair. Now that she had a moment to take a good look at her, Viv noticed that Shelley's hair was too brassy, the skin on her legs was dimpled, her throat was crepey, and there were lines along the side of her mouth. Shelley had to be at least fifty.

"Pleased to meet you," Viv said. Shelley clasped Viv's outstretched hand for a second before dropping it. "Tom didn't mention he had a fiancée."

"He can be as close-mouthed as a clam," Shelley said, exchanging a look with him.

"How was work today, darling?" Tom quickly asked.

Shelley picked up a cherry tomato from the salad and popped it into her mouth. "Pretty slow." She wiped a trickle of juice with her hand. "People must have been outside enjoying the weather." She smiled at Tom. "I'm starving, Daddy."

"How about I get your steak started?"

"That would be great." Tom leaned forward for a kiss before heading for the house. "I'd love a beer, too, while you're in the kitchen," she called after him.

"Will do," he replied. When Tom opened the patio door, Bruno and Peg burst outside. They trotted over to Viv first, and then Bruno sniffed at Shelley. She pushed the terrier away with a grimace.

"I saw him last night when Tom brought him home. I can't stand the sight of that thing, hopping around on three legs with those ugly stitches. I suppose that's why you're here – to see the dog?"

Viv held out her hand and Bruno limped over to rest his chin on her leg. Viv stroked his head. "Good boy."

"I've been looking forward to meeting you, Viv." The smile returned to Shelley's face. "Tom talks about *you* all the time. Your father had heart surgery, right?"

Viv nodded. "An angioplasty."

"How's he doing?"

Tom stepped back outside, switching on the barbecue and setting Shelley's steak down on a shelf before handing her a beer.

"Thank you, Daddy," she said.

"You're welcome." He returned to the kitchen while Peg and Bruno settled on the grass a short distance from the women.

"Dad's doing fine, thanks. He'll be back to work tomorrow."

"That's good. Then they won't be needing your help with the house anymore, right? Tom said that you were painting and tiling. I've never done any of that sort of work myself." She held up a hand to inspect her long, pink nails.

Probably artificial, Viv thought. Out loud she said," So, what do you do, Shelley?"

"I'm the assistant manager of Tooley's Fine Gifts and Sweets. We're located downtown. Have you ever been in the store?"

Viv shook her head. "Sorry. I don't get to Oakville very often."

"Well, if you ever want to visit, I can get you a discount on the china. We've got some lovely place settings and figurines, including all of the Disney princesses. They're adorable."

"I bet. Thanks."

Tom came out of the house with the potato salad, bread, a plate, and cutlery. He placed them on the table and put on Shelley's steak to cook. Viv could hear the sizzle when the meat hit the grill.

"Mmm, don't you just love the smell of barbecue? It's my favourite smell in the entire world." Shelley beamed at Tom as he sat down between the two women. "And Tom sure knows his way around a barbecue, don't you, Daddy? He's pretty good at most things, if you catch my drift." Her smile was packed with sexual innuendo as she winked at Tom. Viv wanted to gag.

"I got to admit, I'm pretty good with a steak." He nodded at Viv. "Viv brought us dessert."

"Oh? What'd you bring?"

"Banana cake. It's an old family recipe." Just not her family's.

"Sounds delicious." The smile on Shelley's face was brittle.

Viv was wondering what excuse she could make to leave when Shelley said, "Isn't Tom wonderful, taking in a cripple with all his other strays? I'm sure that most people would have put a dog like him down. I wonder if that still wouldn't be best for the poor thing." She looked at Bruno with a shiver of distaste before turning back to Viv.

"And you, sugar, driving all the way from Toronto just to see how the dog's doing." Shelley looked at her watch. "My, it's going on seven. How long a drive is it back to Toronto?"

"Not long." Viv settled more comfortably into her chair. Who was this woman – Cruella de Vil? With Tom being such an animal lover, surely he wouldn't be pleased to hear that Shelley wanted Bruno put down. "Now, tell me about your wedding plans, you two. I want to hear all about them."

Thirty minutes later, Viv had learned that Tom wanted a Thanksgiving wedding while Shelley was holding out for Christmas ("Wouldn't I look divine with a fur-trimmed hood?"), Tom wanted to hold the ceremony at the farm while Shelley wanted to be married in New York City ("We could see the Rockettes!"), and Shelley wanted Tom to sell the farm so that they could live closer to downtown ("Do you really want me to have to commute half an hour a day, Daddy?").

That was enough for Viv. Didn't Tom see what a selfish, shallow, unfeeling monster his fiancée was? When Shelley got up to take in the leftover food, Tom turned to her.

"Nice of you to take such an interest, Viv. Shelley likes to talk about all this wedding stuff, but she doesn't have a lot of women friends."

I'll bet. "It's my pleasure, Tom, although it sounds as if you two have a lot to sort out."

Tom chuckled. "Shelley will probably get her way. I like to make her happy when I can. She hasn't had an easy life, what with her husband leaving her with two young kids when they'd only been married five years. He skipped out on the support payments, too. Shelley had to work two minimum wage jobs to keep a roof over their heads. She did all right by those kids, though."

"What a trouper. But Tom, don't you want to get married here so that your family can come?"

He looked wistful. "Sure, if I could, but they'll understand if we elope to New York. Shelley's always wanted to go there."

Viv shrugged. "It's too bad you have to choose between your family and Shelley." Tom peered at her as Shelly came out carrying Viv's cake tin.

"I washed this out so you can take it home, Viv. You don't want to have to make a special trip back just for a cake pan." She leaned against Tom and held it out with a simper.

Viv smiled just as sweetly as she rose from her chair to take the pan. "That was thoughtful of you, Shelley. Although Tom and I made a deal that I'm going to help him finish the house in exchange for riding lessons." Shelley looked suspiciously from Tom to Viv.

"Although I probably won't be out until next week," Viv continued. "We both have a lot to do, what with Tom finishing the house with Daddy – I mean Dad – and it being the last week of school. But I'll see you next Monday, bright and early."

Tom rose to his feet. "That'll be fine. And I appreciate you coming out to see Bruno and bringing the banana cake. It was good, wasn't it, Shelley?"

"I haven't had any yet."

"I'll be sure to give you the recipe, since Tom likes it so much. It was nice meeting you, Shelley. See you later, Tom." Viv stepped across the grass to the dogs, where she patted Peg and squatted to give Bruno a careful hug.

"See you soon, Bruno," she said. "You take it easy until that shoulder heals."

Tom strolled up behind her and said, "I'll walk you to the car."

Viv smiled up at him. "Thanks."

"Bye, sugar," Shelley called.

Viv followed Tom through the gate, where they were quickly surrounded by the other dogs. Tom slammed it shut behind them, took Viv's elbow, and escorted her to the car. There was a silver Corolla parked beside Daisy.

"Did I miss something here?" he asked.

"What do you mean?"

"There was something going on between you and Shelley. You don't seem to like her very much."

"Maybe not." Viv paused beside the car. "I don't think Shelley and I are going to get along very well."

He frowned. "Why not? You barely know her."

"Because she doesn't like Bruno." Viv opened the door and slid in, banging it shut behind her. She had left the windows down, and there were flies buzzing around inside. She swatted at them with her purse.

Tom leaned against the side of the car. "Shelley's not used to dogs. She doesn't have any pets, unless you count her two horses."

Viv turned the key in the ignition. "Neither did I, but all of a sudden, I've got a dog and a cat. I guess either you're the kind of person who likes animals, or you're not. Of course, if you're going to sell the farm and move to Oakville, you'll have to get rid of some of them. Especially the horses."

"Who said I'm selling the farm?"

"You're not? I thought you liked to give Shelley her own way."

"Don't put words in my mouth, Viv. Especially not about the farm. I told you, it's going to my youngest. And I'm not getting rid of my animals."

"Good for you. You stick to your guns, Tom. Don't let Shelley run roughshod over you."

"Who said that she was?"

Viv put the car in reverse and started to back up, forcing Tom to move out of the way.

"Obviously you two have some serious issues to work out before you get married. But don't worry, I'm sure you'll figure them out. With the help of a good counsellor, maybe."

"What are you talking about? We don't need counselling."

Viv shifted the car into drive and paused. "You've got my number. Let me know if you need anything. Otherwise, I'll see you next Monday. Bye."

Viv glanced in her rear-view mirror as she drove away. Tom was standing in the middle of the driveway with his hands on his hips, shaking his head. She smiled as she motored back to Toronto. That would give him something to think about.

Chapter 26

Viv and Julie decided to celebrate the end of the school year the following Friday night by having drinks at the Shoe Horn. Sabrina agreed to meet them there, but arrived half an hour late directly from work. Julie and Viv stood to hug her.

"It feels like I haven't seen you two in ages," Sabrina said. "Did you order me a drink?" The waiter arrived to hand her a martini. "Fabulous. So, congratulations on the end of the school year."

"Here's to surviving another one," Julie said. They clanked their glasses together and sat down.

"Now you've got the whole summer off, you lucky dogs," Sabrina said.

"For which we don't get paid," Julie replied. "But never mind. I've been trying to talk Viv into going to the beach with Olivia and me. Maybe she'd like to try dating a beach bum for a change."

Viv took a deep breath. "Actually, ladies, I've had second thoughts about continuing the dating do-over. I've had a life-altering experience, and it's made me think that I'm the only one who can find me a husband."

"What?" the other two women squeaked. They exchanged an uncertain look. Sabrina said, "But Vivvie . . ."

Viv held up her hands. "Listen, I'm not going to be happy with the kind of man you two would choose for me. I'm not like you. You're into your career, Sabrina, and Julie, you're much more independent than I am. Once I've found the right man and started a family, I'm going to give up teaching and stay home to look after them."

Her remark was met with silence. Sabrina sighed. "Feminist throw-back."

Julie shhh'd her. "Viv and I were just talking about this last week. She doesn't want to date any more suits."

"That's right," Viv said. "No more lawyers or businessmen. I want a maverick. Someone who doesn't have to prove his self-worth by the size of his bank account."

"Someone more like Tom," Julie said.

"Who's Tom?" Sabrina asked.

"The contractor working for Viv's dad," Julie replied. "Only, he's old enough to be her father."

"Definitely not!" Sabrina said.

"Tom's only fifty. Brad Pitt's forty-nine. Would you turn him down if he asked you? And what about Tony Randall? He married a woman fifty years younger, and they had two children and were very happy together."

"Viv," Julie shrieked. "Not Tom!

"I'm not saying that I want Tom to be more than a friend, but he's got a lot going for him. He's handsome, strong, and patient. He cares about his family and tradition. And he's also kind to animals. He took in Bruno."

"Who's Bruno?" Sabrina asked.

"The dog Viv ran over with her car," Julie said.

"I did not run over Bruno!"

"Look, I don't give a damn about the dog," Sabrina said. "It sounds like you're looking for a father figure."

Julie nodded while Viv sputtered, "That's not true!"

Sabrina grabbed Viv's hand. "I know things are bad between you and Gabe right now, hon, but you'll make up soon. Don't try to replace him with this Tom, I'm begging you."

Viv wrenched her hand from Sabrina's grasp. "I'm not. And this is exactly why I don't want you and Julie trying to find me a man anymore. You just don't understand me. I want someone different, someone who makes me feel good about myself." She glowered at Sabrina. "Someone I can trust."

Sabrina sat back in her chair and folded her arms over her chest.

Viv's expression softened. "I don't want to fight with either one of you. And Tom may not be the man for me. It's just that, we were dancing on his patio last weekend, and I had these feelings for him. I don't know where it's going, but I'm not going to rule out someone who's wonderful just because of an age difference." She grinned mischievously. "Besides, it worked for Audrey Hepburn and Humphrey Bogart."

"Who?" Sabrina asked wearily. Viv described how the characters' May-December romance had triumphed in *Sabrina*.

"I don't know, sweetie," Julie said.

"I've got to start trusting my instincts," Viv replied. "I'll know if it's right. Now, if I can just get rid of Tom's bitch of a fiancée."

"Who?" Sabrina and Julie shrieked, and the squabbling started all over again.

When Viv pulled into Tom's driveway at nine o'clock on Monday morning, she noted a silver Corolla parked outside the garage.

"Oh no, what's she doing here?" Viv grumbled. "That sure puts a damper on things." She parked beside Shelley's car and got out with the pumpkin bread she had baked for Tom the night before. The dogs surrounded her, barking a greeting, and Viv spotted Bruno among them.

"Bruno! Look at you right in there with all the other dogs. What a brave boy." She bent to take a closer look at him, and he licked her nose. "Hey, your stitches are out! Good for you. Look, I've got treats." She pulled a pouch from her purse and distributed bacon-flavoured nuggets to everyone. If the way to a man's heart was through his stomach, then it had to be the same with his dogs. And Viv wanted Tom's dogs on her side.

She was walking up to the house when Tom strolled out on the porch.

"Viv! Good to see you, darling. All ready to work?"

"You bet." She pirouetted, showing off her faded t-shirt and dingy jeans. As she climbed the stairs to the porch, he pointed at the foil-wrapped package in her hand.

"What's that?"

"Pumpkin loaf. I thought we might enjoy some during our coffee break."

Shelley appeared in the doorway behind Tom. "That's so kind of you, Viv." She was dressed in a low-necked tank top and white cotton shorts.

"Shelley, I didn't expect to see you today," Viv said.

"It's my day off." She smirked. "I thought I'd help out. You know what they say: 'Many hands make light work,' and all that. The sooner we finish, the sooner Tom can take some vacation time. We're going fishing, aren't we, Daddy?"

Viv rallied with a sunny smile. "Well, what do you have in mind for us today, Tom?"

"Shelley's helped me choose paint colours, so you two can paint the living room while I sand the dining room floor."

"Sounds fine to me," Viv said.

"I'll just put your loaf in the kitchen," Shelley said, snatching it from Viv.

Tom led Viv to the living room and poured paint into two trays.

"I just saw Bruno outside with the other dogs," she said. "His stitches are out. He looks good."

"Yep, he's coming along nicely. I taught him how to climb the stairs last week, so he and Peg are sleeping in my room now."

Viv stifled a smile. *Bet Shelley loves that* she thought. The older woman entered the room. Viv got busy taping the trim while Tom showed Shelley how to use a roller brush. Viv was pleased to see that she could paint a wall in half the time it took Shelley. Two hours later, Shelley was finishing the second coat on the final wall while Viv did the brush work next to the ceiling. Shelley ran out of paint and was getting more when she bumped Viv's ladder with her pole. The ladder rocked, and Viv's paint tray spilled some of its contents on Shelley's head. Viv slapped her hand over her mouth, trying not to laugh.

Shelley glared up at Viv, paint dripping down her hair and onto her clothes.

"I am *so* sorry," Viv said.

"You did that on purpose."

Viv held up her brush. "Scout's honour, it was an accident. Just like you almost knocking me off my ladder."

Tom walked into the room to find his fiancée with a red face and blue hair.

"What happened?" he asked. Shelley turned to glare at him. "It doesn't matter," he said hastily. "You'd better leave those clothes in the kitchen sink while you take a shower."

Shelley pulled the shirt over her head as she stalked out of the room. A minute later, she stomped down the hallway and up the stairs dressed only in her bra and panties, her blue hair tied in a knot on her head. Viv snickered, and Tom frowned.

"What? I didn't do it on purpose."

Tom shook his head, and Viv burst out laughing.

"Come on, you must admit that it was funny."

"Not a bit," Tom said, but the corner of his mouth twitched.

Viv scrambled down the ladder. "I'll make it up to her. I'll wash the paint out of her clothes and hang them out to dry on your clothesline while she showers."

"All right. While you do that, I'll make lunch."

Viv scrubbed Shelley's clothes while Tom sliced crusty rolls and assembled ham, cheese, lettuce, and tomato into sandwiches.

"So, I bet the house you and Daddy were renovating ended up looking great," Viv said.

Tom nodded. "Your dad had a real estate agent through last week. The agent said he had a client or two who might be interested, and thought that the house would be gone in no time."

"I'll bet Daddy was glad to hear that."

"Sure. He's already got his eye on another house in the neighbourhood."

Viv shut off the water and turned to stare at Tom. "Geez, maybe he should take a breather before starting another reno. He's got to start slowing down." She twisted the water out of the clothes more emphatically than required.

"Maybe you should tell him that."

"I'm not ready to talk to him yet." She unrolled the clothes again and shook them out. "You got any clothes pins?"

"In a bag at the top of the basement stairs."

Viv found the bag of pins and left the house to hang up the clothes. When she returned to the kitchen, Tom wasn't there. She found him on the patio with the food and another pitcher of lemonade. He poured her a glass while she slipped into the chair next to his.

"Thanks. So, how are things between you and Shelley? Did you sort out your wedding plans yet?" Tom glanced at her before taking a bite of his sandwich, and Viv selected one for herself.

"We're getting married on the farm at Christmas," he said.

"Oh, a compromise. That was big of Shelley."

Tom put his hand on Viv's. "You should stop sniping at Shelley. Once you get to know her better, you'll see that she's a fine woman."

"I haven't liked what I've seen so far."

"You seem to bring out the worst in her."

"Maybe I bring out her true nature." Viv shrugged. "It's probably because she sees me as a threat."

"Why would she see you as a threat?"

Viv glanced down at the table, away from his searching eyes. "Because she knows I'm attracted to you." There, she'd said it, and now she couldn't take it back.

Shelley walked out onto the patio, her wet hair dangling on her shoulders. She was wearing one of Tom's shirts over a pair of tight-fitting jeans.

"There you are. Having lunch?"

Tom stood up to greet her. "Come and join us." Shelley sat next to him and picked up a sandwich.

"Pour me some lemonade, Daddy. I'm parched." Tom poured out a glass, and as he passed it to her, Shelley glanced up at his face.

"Something wrong? You look kind of tense."

"We've just been discussing some family trouble," Viv said.

"Your dad hasn't had another heart attack, has he?"

"No, nothing like that. Just an argument between my dad and

me. Tom's been playing peacemaker."

Shelley patted his cheek. "That's my fella. You can always count on him."

Tom grimaced, and Viv kicked him under the table. He stood up hastily.

"I'm going to make some coffee. Be right back, ladies."

"Really? It's so warm today," Shelley called after him.

"Some people just need their caffeine," Viv said. She hopped to her feet. "I'm going to get the pumpkin loaf."

In the kitchen, Tom was scooping coffee into a filter. Viv touched his back, and he started, spilling coffee onto the stove. He whirled to look at her, his eyes growing troubled.

"What do you want from me, Viv?"

She responded by laying her hand on his forearm. Tom gazed down at it, but didn't pull away. Viv ran her hand up his arm and rested it on his shoulder. Their eyes met, and she slipped her hand behind his neck, slowly, gently, drawing his head down. Tom's eyes closed as Viv kissed his cheek, letting her lips linger on his skin. He sighed, and Viv's mouth became greedy as she kissed his lips.

The whistle on the kettle hissed, and Tom broke away. They stared at each other as the kettle's hiss became a scream.

"I'd better get the pumpkin bread," Viv muttered. She walked to the saw horses while Tom took the kettle off the burner. Unwrapping the loaf and picking up a knife, Viv sawed several slices onto a plate with shaking hands. Tom pressed up against her back.

"I've got a fiancée," his voice rasped.

"You should have mentioned her before," Viv said, turning.

Tom's eyes bore into hers, and he pulled her into his arms. Viv clung to him. They held each other for several moments, and then Tom kissed her hair and let his hands drop to his sides. Viv's eyes glittered with tears.

"I should take the pumpkin bread out," she whispered. "Shelley's waiting." Tom nodded and stepped back to make room. Viv picked up the plate and rushed across the kitchen to the patio door.

Back out in the warm air, Viv paused to lean against the wall and take some calming breaths. Fixing a smile on her face, she strode across the patio to Shelley.

"Here we are." She thumped the plate down on the table harder than she had intended. "Hope you like it."

"It looks delicious," Shelley said. She broke off a chunk and popped it into her mouth. "Mmm."

"Glad you like it." Viv collapsed in the chair next to Shelley and began fiddling with her ring.

Tom walked outside carrying steaming mugs. "Coffee's ready." He placed them on the table and sat down on Shelley's other side.

"So, what are we going to do this afternoon?" Shelley asked.

Tom was looking at the yard and didn't answer. She glanced up at him.

"Tom?"

"Sorry. I thought I'd sand the hallway floor. You ladies don't want dust getting into your paint, so why don't you take the afternoon off?"

Viv glanced at Tom and away again. Was this his way of getting rid of her? No, enough of her insecurities. They had shared something very powerful, and now he just needed time to think.

"Well, I must say I'm relieved," Shelley said. "Painting was harder work than I expected, and I just got clean." She turned to Viv. "But it's a shame you came all the way out here for only a couple of hours' work. Why don't I give you a riding lesson?"

Viv was surprised by Shelley's generosity. She hesitated, not wanting to insult Shelley by turning her down, but not trusting anyone but Tom to give her a lesson.

"So?" Shelley said.

"It's so warm. I wouldn't want to tire you out."

"Don't worry, I love the heat. Can't get enough of it."

"I don't know . . ." Viv looked imploringly at Tom.

"Viv's only had one lesson in the riding ring," he said.

"No problem. We'll take it nice and slow. She'll be in good hands, won't she, Daddy?"

Tom looked away. "You can ride Jenny, Viv. You'll be safe on her."

"Sure," Viv said doubtfully. She felt as if Tom had let her down. "That's really kind of you, Shelley."

"Not at all. It's the least I can do for all the work you're putting into the house. Why not let Tom get back to it while we head down to the barn?"

"Just as soon as I clean up," Viv said, rising. Stalling might give her time to think of an excuse to skip the lesson.

"Don't worry about that. I'll clean up later," Shelley said. She rose to her feet. "Shall we?"

With one last glance at Tom, Viv followed Shelley to the patio gate. As soon as Shelley had opened it, the barn dogs surrounded them, glad to be included again. Shelley pushed past them and strode across the drive with Viv and the dogs trailing behind her. When they had all reached the barn, Shelley let Viv squeeze through the door and slammed it closed behind them, shutting out the dogs.

"I'm sick of that mob always underfoot," she muttered.

There was something about being separated from the dogs that made Viv feel uneasy. She flinched when Shelley took her arm.

"I didn't really bring you here for a riding lesson, Viv. It's time you and I had a talk." She towed Viv to the couch, where Tinks and Mitzie were curled up having a nap. They raised their heads inquiringly, and Shelley swatted at them. Mitzie hissed before both cats jumped down.

"Sit," Shelley ordered. Viv obeyed, and Shelley sat next to her, uncomfortably close. "So, what are you trying to pull with Tom?" she demanded.

Viv shrank back. "What do you mean?"

Shelley snorted. "Don't play all innocent with me. He's been talking about you for a month, and the two of you were acting pretty guilty on the patio just now. I'm not blind, you know."

Viv shook her head. "You're imagining things."

"What do you take me for, one of your silly Toronto friends?" She shoved her face next to Viv's. "I'm a lot tougher than you, sugar. I've worked hard to make Tom love me, and I'm not giving him up. So you just take your tight little ass back to Toronto, and don't ever come back, do you hear?"

She grabbed the front of Viv's t-shirt and hauled her to her feet. Viv was frightened and shoved Shelley hard, forcing her to stumble back. Shelley's face turned red and her eyes bulged. She started forward with her hand raised, and Viv's arm sprang up in defence.

Someone whimpered behind them. Viv glanced over her shoulder to see who it was. Riley, the black cocker spaniel, was trying to squeeze behind the feed bins. Viv looked at Shelley, and saw her scowl.

"Shit, another one of those fricking dogs! I've had it with them," Shelley shouted. She grabbed the broom resting against the wall and stomped toward the cowering animal. Riley was frozen with fear and couldn't move.

"Don't you touch him," Viv screamed. She raced after Shelley and grabbed the back end of the broom as the other woman swung it into the air.

"Let go!" Shelley shrieked.

"No!" Viv seized the handle, pulling Shelley closer, and kicked her as hard as she could in the ankle. Shelley howled, jumping on one foot, before wrenching the broom from Viv's grasp and tossing it over her shoulder. She shoved Viv backward, knocking her to the ground, and jumped on top of her. She was about to punch Viv in the face when Tom appeared out of nowhere and dragged Shelley away. Viv rose on her elbows, panting, as Tom struggled to hold Shelley back. Finally he picked her up, slung her over his shoulder, and stalked out of the barn with Shelley still screaming obscenities.

Viv looked at Riley, who was shivering beside the bins. She rolled over and held out a hand to him.

"Riley, it's okay boy," she said, but he wouldn't look at her. Crawling to him on her hands and knees, she reached out to touch his head. He glanced up at her then, the whites showing around his eyes, and shrank back.

"Everything's all right." Slowly, Viv picked him up and cuddled him, the terrified animal shuddering in her arms. She stroked his head and murmured to him while hearing a car door slam and an engine start up.

"Don't worry, nobody's going to hurt you," Viv soothed. Riley whimpered and panted.

Tom returned and sank down wearily on the packed earth beside them. "You all right?" he asked Viv.

"I'm fine. Where's Shelley?"

"I told her to leave – permanently. I can't stand meanness in a person, either to another person, or to an animal."

"I'm so glad," Viv said. She glanced down at the quivering dog in her lap.

"Here, give him to me," Tom said, holding out his hands. He took the dog from Viv and cradled Riley against his chest.

"It's all right. It's all right, boy," he said over and over while stroking the dog's back. Under Tom's familiar touch, Riley's breathing slowed and his tense body relaxed. Viv smiled as the dog tentatively wagged his tail.

"Good boy," Tom said. "Want a treat?" The cocker spaniel's head shot up, and he stared at Tom. "Where do we keep the treats, Riley?" The dog jumped out of his arms and trotted to the cupboard where the pet food was stored. He sat down and gazed at Tom. Viv hung back while Riley got his treat, and heard whining and scratching at the barn door. She looked inquiringly at Tom.

"I kept them out. Didn't want it turning into a riot, the way Shelley was carrying on in here." He opened the door and the dogs bounded in, sniffing at Viv before leaving to check out the rest of the barn. Riley, fully recovered, joined in.

"Come here," Tom said, holding out his arms. Viv hurried to snuggle into them. Tom pressed her close. "Now that Shelly's gone, do you want to explain what's going on between us? Because I feel like I've been hit by a truck."

Viv smiled and cupped the side of his face with her hand. "It's easy, Tom. I'm just following my instincts." She stood on tiptoe as Tom bent toward her. Just before their lips met, Tom said, "Gabe is going to hunt me down and kill me."

Chapter 27

Moonlight peeked in the bedroom window as the breeze ruffled the curtains. Tom was breathing deeply as Viv crawled out from under his arm and crept off the bed. She was slipping into her jeans when Tom rolled over and mumbled, "What are you doing?"

"Shhh." Viv tiptoed back to kiss the top of his head. His arm shot out, wrapped around her waist, and hauled her back onto the mattress. Viv giggled and squirmed beneath him, but he silenced her protests with his mouth.

When she had been thoroughly kissed, Viv whispered, "I have to go home."

"Why? It's the middle of the night."

"No, it's not. It's before midnight. I have to feed Constantine. He hasn't had his dinner yet."

Tom groaned and rolled off, tangling the sheet around him. "I'll go with you."

"No you won't." Viv pushed him down and straddled his chest. "You have to be here first thing in the morning to feed the animals." She bent to kiss him, and his hands slid through her hair and grasped the back of her head. Several seconds later, Viv placed her hands on his shoulders and arched away.

"I'm never going to get out of here if you keep doing that." She removed her right leg and climbed from the mattress.

"Bring Constantine here."

"With these guys?" She pointed at Bruno and Peg, who were lying on their dog beds in a corner of the room. Their heads were up and pointed at Viv.

Tom leaned on one elbow. Viv liked the look of all that bare skin

227

and muscle rising up from under the sheet, and fought the urge to climb back on top of him.

"Sure. I'm good with animals, remember? We'll make certain the rest of the dogs stay in the barn. He'll only have to get used to Bruno and Peg." Two tails beat at the mention of their names.

Viv paused to consider. "Well, we could try, I suppose. I remember seeing a cat carrier in Fred's attic somewhere."

"Good." Tom lay back against the pillows, his arms behind his head and his hair streaming over his shoulders. "Because I expect you to spend the summer here with me." He gave her a slow, roguish grin, and Viv shook her head.

"Oh, no, I am not crawling back into that bed with you." He held out his hand. "Uh-uh. I'm driving back to Toronto to feed Constantine, where I will spend the rest of the night in my own bed. I'll be back tomorrow with the cat and our stuff." She paused, her smile fading. "If you're sure about this, Tom. We're not going too fast, are we?"

He patted the bed, and she sat down beside him. He pulled her backward to cradle against his chest.

"We're going faster than a shooting star, but that's all right. You're not afraid to take a chance on me, are you, Viv? Because I've never been surer of a woman in my life."

Viv's fear evaporated as she felt his body behind her. "Not at all. I thought we were destined to be together the first time I saw you." She turned toward him and he kissed her, his fingers tracing the side of her face.

"I seem to remember you were pretty ticked with me that day," Tom said. "Your father had heat stroke, and you didn't want me driving him home."

Viv tweaked his nose. "Okay, maybe the second time I saw you, smarty." She leapt off the mattress before he could grab her again and scurried to where she had abandoned her shoes. Stepping into them, she said, "Constantine and I will see you in the morning. Try to get some sleep so that you're extra well-rested. I'll be expecting a replay of tonight."

"Yes, ma'am. Except that I can think of one or two new things

I'd like to try."

She ran over to peck a quick kiss on his mouth. "Hold that thought."

Slipping into the routine of the farm was easier than Viv had expected. She spent each day working beside Tom, and every night wrapped in his arms. Not that she avoided her duties in Toronto; she visited Fred's house twice a week to ensure that all was well, but hurried back to the place that was beginning to feel like home.

Life in the farmhouse was a bigger adjustment for Constantine. He spent the first week hiding under the bed, hissing at Bruno and Peg whenever the curious dogs eyed him at ground level. Viv was finally able to coax him out, and then the animals only had to be separated when it was Constantine's playtime. The dogs never did get used to the Siamese's antics as he chased the laser pointer's red dot. Sometimes Constantine preferred Tom's lap, purring as those strong hands stroked him, and Viv pretended to be hurt.

During Viv's first week, they harvested the hay. She drove the tractor that towed the baler while Tom arranged the hay on the wagon. The harder part came next, when the bales had to be taken off the conveyer belt and stacked in the stifling hay loft. Tom and his neighbour did that, while the neighbour's brawny son helped Viv load the belt from below. As a joke, Tom presented Viv with a t-shirt that said "Small but mighty," and Viv wore it proudly to do her chores. She also learned how to stain furniture, sand floors, use a power saw and a tile cutter, and install kitchen cupboards.

Viv even became comfortable on Jenny's back, riding alongside Tom and Champ on the trail that cut through the acreage. Bruno and the other dogs always accompanied them, Bruno's stamina keeping pace with Viv's endurance in the saddle. Viv loved all the dogs, even the malodorous Hoover, but Bruno held a special place in her heart because he had helped to bring her and Tom together.

One memorable day toward the end of July, Tom and Viv attended a performance at the Stratford Shakespearean Festival with his mother. Viv had been looking forward to the meeting until Tom told her not to worry, that he had given her a special build-up with his mom.

"What do you mean?" Viv had asked.

"Well, darling, Mom does think of you as a home-wrecker."

Viv's eyes had opened wide with surprise. "You've got to be kidding! How am I a home-wrecker?"

"Mom liked Shelley. She thought Shelley overcame a lot of adversity to raise her kids. Then you came along and broke up our engagement." Tom shrugged.

Viv was speechless. "But does she know what a terrible person Shelley was?"

Tom took her in his arms. "I explained all that, and Mom's willing to give you the benefit of the doubt. But she's old-fashioned, and she still sees you as the woman who came between her son and his fiancée."

"What am I going to do?"

"Nothing. Just be yourself, and everything will work out fine. Be glad that Shelley and I weren't married. I don't think Mom would ever have warmed up to you if you had been the cause of our divorce."

The visit with Tom's mother turned out well, but it got Viv thinking. What if Tom had been married to Shelley? Would she have been willing to come between them if Tom had been truly miserable? Were Daddy and Magda so different from her and Tom?

After a sleepless night, Viv said to Tom, "I'm ready to see Daddy, but I'm scared. Will you come with me?"

Tom smiled. "Be glad to. I'm proud that you're taking the first step toward a reconciliation."

"Well, don't be until we see how things go. I'm still not happy about Daddy bringing his mistress into our house."

Viv called straight away to arrange a visit for that evening. When she told Tom about it, he asked, "Are you going to tell Gabe about us tonight, too?" Viv smiled; Tom looked so apprehensive.

"Of course, unless you think it's going to give him a heart attack on top of everything else." They were sitting on the patio after breakfast, enjoying a second cup of coffee. The dogs were lying in the shade under the trees except for Bruno and Peg, who were under the table at Tom and Viv's feet.

"Before you see your dad, there's something we need to talk about," he said. "I've been keeping this under my hat, wondering how to broach it to you."

Viv's stomach tensed, but in a light-hearted voice, she asked, "You're not a murderer or anything, are you?"

Tom took her hand. "No, darling. Hell, there's no way to do this except to come right out and say it. I've had a vasectomy."

Viv was stunned. As much as she wanted to be with Tom, she wanted to have his children. She stared at him with a blank face as he squeezed her hand.

"I did it after my wife and I were done having kids. I never thought of having a second family, and my wife didn't want to stay on the pill until menopause. I've already called my doctor about reversing it. He says that the procedure works some of the time, but not always. There's no guarantee, Viv. I want to prepare you for the worst because I know how much you want a family." His eyes searched her face as his grip tightened on her hand. "I hope it's not a deal-breaker."

Viv's heart melted at his anxious expression. "Of course not. I love you. I would never give you up. You'll have the procedure and everything will be fine. If not, we'll cross that bridge when we come to it."

Tom let out a long breath. "Whew, I'm sure glad to hear you say that. I've been wondering how to tell you since the first night we were together. I've been a real coward, holding out on you like this."

Viv stroked his face. "It's all right, Tom. You're stuck with me."

Viv didn't refer to the vasectomy for the rest of the day, but it never left her mind until they were in the car headed to Toronto. Then all she could think about was what she would say to Daddy and Magda.

It was Tom who finally rapped on the door while Viv paced nervously on the porch. The door opened, and Viv saw her father with an unreadable expression on his face.

"Viv." He looked past her to Tom. "I didn't expect to see you here."

"I asked Tom to come, Daddy." Viv walked into the house and hugged him. Gabe hugged her back, but he felt stiff in her arms.

"Where's Magda?" she asked.

Gabe stepped aside, and Magda appeared behind him. Fear and sadness mingled in her face, and Viv realized how much she had hurt Magda. She ran straight into Magda's arms.

"I'm so sorry. I should never have said those terrible things to you," Viv said in a shaky voice. "You were always there for me when I was growing up. I'm sorry I let you down."

"That's okay, beautiful girl," Magda said. She stroked Viv's hair. "Your father and I should have told you before you heard it from your mother's lips." She released Viv to beam at Gabe. "See, I told you everything would be all right."

Viv turned and saw her father coming toward her with an expression of sheer relief on his face. He hugged her close and murmured, "Thank you, Peaches." When he released her, he had to turn away to wipe his eyes.

"Look, it's the cowboy. Come in," Magda said. She took Tom's arm and towed him into the kitchen. "Let me get you a drink. Are you hungry? I've got stuffed peppers I can heat up in a jiffy."

"No thanks, Magda. We barbecued some hamburgers before we came. Great to see you, by the way. Been keeping Gabe out of trouble?"

"No, he never listens to me. Good that Viviane's back to keep him in line."

They settled in the family room, where Magda brought cold stuffed peppers and a bottle of vodka. Gabe poured the drinks, and he and Magda toasted them, saying, "Na Zdrowie!"

Viv turned to Tom and said, "That means, 'To your health.'"

Tom repeated the toast, and they all drank. Setting down his glass, Tom said, "So, what have you been doing, old man?" They spent a pleasant hour chatting about Gabe's next renovation project and the work Viv and Tom had been doing on the farmhouse. When it was time to leave, Viv kissed Magda, and Gabe walked Tom and

Viv to the door.

"I'm so glad you came tonight," her father said.

"So am I, Daddy."

Gabe turned to Tom. "Say, would you mind if Viv and I had a moment alone?"

"Sure. I'll wait in the truck." Tom shook Gabe's hand and climbed down the porch stairs as Viv and her father sat.

"Is there something going on between you and Tom?" Gabe asked. "I mean, I'm happy he brought you tonight, but our conversation was kind of personal for him to be hearing, don't you think?"

Viv took her father's hand. "Tom's not an outsider, Daddy. We've become very close. As a matter of fact, Tom and I are going to be married someday. I guess it must come as a shock to you, but it all happened so fast."

Gabe stared at her glowing face in the light of the porch lamp. Viv could see that he was dumbstruck and kept silent, realizing that he needed time to get used to the idea.

"I don't know what to say, Viv."

She patted his arm. "I know there's a big age difference, but it's okay. Tom's in the prime of his life, and I couldn't find another man more right for me." She grinned. "He's a big improvement over Kyle, don't you think?"

But Gabe shook his head. "Have you given this much thought, Peaches? Where are you going to live, for example?"

"At his farm. We're making the house beautiful. I can't wait for you to see it."

"But what about your teaching?"

"I'm going to give it up once we start a family. I'll commute to Toronto until then. No career could be more important to me than my husband and children."

Gabe looked down at his hands clasped on his knees. Viv knew that he was worried about her, but there was another matter she needed to discuss before she left that night. She wouldn't know true peace until she had the answer.

"Daddy, before I leave, I want to ask something about you and

Magda, if you don't mind."

He looked up, startled. "What is it?"

"Why haven't you two ever married? You could have divorced Mother."

"Right. I didn't get a chance to tell you before. Magda's married."

Viv stared back at him. "What?"

"To a neighbour in Poland. When his wife died, Magda's parents thought that she should marry him so that there would be someone to look after his children. Magda's parents and the neighbour were old friends, see? But he was abusive. After putting up with him for seven years until the youngest kid grew up, Magda ran away. A cousin helped her get a passport and scrape together the money for her airfare.

"When I first met her in Toronto, she was working as a cook at a little hole-in-the-wall restaurant, saving up the money to pay the cousin back. When we knew how we felt about each other, we wrote to Magda's husband about a divorce, but the letters came back unopened. We hired a lawyer, but the husband wouldn't cooperate, and the red tape to get the divorce was unbelievable. So we decided to wait until the old bastard died. He's eighty-four now. The cousin says his health is lousy, and that he could go any minute."

Viv shook her head. "Poor Magda."

"Look, just for the record, I swear that Magda and I were never intimate while we were all living together. Not that I'm a saint, but it was against Magda's beliefs. It might have been a mistake, bringing her into the house, but she was a good woman, and I knew that she would love you and treat you well."

"She always did." Viv grinned. "I'll bet the two of you were relieved when I moved into residence." Gabe laughed and took her hand. "So, have you talked to Mother about a divorce?"

Gabe nodded. "It's just about done. That was one of the reasons for her visit this spring. As soon as Magda's husband dies, we'll be down to the church before you know it."

Viv leaned forward to hug him. "I hope that's soon, for both your sakes. Magda deserves the security of a marriage certificate after all these years."

"I'm sorry that you had to find out about this from your mother," Gabe said. "I had hoped that Magda and I would get married without you ever finding out."

"I don't have any hard feelings, Daddy." She kissed his cheek and stood up. "But I've got to go. Tom's waiting." She waved at the truck in case he was watching, and Gabe stood up.

"Look, Peaches, you be careful with Tom. I'm still not sure that I like the idea. I don't want you getting hurt again."

Viv kissed his cheek. "I know this must come as a shock, but please don't worry." She smiled. "See you soon."

Viv skipped down the steps and turned to wave before jogging across the lawn to join Tom.

"See you," she heard her father call after her. "But please, Viv, be *careful*."

Chapter 28

A week later, Viv and Tom were installing the kitchen counter backsplash when Viv's cell rang. She spoke for a couple of minutes, switched it off, and looked up at Tom with a smile.

"It's Daddy," she said. "He wants to see the house. He should be by in an hour." She clasped her arms around Tom's back. "I'm so glad. Maybe he's coming to give us his blessing. Not that we had an argument the other night, but he seemed so worried."

Tom kissed her. "I'm happy for you, darling. I'd hate to come between you and Gabe."

Viv eyed the kitchen. The cabinets and the counter were installed, plus the island. They still needed to buy a dishwasher, but the work was mostly done.

"Just help me tidy up a bit before I run upstairs to take a shower. I'm glad I made peanut butter cookies last night. They're one of Daddy's favourites."

"Mine, too," Tom said. He looked as if he were the happiest man in the world. She couldn't believe how blessed she was to be with him.

Gabe arrived an hour later, right on time. Viv and Tom were sitting on the porch swing waiting for him with the dogs at their feet. As Gabe drove around to the garage, they gathered on the drive to greet him.

"Hi, Daddy." Viv kissed him, and he and Tom shook hands.

"Wow, what a menagerie you have here," Gabe said. "Viv never even had a pet growing up. This must be Bruno." He pointed to the terrier standing guard at Viv's side. He was protective of her around strangers.

"That's him," Viv said proudly, patting the dog's head.

Gabe gestured at the farm. "Sure is a beautiful spot you've got here, Tom."

"Come on, we'll show you around." Tom clapped a hand on Gabe's back and led him into the house.

With the dogs secure on the porch, Viv and Tom showed Gabe the work they had accomplished on the first floor. He admired the wide, refinished floor boards, the fresh paint, the open-style kitchen and dining room, and the restored woodwork.

"You don't see features like this in new houses," he said, sliding out the leaded glass pocket doors leading into the dining room. "Everything looks terrific. You must be very proud."

"I am," Tom said. "The place got kind of run down while my dad was sick, but I didn't want to do the renovating until after Mom left."

"Can I get you a coffee, Daddy? I made peanut butter cookies," Viv said.

"That sounds great, but why not let Tom show me the barn while you make the coffee? I'd like to see his horses."

"Sure," Viv said. "There're only two of them, now that the boarder's left." She arched her eyebrows at Tom; her dad didn't know anything about Shelley, and Viv didn't want Tom mentioning her. Her father had enough to digest for now.

"What kind of horses do you have?" Gabe asked. He and Tom left the house while Viv started the coffee and arranged cookies on a plate. She was going to put placemats on the island, but decided that that would be too fussy. Twenty minutes later, the coffee was ready and Tom and her dad still hadn't returned. Viv sat on a kitchen stool, picking at a cookie. What was taking them so long?

When she heard a car start up and drive past the house, Viv flew down the hallway to the front door. She was just in time to see her father's car turn onto the road with Tom watching from the porch. She threw open the screen door.

"What happened? Why is Daddy leaving?"

Tom's mouth was pressed into a straight line when he turned to look at her. "Your father had a talk with me in the barn. Turns out, he's still concerned about you marrying me." He put an arm around her shoulders. "Is that coffee ready? I sure could use some."

"It is. Come on." As they headed down the hallway, Viv said, "I'm sorry if he gave you a hard time. Is he worried about something else, or is it still just the age difference?"

Tom sat down on a stool while Viv poured them each a coffee. "He's concerned about my ability to provide for you after I'm gone."

"That's silly. I can always go back to teaching." She smiled. "Don't let it worry you. He's just being overly protective. I'm still his little girl."

"Well, hell, I hate to admit it, but he got to me. I'm a carpenter, Viv, not a banker. I don't have an RRSP or a pension, although I earn a decent living. As Gabe pointed out, the farm isn't big enough to generate a living. We would need at least two hundred and fifty acres for that. The money you'd realize from the sale wouldn't last long enough, either."

"I told you it isn't a problem, Tom. I can take care of myself."

But he shook his head, muttering under his breath. "When I told him about the vasectomy . . ."

Viv stared at him with her hands on her hips. "Did you have to tell him that? I can't believe you let that slip. He's worried enough as it is."

"What, was it supposed to be a secret? What happens if the procedure doesn't work and I can't give you children? Did you want to keep that from Gabe until after we were married? He'd think I was trying to pull a fast one on you."

"It's none of his business. That's between you and me." She shook her head and tossed the cookies back into their plastic container.

"That's not how your dad sees it. He's good and mad now. He wouldn't even come into the house to say goodbye to you." Tom got up from the stool. "I don't like it, Viv. I don't want the two of you falling out again. I saw how upset you were last time."

Viv whirled to glare at him. "Well, it sounds like you did

everything you could to put a wedge between us! How am I supposed to fix this?"

Tom stared back at her, his face doing a slow burn. "Look, there are problems between us that just aren't going to go away. I'm nineteen years older than you. Odds are, I'm going to die long before you. Hopefully, when that happens, you won't have a bunch of kids to raise on your own. If you do, you won't be able to stay at home to look after them, the way you've always wanted. That is if I can give you kids. If you don't have your dad on your side, who's going to look out for you? I can't let that happen."

"Look out for me! Let that happen! Who the hell do you think you are, Tom? I will not be treated like a child, not even by you. Especially not by you!" She stormed past the island to leave the kitchen, but Tom blocked her way.

"So now what?"

"I don't know. Maybe you've broken things so badly that they can't be fixed."

He stared at her, his eyes angry. "I can't believe you'd give up on us so easily."

"Give up?" Now she was furious. Everything had been fabulous between them until he had screwed up so royally. "I'm not the one who had the vasectomy and told Daddy about it. Oh, just get out of my way!"

She couldn't stand being in the same room with him. She pushed past him and ran down the hallway, racing up the stairs with Bruno clattering after her. She slammed the bedroom door behind them and collapsed on the bed, so upset that she felt sick. The dog whined and laid his head in her lap, and Viv reached down to pat him. She sat like that for a long time, replaying the argument in her head and trying to think of a way around their problems.

But what Tom had said was true. There were some things in their relationship that they couldn't change. If they couldn't live with them, where were they headed? She groaned; her head was throbbing. She found her purse, took a couple of headache tablets, and lay down to rest.

When Viv awoke, the room was dim. She glanced at the clock; it was after seven. Where was Tom? Why had he left her alone all this time?

She opened the bedroom door and Bruno ran out. Constantine was waiting in the hallway and twined around her legs, meowing. Peg appeared at the top of the stairs. Obviously they hadn't had their dinners yet. She went downstairs and fed the three animals. Tom wasn't in the house. She walked out to the barn, and the other dogs bounded toward her. Looked like Tom hadn't fed them, either, or the cats. She checked the tack room after feeding the animals and saw that Tom's saddle was missing. He'd probably gone out for a ride.

She sat down on the porch swing, pushing herself back and forth with the toe of her shoe while waiting for Tom to come home. He'd have to come back soon, or it would be dark. But the shadows lengthened across the yard and still he didn't come. At eight thirty, she got up and went into the house, banging the door behind her. Stupid man. Why didn't he come home and talk to her? He was the one giving up, not her.

Viv had a sandwich and a glass of milk for dinner, and then killed the rest of the evening on her computer. At eleven o' clock, there was still no sign of Tom, and she was really worried. What if he had hurt himself? She was about to go find a flashlight when a text came in from her neighbour. Tom had dropped by for a beer, and asked the neighbour to tell her that he was going camping for a few days. Viv gritted her teeth. Of course, Tom didn't text, but why hadn't he called her? Taking off like this was just infantile. Well, she wasn't going to sit here waiting for him.

She texted the neighbour to tell Tom that he'd better come home tomorrow because she was going back to the house in Toronto. She'd planned to move back the last week in August in preparation for the start of school. It didn't make sense for her to commute during the term, so she was going to stay in Toronto during the week and come home to the farm on weekends. Only now she was returning a few days early. She waited for a response, and the neighbour texted back just two letters: "OK."

OK? That just made her blood boil. What a jerk Tom was being!

Why had she thought that his taciturnity indicated strength? He was lousy at communicating, that's what it meant. She got out her suitcases and started packing because she was too keyed up to go to bed. Too bad she couldn't drive back to Toronto tonight, but someone had to feed the animals breakfast, and she couldn't rely on Tom. At two o' clock in the morning, she finished putting her things together and went to bed.

Chapter 29

"Julie, can I talk to you? I've got a problem." It was the third week of school, and Julie was on yard patrol at morning recess. Viv wanted to talk to her friend privately, so this was a good opportunity.

"Of course." Julie waved at one of the kids who had been in her class last year, and turned back to Viv. Julie had grown her pixie cut out over the summer, and her hair was combed back in soft waves. "What's up?"

"My period's six weeks late. You know I'm regular like clockwork. I'm scared."

Julie's eyes grew large. "Do you think you're pregnant?" she whispered.

"No, how could I be? I told you, Tom had a vasectomy. I think something's wrong with me."

"Like what?"

"I don't know – cancer?"

"Don't talk crazy. A lot of things can throw your cycle off. Have you made an appointment to see your doctor?"

"Yes, for after work today. Can you come with me?"

Julie pulled her cell from her pocket. "Let me call my nanny to see if she can stay late."

Julie's nanny said "no problem," so the two friends went to Viv's appointment together. When Viv returned to the waiting room, looking shocked after seeing the doctor, Julie stood up.

"Oh, no," she whispered, dragging Viv into the chair beside her. "What is it?"

"The doctor did an internal. I have to get a blood test to confirm it, but he says I'm pregnant."

"Viv!" Julie shrieked. She threw her arms around her friend and rocked her from side to side. The woman sitting on the other side of the waiting room smiled. "I'm so happy for you, sweetie." When Viv didn't respond, however, Julie pulled back to study Viv's face.

"You're happy, too, aren't you?"

"This can't be happening. Tom said he'd had a vasectomy. Why would he lie about a thing like that?"

"Oh, Viv, don't think the worst. Come on, let's get the blood test taken care of."

Julie escorted her down the hall to the medical lab, where Viv's blood was drawn. When the women were outside again, Julie asked, "It couldn't have been anyone else, could it?"

Viv shook her head. "No. I've only been with Tom since Kyle and I broke up. I went off the pill to give my body a rest, and Tom used a condom when we were together. Until he told me about the vasectomy, that is. Why would he lie about a thing like that? He was afraid I wouldn't marry him if he couldn't give me children."

They paused at the streetcar stop, and Julie took Viv gently by the shoulders. "You don't think he was using it as an excuse not to marry you, do you?"

Viv shook her head, her face stricken. "No. Tom might have had his faults, but he was honest. He'd never have lied to me about a thing like this." But then she clapped her hand over her mouth because she remembered saying the same thing to Sabrina about Kyle. Was she just hopelessly naïve about men?

"I think I'm going to be sick," she moaned. She ran up the lawn away from the streetcar stop and vomited. Julie followed and handed her a tissue.

"Poor Viv. I was just like that during my first trimester," she said.

An hour later, the doorbell rang. Viv was sitting on the couch at home, still trying to absorb what had happened to her. She shuffled to the door to answer it.

"Vivvie," Sabrina said, enfolding her in her arms. "Julie texted me." Viv closed her eyes and clung to Sabrina, the solidity of her friend's body feeling real when nothing else did. After a moment, Sabrina stepped back and towed Viv to the parlour.

She took Viv's hand, and they sat down. "Look, this is all going to be okay. As soon as we get a positive result from the blood test, I'll call your dad. Don't worry, I know just what to say. A girl needs her family around her when something like this happens. I've already called a friend who's on her second maternity leave and got the name of her obstetrician. She says that the doctor's wonderful." Sabrina handed Viv a slip of paper with a name and phone number scribbled on it. "I also know a terrific lawyer, in case you want to sue Tom for child support." She paused, worried by Viv's grey face.

"Have you had any dinner yet?" Viv shook her head. "Come on, let's take care of that right away. You're eating for two now. I'm sure the obstetrician will recommend maternity vitamins, but you'd better start taking a multi-vitamin."

Sabrina stood up, but rather than following her, Viv toppled over onto the couch and started sobbing. "Sabrina, how could he have lied to me about the vasectomy? He loved me. He wanted to have a family with me."

Sabrina patted her friend's back in tight, angry circles. "Like I said before, Viv, you're just a magnet for the worst kind of men. Promise me you'll let me be there when you tell Tom you're pregnant. Julie said she's bringing a bat, and I'm bringing brass knuckles. If there's anything left after your father gets through with him, that is."

Viv cried even louder.

But when it came time for Viv to tell Tom about her pregnancy, her father was the only one with her. Viv was feeling stronger by then and would have preferred going alone, but she couldn't deter Gabe. At least she could prevent bloodshed if things went badly between the two men. She glanced at her father's profile as he drove the sedan. There was something so anachronistic about this situation, her father coming along to force her child's father to do the right thing. Gabe glanced at her and picked up her hand to kiss it.

"Don't worry, Peaches. I don't know about this vasectomy story, but Tom's a decent man. I'm sure he'll want to marry you once he finds out you're pregnant."

Viv sighed. Maybe Tom wasn't the man she thought he was. She had watched the *Sabrina* DVD again, this time cold sober, and noticed how manipulative the older brother had been. Even if she couldn't help having feelings for Tom, maybe she and her baby were better off without him.

When her dad turned up the driveway and she saw the old farmhouse with the sun slanting across the lush lawn, Viv had to swallow back a wave of sadness. It was so homey and welcoming. She had been so happy here.

The dogs swarmed out of the barn to greet them as the car bumped up the laneway to the garage. Bruno spotted her inside and started barking. Viv popped open the door as soon as the car stopped, and hurried out to hug the wiggling dog.

"Bruno, I'm so happy to see you." The dog licked her arms and face, whining with excitement.

"He's really missed you, Viv," she heard a low voice say behind her. She took a deep breath and looked over her shoulder. Tom stood next to the car, tanned and strong, but his face seemed thinner than she remembered. There was a trace of a smile around his mouth, but uncertainty in his eyes.

Viv straightened and turned to him. "Tom," she murmured, apprehension growing within her.

Tom's smile deepened. "It's been a long time, darling. I'm sure glad to see you again."

Gabe slammed the car door and walked around to join them.

Tom held out his hand. "Good to see you, Gabe," he said, but he dropped the hand after seeing the older man's disapproving expression. Tom looked at Viv.

"You said on the phone you wanted to talk. How about we sit on the porch?"

Viv nodded, and she and her father followed him to the house. Viv sat on the porch swing while her father took one of the rocking chairs.

"Can I get you some tea or coffee?" Tom asked.

"No thanks," Gabe said. "Let's get this over with." Tom nodded warily and perched on the railing. "I guess Viv didn't tell you the news over the phone." Gabe glanced at his daughter, who shook her head. He turned back to Tom. "She's pregnant."

If he hadn't been sitting down, Tom would have fallen off the porch. He stared at Viv with shock and disbelief in his face. "You're pregnant?"

She nodded. "Almost seven weeks."

Tom shook his head as if someone had sucker-punched him. With his face darkening, he sprang up and strode the short distance to Viv. "Who's the father?" he growled.

"Now, wait a minute," Gabe said. He rose and went to his daughter's side.

"You are," Viv said. Their eyes locked, and Tom grabbed Viv's hands and pulled her to her feet.

"You know that's not possible."

"It has to be. Something went wrong with your vasectomy."

"In the fifteen years since I had it, no one else has gotten pregnant."

"Are you calling my daughter a liar?" Gabe shouted.

Tom tore his gaze away from Viv to glower at him.

"I'm saying that your daughter was dating two other men shortly before she started up with me. One of them is likely the father, and Viv is lying about how far along she is."

Gabe knocked Tom down with an unexpected right hook. Tom sprawled on the floor while Viv stared. The dogs swarmed around them, barking and sniffing. Tom sat up and fingered his jaw while Gabe paced back and forth, shaking his stinging hand and muttering.

"Been working out, Gabe?" Tom asked.

"Get up," Gabe hollered, rushing back for more. Bernie, the one-eyed beagle, slunk between them, growling at Gabe with his teeth bared. Riley cowered against Viv's legs while the other dogs froze, watching the men intently.

"Stop it, Daddy! You're only making things worse," Viv shouted. She grabbed his arm and looked down at Tom. "Are you all right?"

Tom nodded, but didn't stand. He stared at Viv with his lips pressed together and his eyes sullen. Viv shook her head in exasperation. Why couldn't Tom just talk with her?

"I don't care what you think, Tom Lockhart," she said in a ringing voice. "I suggest you see your doctor and get yourself checked out. Come on, Daddy," she said, dragging him off the porch. "I want to go home." She hustled him to the car, and they climbed inside.

As they drove past the house, Viv looked over her shoulder and saw Tom staring at them from the porch. She sniffed and turned back.

"Don't worry, Peaches. I won't let him besmirch your good name. I'll go to court after the baby is born and force him to have a paternity test." Her father reached the road and turned right, headed for Toronto.

Viv sighed. "Oh Daddy, no one's name gets besmirched anymore when a baby's born out of wedlock." She patted her father's arm. "Thanks for coming today, but I don't want you arguing with Tom anymore."

"But Peaches . . ."

She lifted her finger. "No 'but Peaches!' I'm going to have a baby, and I'm not going to force Tom to be involved in any which way, shape, or form. This is my baby, and I'm going to be just fine."

"Well, if you're sure," Gabe said in a meek voice.

Viv nodded, smiling. "I'm going to be a mother."

Chapter 30

It was a beautiful Friday evening in the first week of October. Viv had eaten an early dinner on the garden bench with a sweater over her shoulders to offset the slight chill in the air. The sky was azure blue, with the first tinges of red and orange leaves in the trees shading the backyard. Someone had lit a wood fire nearby, probably more for show than for heat, and Viv was sniffing the sharp, tangy scent with appreciation.

She went back inside as the shadows deepened and the crisp air became cool to sit on the couch with a science fiction novel. Julie had recommended it; Viv wasn't in the mood for a soppy romance these days. She kicked off her shoes and propped her feet up, Constantine cleaning himself on the chair next to her.

He meowed and jumped down when the doorbell rang. Viv sighed. She had just gotten comfortable. She listened without moving, and thought she heard scratching. Odd.

Getting up, she padded to the door, wishing it had a peephole, and opened it a cautious couple of inches.

Bruno sat on the front mat with a fat red bow around his neck.

"Bruno!" Viv knelt down on one knee to hug the dog, who tried to squirm into her lap. "What are you doing here?"

She gazed suspiciously around the front yard, but no one was there. "Well, if this isn't the strangest thing." She glanced down at the dog again, who was wagging his tail happily, and spotted an envelope clipped to his harness. She plucked it off and saw that "Viv" was written in cursive across the front.

"Come inside," she said to the dog. Bruno limped into the house and spotted Constantine peeking at him from the parlour door. He yipped and hurried after the cat, happy to see his buddy again. Viv sat down on the couch and tore open the envelope.

There were three sheets of paper folded up inside. Shaking out the first one, Viv saw a doctor's name, address, and telephone number in the letterhead at the top. It was a medical form, dated April 2, 1998. "Tom Lockhart" was listed as the patient, and the form gave the details of the vasectomy that had been performed on him that day.

Viv read the information twice, her heart beating faster. It was true. Tom had had a vasectomy.

She dropped the first sheet into her lap and unfolded the second page. It was a report from the same doctor's office with yesterday's date. Viv didn't understand all the terminology – there were words like "recanalization" – but it was obvious that a sample of Tom's ejaculate had been analyzed, and that the sperm count was normal for a man who had not had a vasectomy.

Viv's hand flew to her mouth. Tom had had a vasectomy, but something had grown back, enabling him to father a child. *Her* child.

Her hand trembled as she reached for the last page. It was handwritten, with today's date, and bore Tom's signature.

My darling Viv,

I've been the damnedest fool. You were absolutely right about the vasectomy having failed, and now we've made a baby together. What should have been one of the happiest moments of our lives was ruined because I called you a liar. I should have had myself tested before I said anything, but I saw red when Gabe said you were pregnant. There is no fool like an old fool, and I was scared that you were looking for a father for another man's child. Because it still feels like a miracle that a beautiful, sweet-natured angel like yourself has fallen for a middle-aged crock like me.

I should have trusted you, Viv. I know that we'll always have the age problem, but if I promise never to die, do you think you could give me a second chance? These weeks without you, I feel like the light has gone out of my life, and nothing – not my home, my work, or the animals – will bring joy to my heart again if you don't come back to me.

I hope that seeing Bruno, who misses you almost as much as I do, will help to win you back. That's why I sent him ahead with this letter and the doctor's reports. I'm hoping against hope that you miss your home with me and are willing to start over again. Will you forgive me?

Yours with all my heart and soul.
Tom

Viv clasped the letter in her hand. Tom wasn't a seducer or a liar. He was honest and true, and he loved her. Sure, they'd had a fight, a real doozy, but it would have been all right if they had just talked it out. Tom's unwillingness to talk and her old insecurities had made her doubt his love. Well, it wasn't true! Tom loved her and she loved him and they were going to have a baby together. Everything was going to be fine. And Daddy was going to have to lump it because he was going to be a grandfather!

Bruno hobbled over to the sofa and she pulled him onto her lap. "Bruno, where's Tom?" The dog stared at her with his moist brown eyes and licked her nose. She laughed and hugged him.

"Come on, Bruno. Either Tom's still here, or I'm going to have to drive us out to the farm. Which is it?" She put him down and ran to open the front door. The sun had set and she blinked, peering into the darkness. Before she could turn on the porch light, however, something moved in the shadows.

"It's me, darling. I was prepared to stay all night until I got an answer. What do you say? Will you forgive me?"

She threw herself into Tom's arms and he staggered back a step, holding her tight and laughing. Bruno jumped around his feet and barked while Viv laughed and blinked back the tears.

"It worked," she cried. "Bruno brought us together again."

Tom kissed her tenderly, and pressed his cheek against hers. "I'm sorry for hurting you, Viv. I love you so much."

"I love you so much, too," she sniffled.

He kissed her again before putting her down and reaching into his pocket. Viv could just make out a small velvet box in the light from the open door.

"I was hoping you'd forgive me, so I brought this." He opened the box, and Viv saw a gold band with a diamond surrounded by four pearls. "I hope you like it. I know how special your dad's ring is to you, so I had it made in reverse. I special-ordered it this summer."

He slid the ring onto her finger, where it nestled cozily. Viv gasped and held up her left hand to admire it.

"Tom, it's perfect." She grabbed his shoulders and kissed him. "I've never seen anything so beautiful in my life. Just wait until I tell Julie and Sabrina about this." She dashed inside, Bruno running after her, leaving Tom alone on the door mat. He chuckled, slid the ring box back into his pocket, and followed her into the house.

Chapter 31

It was New Year's Eve, and Julie was holding the party at her house. Tom and Viv were there, Viv wearing a low-necked dress with an empire waist that showcased her swelling stomach. She was curled against Tom on the couch; they were never far apart these days.

Sabrina and her new boyfriend, Matthew Stone, were slow-dancing in a corner of the cramped room. Sabrina had kicked off her metallic pumps with the white bows and five-inch heels, and Matthew's face rested against her auburn hair. He was tall and broad-shouldered with glasses and inky-black hair combed back from a wide forehead. Viv thought he looked like Gregory Peck, and wondered if that had attracted Sabrina to him in the first place. She had made both her friends watch *Roman Holiday*, and Sabrina had commented afterward that Mr. Peck was "sizzling hot."

Julie was cuddled with Kim in an armchair, feeding her melted brie on crackers. They had been inseparable since baseball season had ended.

Josh sat in a rocking chair with Olivia in his arms. The little girl, in a velvet dress with trailing green ribbons, was fast asleep, her head cuddled against Josh's shoulder. Julie had invited him to spend a week at the beach with them that past summer, provided that Josh found his own accommodations. He had rented an RV and stayed at the trailer park. The threesome had gone to the beach most days, wading while Olivia paddled in her water wings, and built sand castles together. Uncle Josh had gone trick-or-treating with them on Halloween night, too, dressed as a giant Tigger, and brought apple cider and mashed potatoes to the Christmas feast. Viv grinned at him; Josh was half-asleep himself with a smile on his lips.

Viv was feeling happy, but tired. It had been a tumultuous holiday season, beginning with an ending: she had said goodbye to her first grade class. Tom had been worried about her driving back and forth to the farm during the icy winter months, and there hadn't seemed much point in staying another term with her due date at the beginning of May. Viv had a project to keep her busy that winter, however. She was going to photograph their dogs and dogs belonging to other foster families to create a fund-raising calendar for Dog Angels.

She and Tom had one less pet these days, however. A couple had given Tank, the pit bull, a "forever" home. Viv had cried as Tank looked out the back window of the van as his new family drove him away, and Tom had wiped his eyes, but they were happy that the big-hearted dog would have the couple's exclusive attention. For them, he would be the "top dog." But she and Tom still had five dogs, six cats, and two horses to console them.

And she had said goodbye to Constantine, too. Fred had not been pleased when Viv had called him in Greece to say that she was pregnant and moving in with her boyfriend, but his indignation had thawed when Viv had Skyped him with a prospective tenant, the first-grade teacher replacing her at school that winter. Fred had even agreed to waive the two-month penalty for breaking the lease as a baby present.

Christmas Eve with her family had been special, but exhausting: Daddy and Magda had finally married. Tom had walked Magda down the aisle while Viv had been her maid of honour. Viv had been extra proud of her father as he and Magda had danced together at the Polish club reception, their friends and relatives cheering. Tom and Viv had stayed overnight in Viv's old room after the celebration, and Daddy had given her an envelope on Christmas morning.

"What's this?"

"Your present. Merry Christmas, Peaches."

Viv had slit open the envelope and read the contents before she burst out laughing. "It's a two-million-dollar life insurance policy. On Tom's life." Gabe had winked, and Tom had just about fallen down laughing.

When he had recovered, Tom said, "Guess I'd better not tick you off in future, darling. Whatever makes you happy, Gabe." The two men had shaken hands while Viv beamed.

Magda had been keen to make it a double-wedding, but Julie and Sabrina had vetoed the idea. They couldn't possibly make it the distinctive event they believed Viv deserved on such short notice. So she and Tom were getting married on Valentine's Day, before she got too huge to enjoy it. And the preparations, in combination with the Dog Angels' calendar, would occupy all of her energy until then, leaving lots of time to rest before the baby came.

"Hey, quiet down everyone!" Sabrina shouted. The music stopped, and Olivia opened her eyes in Josh's lap. "Julie, turn up the sound on the TV." The volume was turned down on an entertainment news program as they waited for the New Year's Eve broadcast to begin. Viv sat up to gawk at the screen.

"That's your mom, isn't it?" Julie asked.

Viv nodded. There was her mother in her white sheath and a flaming red cape with matching stilettoes being interviewed by one of the handsome young male hosts.

"So, the rumours of you selling Rouge Shoes are false?" he asked. Véronique was poised and regal beside him, but the rapacious smile on her lips reminded Viv of a crocodile.

"Definitely. Who knows where such ideas start? I have no intention of letting anyone take over Rouge. I'm much too young to retire, don't you think?" She rested a jewelled hand on the interviewer's sleeve.

"Of course," the mesmerized hunk with cheek bones any enterprising starlet would kill for said with an emphatic nod.

"Besides, there is a joyous event about to occur in my family. One day my progeny will continue my line of haute-couture shoes. Until then, it is nonsense to think that I am stepping down."

"Thank you for denying those rumours, Madame Roux."

"Call me Véronique," she purred seductively.

The young man smiled as Véronique slid her hand up his arm. The program went to commercial.

Everyone looked at Viv, who shrugged and said, "That's my Mom!" Julie and Sabrina laughed, while Tom hugged her.

Sabrina sank onto the couch beside Viv and nudged her. "Told you you'd have a keeper by New Year's Eve, didn't I? You can always trust my feelings." Viv shared a smile with Sabrina before Matthew towed her back to the dance floor.

Viv looked up into Tom's amused face and nodded. "Oh yes, definitely a keeper."

"Happy almost New Year's, darling," he said, bending to kiss her.

"Happy almost New Year's, Tom," she echoed, meeting him halfway.

THE END

Thank you for reading my book. If you enjoyed *The Dating Do-Over*, won't you please take a moment to help other readers discover it by leaving a review with your favourite retailer?

Thank you!

Cathy Spencer

AFTERWORD

Dog Fostering

In *The Dating Do-Over*, Tom fosters dogs through a fictional organization called Dog Angels. This aspect of the story was based upon my family's own experience with Ugly Mutts Dog Rescue, based in Hamilton, Ontario, Canada. We were living in a high-rise apartment then, and while we missed having a dog, we didn't think that it was the right time to commit to pet ownership. Instead, we fostered a well-trained, six-year-old boxer named Marlee. Marlee had a loving disposition, and we greatly enjoyed the weeks we had with her until she was adopted into her forever home.

What does it mean to foster a dog? Ugly Mutts interviewed us to judge our suitability as foster parents and to determine the type of dog that would best fit our home environment. They provided dog food and would have paid for veterinary care, had it been required. For our part, we wrote an assessment of Marlee's personality and took pictures of her, which were placed on the Ugly Mutt's website to facilitate adoption. We also met the family who eventually adopted Marlee.

There are many fine organizations which rescue both cats and dogs from pet mills, pounds without a no-kill policy, or from families who can no longer look after them. We found Ugly Mutts Dog Rescue on the internet, but your local pet store or veterinarian may also be able to help you find similar organizations.

Check out Ugly Mutts at http://uglymutts.com.

Tripawds

The Tripawds blogs gave me lots of helpful information on what I could expect after my fictional dog, Bruno, had a leg amputation.

Tripawds is the largest online community for three-legged animals and their people. The Tripawds mission is to maintain a community of support for those faced with amputation for their dogs, cats or other animals by providing helpful information and educational resources, and by creating a platform for discussion. Find blogs, forums, resources, advice, and support at http://tripawds.com.

The Distillery District

The Distillery District, located at 55 Mill Street, Toronto, Ontario, is a national historic site that was once The Gooderham and Worts Distillery, and represents the largest collection of Victorian industrial architecture in North America. Today it is an internationally-acclaimed village of shops, galleries, studios, restaurants, and theatres. For more information, visit The Distillery District website at http://www.thedistillerydistrict.com.

World's Best Banana Layer Cake Recipe

My high-school friend, Pam, gave this recipe to me about thirty-five years ago. She requested it for her birthday every year when she was growing up. I'm sure you'll enjoy it as much as I have.

1½ cups sugar
¾ cup margarine or butter
2 eggs
2½ cups cake flour
1 tsp vanilla
1¼ cups ripe bananas, mashed (about 3 medium)
¼ cup sour milk
1 tsp baking soda
½ tsp baking powder

Cream margarine in a bowl at high speed for 2 minutes.

Add sugar gradually at high speed until consistency of whipped cream. Scrape sides of bowl.

Add eggs one at a time. Beat one minute on low after each addition.

Add sour milk and vanilla to bananas.

Mix together flour, soda, and baking powder. Add alternately with banana mixture to margarine and egg mixture. Work quickly and don't over mix. Scrape sides of bowl and beat half a minute longer.

Pour into two well-greased 9" layer pans. Bake at 350°F for 30 minutes or until an inserted toothpick comes out clean. Ice when cool.

Note: For an added touch of moistness, ice the bottom layer and slice a banana on top before adding the top layer.

Award-winning author Cathy Spencer is married to a singer/actor/teacher. He didn't actually say "marry me and see Canada" when he proposed, but that's practically what happened. They have lived on the west coast in Vancouver, on the east coast in St. John's, in Calgary, and are currently living in Ontario.

Cathy writes both romance and mystery novels. *Framed for Murder*, winner of the 2014 Bony Blithe Mystery Award, is the first in the Anna Nolan series, a cozy mystery with an amateur sleuth set in the Rocky Mountain Foothills of Alberta. The second novel, *Town Haunts*, takes place at Halloween, while the third, *Tidings of Murder and Woe*, will be released in time for Christmas 2014. Aside from the mystery series and *The Dating Do-Over*, Cathy has written a regency romance entitled *The Affairs of Harriet Walters, Spinster*, as well as two short story collections, *Tall Tales Twin-Pack, Mysteries* and *Tall Tales Twin-Pack, Science Fiction and Fantasy*. Connect with Cathy at her website: http://cmspencer.blogspot.com.